"*What Burns Away* is a beautifully crafted narrative wrapped inside the trappings of a tense thriller. The upheavals of new motherhood followed by a difficult move to the Midwest lead Claire Spruce to seek out the remnants of her former self—a search that takes the form of a dangerous venture with her first love. The impulse to race to the conclusion of Melissa Falcon Field's gripping debut is tempered by the desire to savor the gorgeous prose along the way."

—Jean Reynolds Page, author of *A Blessed Event*

"*What Burns Away* leaves behind a scorch mark as a warning to her readers: watch what you wish for."

—Dina Guidubaldi, author of *How Gone We Got*

what
burns
away

MELISSA FALCON FIELD

Published by Sourcebooks Landmark, an imprint of Sourcebooks, Inc.
P.O. Box 4410, Naperville, Illinois 60567-4410
(630) 961-3900
Fax: (630) 961-2168
www.sourcebooks.com

Library of Congress Cataloging-in-Publication data is on file with the publisher.

Printed and bound in the United States of America.
VP 10 9 8 7 6 5 4 3 2 1

For Noah, who teaches me everything.

"She is made out of yesterdays."

—James Salter, *A Sport and a Pastime*

PART 1

CHAPTER ONE

MEMORY

I F I'M HONEST, I CAN ADMIT THAT EVEN BEFORE THE flash point, all was not well. Even back during Miles's cardiology fellowship and my own research on the gouged ozone layer over Antarctica, back when I was considered an expert at something, back when Miles and I were still in the infancy of our marriage—even then the past had begun to instigate trouble.

Because weather patterns are the way my mind delineates time, I know it was two days into the Blizzard of January 2005, a Category 4 storm with Arctic conditions that lasted three days and dumped thirty-six inches of snow over New England. Maybe the storm itself brought on the memories, but I'll never be sure.

What I do know is that throughout the day, I'd grown lonesome at work the way I always do after a snowfall, the isolation made worse by impassable roads. Miles was stuck at work too, so I stayed at the lab to wait it out, where, hunched over satellite depictions of a warmed and brutalized troposphere, the recollections penetrated my concentration like meteoroids ripping through the atmosphere.

And there in the lab, seven years ago now—before our son, before the move—came sensations like flashes of light. The snapshots were from my girlhood when, had I been braver or more attentive, I could've helped stop things before they spun out of control. The first images were my mother setting Dad's beer can back on the table, the slam of the door, the memory of her slight frame running out into the early dark, the starless night, and fog so dense it left dew on my teenage skin. Then, out in front of her, the outline of the big, white house, 101 Quayside Lane, rising from the haze like a vessel.

I could feel the impression of my moon boots across snow-covered sand, could hear the panting of my breath. I sensed my arms pumping while I chased after my mother. Next, I saw the gravel footpath to the house, then my mother's profile before she disappeared beyond the enormous oak door. As I waited, the wind grew wild off the water; I could feel it in my hair. The snow squalled, and behind me Long Island Sound thrashed at my heels.

To stop more of the visions from coming, the horror of what I knew followed, I left my bench at the lab, abandoned the ozone reports I was working on, and ran outside into the blizzard, where I stood as an adult—not that frightened teen-age girl, but the woman she had become. I let the cold fill my lungs and exhaled deep smoky breaths; flakes soaked through my lab coat and sopped my hair. I stood there who knows how long, while snow whipped up from the drifts until everything went numb.

And from that moment forward, I tucked away the magne-tism and loneliness encased in those memories, hiding them from Miles, from myself even. But over time, the power of that indiscernible past escalated, and my longing to right it became comparable, I estimated, to the desperation of the little girl in an old Khoisan legend I've always loved. Under the dark seclusion of the Kalahari sky, the girl grew rash after years of isolation. One day she reached into a blazing fire, grabbed a fistful of red-hot embers, and tossed them to the heavens, delivering the Milky Way galaxy from her fist. Its twinkle of light became her rescue, making the desert around her passable for travelers in southern Africa and forever saving the girl from her solitude.

After talking through it with Miles and my counselor, Anna, these past twelve weeks, I see now that my loneliness gained quiet momentum in the same hushed way our marriage began falling apart. I had grown unrecognizable to myself, invisible in my own darkness—and yes, like the little Khoisan girl, I stuck my hand into a fire, wanting desperately to be found.

And found I was again, on the morning of my fortieth birthday, when Miles and I were barely unpacked from a move to Madison, Wisconsin. Then, too, the snow fell fast. But I was spared the worst of my memories by the rousing call of my sixteen-month-old son.

It was six thirty, maybe seven, and Jonah's voice woke me. Gravelly and amplified through the baby monitor, he shouted: *"Come!"*

In my half sleep, I suppose it was the word that conjured up the image of my estranged mother who, in her own fortieth year, thumped a rose-colored roller bag, the same color as her lipstick, down the front stairs and out the door.

I was fourteen when she stepped from our stoop, a long, thick ponytail swinging behind her, while my father, my sister Kara, and I watched her hurry along the brick walk to the end of our charred driveway still tagged with yellow crime scene tape. Waiting for her, a car we had never seen before idled in front of our house. Mom paused once she reached it, turned to face us, and waggled her fingers good-bye.

The gesture suggested something playful, and although her expression was veiled by the haze, I remained hopeful, expecting her to retrace her steps back to us, imagining the warmth of her lips blotting my cheek and the collapse of her thin frame into the meaty arms my father held out to her. His voice had already gone hoarse from hollering, over and over again: "Kat, come back!"

But she went. Ducking into the passenger's seat, she clutched the rose-colored bag to her chest, while the driver of the car stole her away. From the steps, Kara and I watched as the tail-lights disappeared into the haze, while Dad called our mother home long after she was gone. Once he went silent, Dad slid down the doorjamb and quietly wept into his hands.

Jonah beckoned me back into real time and out from that reminiscence of my father with his plea: "Come! Mama, please?"

I kicked off the down comforter and studied the snowy Midwestern dawn, noting the cumulonimbus clouds that rolled past my window.

Jonah hollered again, his breathing gone fierce: *"Mama! Come!"*

I tied my hair back, wondering where my own mother was

that morning, briefly considering what I would say if I ever saw her again. Then I eyed my husband through the open bathroom door, watching as he tapped his razor against the edge of the sink.

Miles kept his back to me. A new breadbasket of weight pooled at his waist, and I studied his face in the mirror. His steady surgeon's hand took a straight edge to the beveled cleft of his chin.

All desperation and hysterics, Jonah screamed. *"Please, Mama!"*

Miles turned to face me as I stood, a dollop of shaving cream above his lip. "Claire, go get the baby."

And as I shrugged into my robe, I wondered if my fortieth year would be the one during which I would leave Miles, finally surrendering to a dissatisfaction I could never quite explain, assuming it was better to go while Jonah was still so small he'd never remember.

But I pushed that impulse away, not allowing myself to imagine the ways that scenario could play out, still haunted by my own mother's departure, her act of selfishness the first domino in what became a chain reaction with inescapable fallout.

In my slippers I shuffled across the master bedroom, running my fingertips along the dark wood paneling lining every wall of our cold, dim rental house. Passing the angular built-in dressers that boxed us in, I felt the loss of the sunny, newly renovated home Miles and I had sold back East only months before, a place we surrendered for a mere quarter of its worth, when our faith in each other seemed to collapse right along with the housing market.

My husband, the steadfast Dr. Miles Bancroft, stood shirtless and toweled his face dry. Leaning through the bathroom door frame upon my approach, he stopped me for a kiss. "Claire Elizabeth Spruce," he said. "Forty! Have a perfect birthday."

Apathetic in response, I continued past him toward the nursery. There, Jonah shook the rails of his crib like an angry convict, settling once I hoisted him into my embrace.

"I'm here, baby," I whispered.

We nuzzled against each other, and I remembered how hard he was to bring into the world, how my overwhelming love for him had unhinged me for a time. I wondered, as I still often do, how I had managed to live an entire life without my little boy.

Jonah clasped his arms around my neck, pressing his feet against my ribs.

I kissed each one of his ears, our morning ritual.

"Look," I said. We swayed a minute, and I pointed out the nursery window to the mounting snowfall. With the cold front moving off Lake Mendota, I estimated that there would be even more accumulation for Madison and south-central Wisconsin than the weather stations had predicted.

Lacking my interest in the elements, Jonah furrowed his brow and patted my face, demanding breakfast like he still does nearly every morning: "Mama, yummies!"

We headed downstairs to the kitchen, and with Jonah tight in my grip, I recounted all my non-fortieth birthdays—the years of Carvel ice-cream cakes, their pink and white frosting, and that one redundant wish for the things that could never be brought back.

Moving into the monotony of our morning routine, the breakfasts and lunches yet unmade, I recollected the bent light of tiny wicks over four decades, noting that it was twenty-six years since my mother left, her actions changing everything, and how it was Dean who lit my candles once she was gone, before he went south, his warm breath in my ear, singing, "Happy, happy birthday, Claire!"

Dean D'Alessio, my first love, lived one block from my family on the other side of Willard Street, in a blue raised ranch identical to my parents' except for the aluminum awnings his mom had added as a bonus. From our cookie-cutter back porches, we grew up listening to Long Island Sound erode the Connecticut coastline while gulls barked above the power lines that stitched his side of the street to mine.

I noticed Dean for the first time on a November snow day in 1985, following Thanksgiving break. Having grown tired of the surplus turkey stew and stuffing that lined our refrigerator in Tupperware, I left my eleven-year-old sister, Kara, behind to watch Bugs Bunny and headed out to Micucci's corner store with a pocket full of change.

I sank deep into the snow along our footpath and, as I trudged by, I watched Dean. He glanced up at me while busting apart the last of the ice in a bank blocking a neighbor's driveway. He launched a shovel into the bed of his pickup truck, then pulled his winter cap low over his brow, just above his eyes. His frame was taller, bulky even, in comparison to the sinewy boys in my freshman class, and he stood with an air of resilience.

Shivering at the curb, I waited for the light at the crosswalk.

"Hey!" he shouted in my direction, moving closer to where I stood.

I peered over my shoulder, and his chiseled features vaguely hidden under the start of a beard came into view.

"What's your name?" he asked, locking me into the intensity of his stare.

Unnerved and excited, I answered in a near whisper, "Claire."

"Pretty name." He nodded. "For a pretty girl."

And just then, as the walk signal beeped, he turned back toward his truck, jumped in, and drove off.

I glided across the street, and the twinge of something triumphant welled up inside me. Unable to stop myself, I glanced back, just once, to catch only the red taillights of his truck.

But as I finished my slice of pizza a few minutes later under the corner store's awning, listening to Mr. Micucci belt out a baritone version of "Come Back to Sorrento" while he tossed pies into the air, Dean looped the block, rolled down his window, and hollered my name.

I gave him a tiny, awkward wave, holding in a giggle, and from that moment forward, Dean D'Alessio became my secret crush, until nearly two months later, the morning of January 28, 1986.

On that January day, as I carried my papier-mâché model of Halley's comet through the slushy brown snow, headed to science class to watch the space shuttle *Challenger* launch from Kennedy Space Center, I was thinking about letters. There was the letter I stole off my father's dresser and the letter I'd received from Christa McAuliffe, the thirty-seven-year-old high school teacher from New Hampshire selected from 11,000 applicants to be the nation's Teacher in Space. I had one of the letters in each of my coat pockets and had just dropped my sister off at middle school when Dean D'Alessio pulled up to the curb and offered me a ride.

"Claire," he called. "Give you a lift? You don't want to ruin your project in the snow."

His acknowledgment of my science model made me feel childish. "I guess," I said. "Sure."

Dean got out of his truck, took the sequined comet from my hands, and held open the passenger door.

I had just turned fourteen that January, and my parents had begun lecturing me at the dinner table about never getting into a car with an older boy. Knowing full well that they would disapprove, I climbed inside with my face flushed, glitter falling everywhere.

As he set the model back in my lap, Dean rested his hand on my knee, and the heat of his touch unlocked something inside me.

I chewed my cuticles and asked him, "Are you in school?"

"Quit when I was sixteen. Been out a year, just got my GED. I don't miss any of that bullshit." Dean lit two cigarettes off a match. "Smoke?" He held one in my direction.

I rolled the filter between my fingers but never brought it to my lips. I had smoked before, behind the public library with my neighbor Staci DiMaggio and her big brother Tony, and I knew I didn't like the way it made my mind go tippy. I cared more about the teardrop shape of the match's flame and the smell of the rolled paper's first burn. But instead of saying no to Dean, I toyed with the ember he'd handed to me, flicking it against the ashtray like Dad did when he gambled at cards.

Ahead of us the light was faint, a muted winter sun. I arrived at school two hours late that January day because Dean took me to the creek, the place we would go to park until the end of winter, when warmer days changed the places we could be alone together.

The creek varied in width and revised its course over the months we spent beside it—cutting wider with the spring thaw and rains, then leaving an actual bank come summer across which the blue crabs would scurry as we sunbathed.

The water ran from the tidal marsh into Long Island Sound and separated our neighborhood beach, Hawk's Nest, from the bird sanctuary and the private strand on the other side. From the cab of Dean's truck, I learned to spot the piping plovers bobbing on the branches of ocean roses before they buried themselves amid the sea grass to nest. At low tide, when the weather warmed, we rolled up our jeans, darkening the cuffs of our pant legs in our attempt to wade across. At high tide, the creek was over my head, up to Dean's chest. But on that first day, it was frozen along the edges, glazed with a thin layer of ice that would have cracked like peanut brittle under the slightest pressure.

Before my classes that first morning together, he'd simply asked, "Can I kiss you?"

In my moon boots, with a papier-mâché comet in my lap, I looked up to the sky as if the answer could be found there and said nothing.

Dean took my chin in his fingertips and guided me toward him for a kiss. He smelled like menthol cigarettes, Juicy Fruit gum, and the coffee he sipped from a thermos that made him seem old.

In the cab of his truck, we shed layers of our clothes and kept the heater on high as our bodies drew close. Beside him, my pulse banged against my wrist, my chest, inside my ears, and I wondered if Dean could hear the noise.

But unlike my previous sloppy make-out sessions with other boys among the *National Geographic* magazines at the public library, I lost myself beside the creek with Dean.

His touch somehow emancipated me from my insecurities and left room to fill that space with desire. With him, I grew gutsy, not just about skipping class, but also about what it meant to yearn for more. I had not known that feeling before and it came as a surprise to me. But Dean knew. He was older and understood what girls wanted, even when they didn't.

From the moment his calloused palms slid over my skin, I wanted it to happen again. His touch was like a small lamp illuminating a big house of dark rooms—and I wanted, desperately, to feel my way back to that light.

The morning before Dean picked me up, I had been struck by an unfamiliar and blooming emptiness after discovering a sealed letter left on top of my father's dresser. The envelope had Dad's name, Peter, written in Mom's loopy cursive. It was unusual for her to correspond with any of us in writing, and given the weighted silence between them, my curiosity rose. So, I had folded it in half and slipped it into my coat pocket, opening it after I escorted Kara to school. The letter read:

January 28, 1986

Peter,

Last night was just another example of how, even when you are in the room, I feel deserted. I need someone who makes me feel wanted and less alone. I'm very sorry, but I just can't do this anymore. I'll try my best to make this easy on you and the kids. We can work out the details later. I plan to talk to a divorce attorney sometime this week, but I don't want there to be any surprises.

Kat

My stomach had churned with fear and hurt. I'd taken my mother's words to mean that if she didn't want my father, then she didn't want any of us. From the second I crumpled the note and stuffed it back into my coat pocket, the entire world became suspect.

But there in Dean D'Alessio's truck, with the defrost blowing a hot stream of air on my face and feet, I wanted to get closer to the center of something that felt good, to move away from the injury of my mother's letter and the fear my stomach sickened with upon reading her words, so I took his hands and held tight as he guided our interlocked fingers down the front of his jeans.

And as chance would have it, while eating cereal with my husband and son in Madison on my birthday, an entire lifetime since that moment, I logged into my Facebook account for the first time in months. Among the birthday wishes, I was shocked to find a brief message and accompanying friend request from that old love, Dean.

Claire Spruce, is it you, after all these years?

After reading the message, I studied the thumbnail image of a man I'd never dared search for, always stopping myself from imagining his hulking frame, but there he stood on a mountain summit, something familiar in his posture, thrusting a ski pole into the air.

Crosswise from me sat Miles, who slurped his coffee and studied stacks of EKGs without any awareness that our son had dumped his milk across the kitchen table.

I closed the lid to my computer, searched for paper towels to sop up the mess, and pulled Jonah into my lap. The smell of his hair suggested maple syrup, and I nibbled the sticky finger he held to my lips, thinking about that photograph of Dean.

Tempted to send Dean an immediate response, I considered the time. Story hour at the public library was in twenty minutes, and getting there would take longer than usual with the falling snow, so I would wait to give the correspondence my full attention, when I wasn't rushing—once Miles was gone and Jonah was down for his nap. Eager to respond, I read the request again, lingering a second longer over the words. "Is it you, after all these years?" And with that one question,

I envisioned Dean D'Alessio removing me from all that had frayed between Miles and me.

But things weren't always unhappy between Miles and me. We used to laugh together until we were breathless on the stretch of coastline down the lane from our turn-of-the-century farmhouse in Mystic, Connecticut. The expansive front porch and gorgeous framework of the place were obscured under a peeling, gray hide against which we leaned twenty-four-foot ladders and from which we skinned a hundred years' worth of paint. We were newlyweds and new homeowners, blissful and madly in love.

Those hot days of late August 2005, only a few weeks into our marriage, I was thirty-three years old, and while I stood on the top rung scraping a chisel over the clapboards, Miles steadied himself on the rooftop. From my vantage point, I studied his meticulous doctor's hands reconstructing the pebble chimney as a gentle rain fell over us. Knowing the surface beneath Miles's work boots had grown slick, I worried he might lose his footing and slip down the steep pitch of the copper roof, believing wholeheartedly that I would go undone if I had to live one moment of my life without him. I had found, I believed, the person I was meant to build not only a home with, but also a life, and it seemed I could never hold him close enough.

Through the year of restoration, my love for Miles only grew stronger, and I could feel the ache of it somewhere at the center of me, my desire for him throbbing like the exhausted muscles under my skin. All day, wearing tool belts and climbing ladders, we encouraged and challenged each other, resting only for lunches, devouring sandwiches a yard long, gulping down gallons of iced tea. We were a solid, unyielding team, and the house became an example of what we could accomplish together.

One freezing Sunday morning a month before Christmas, our goal, overly optimistic, was to have the kitchen primed and ready for a holiday meal. But watching Miles fuss over the base coat, dabbing the tiniest crevice with bristles, I saw his detailed process as a complete waste of time.

"At the rate you're working, we'll have the primer done by St. Patrick's Day," I teased.

Miles turned to me, brush in hand, and painted a white splotch on my nose.

"Watch it," he warned.

Responding to the threat, I ran a roller drenched in paint over the side of his face and grinned wickedly.

In retaliation, Miles chased me, half a gallon of primer in hand, hollering, "You're about to get it, my dear!"

Protecting myself, I pulled the drop cloth out from under Miles's feet, which sent him to the floor and the can into the air, splattering both our faces with white.

Stunned, blinking like two characters in a pie scene from an old television sitcom, we tumbled to the floor, giddy with laughter.

After a moment, Miles stood, drenched in paint, and ran his fingers over my lips, searching for a clean spot to kiss before he picked me up and carried me over the threshold and into the bathroom shower he had tiled himself.

With a pair of shears, he cut me from my paint-soaked

clothes. Under the warm water, the paint ran from my hair in a milky stream. He pulled my body against his, kissed my neck and shoulders, and moved his hand between my legs, both of us frantic with desire.

"I love our life," he whispered, and I paused, hoping I could forever love it back.

I whispered, "It's the perfect life. Let's take good care of it."

Then, I eased us into the basin of the tub, straddled his lap, and moved him inside me, while the water rained over us. In that moment, I never wanted the house to be finished or the days constructing it to end.

But by the close of that second summer in Mystic, the house was completely prepped, everything but the trim painted sage green. With extra time on our hands, we started taking morning swims, running barefoot past the swing on the portico, and racing beyond my raised gardens filled with tomatoes to the sandy lane where the sea grasses had thickened alongside the dunes, out onto our private stretch of shore.

And there, as predictable as the tide, we'd encounter a pair of pugs always dressed in seasonal attire headed toward the surf. Our middle-aged neighbors outfitted their dogs, Pansy and Sebastian, as daisies in springtime, complete with petal headbands. Then, as the days grew long and muggy, they refashioned the pitiful little animals into gigantic bumblebees, with black-and-yellow T-shirts and battered wings bobbing behind them until Labor Day. Come fall, the dogs had their final metamorphosis, turned into apprehensive-looking jack-o'-lanterns who scuttled after sandy tennis balls in orange cable-knit sweaters.

Every time Miles and I caught a glimpse of them, pink tongues hanging from their dark lips, we debated how much humiliation a dog could stand and then how much humiliation we might one day tolerate from each other. For us, during that first year of marriage, the absurdity of Pansy and Sebastian was the worst we could ever imagine.

Standing on that stretch of beach, Miles told me, "I love how you just get it. Why I find those damn dogs so ludicrous." He was drying his tanned face on a towel after a swim. "And you'll get this one too," he said, as the pug twins darted by us in yellow-and-black T-shirts. He gestured toward the dogs' owners, Ned and Sheila Whitaker, wielding metal detectors over the sand.

"Check out Ned's shorts," Miles whispered. "He and Sheila are even worse off than the pugs."

We watched Ned stroll ahead of us, a cascade of pocket change falling from some forgotten hole in his tartan shorts and onto the sand. A few feet behind him, his wife, oblivious, whirled her metal detector over his path, sending the thing into the computerized song of a slot machine and her down on hands and knees, digging for treasure.

We watched our neighbors cackling like seagulls, amused tears welling in our eyes, as Sheila called to Ned. She wanted to show him her riches, not a clue in the world that they'd come from his pocket.

Miles reined me in to kiss the joke from my lips. "That's gonna be us," he said. "And I wouldn't want to grow demented with anyone but you."

As he held me close, the cold coming off his body from a swim, I let Miles's wet trunks soak through my clothes. I was happy then, happier than I had ever been in my life. I trusted that the strength of our love propelled not only our laughter, but also our mutual career successes—both Miles's clinical accolades and research distinctions at UConn's medical center, and my frontline investigations into global warming at the school's Atmospheric Resources Laboratory. Our combined honors were more than we had imagined for ourselves, or each other, and like the house, those achievements were something we worked at building together.

But somewhere in the seven years of our marriage, Miles and I stopped finding each other. We stopped working cooperatively; we stopped encouraging each other professionally; we stopped rejoicing in the ridiculous. As soon as our laughter vanished, so did our casual everyday intimacy—the way we reached for each other in the morning, shuffling through sleepiness to the coffeepot, or how we brushed up against each other on the way back from the mailbox. That kind of routine touch had become mislaid.

After we moved into our modern rental house in Madison, Wisconsin—where there were too many floor-length windows and doorways to keep the cold out, where Miles stood waiting in his lab coat and his mismatched socks, awaiting the kind of send-off I was too lonely and homesick to give him—the awkwardness of what was missing between us brought forth a deep sadness in me. There was no argument, no unforgivable exchange of words, no discussion, just a sense that what held us together was coming unstitched. Fraught with uncertainty about what that meant, I couldn't bring myself to move toward him.

Maybe because Miles had become so preoccupied with his work, he failed to recognize how hard the relocation for his clinical research and job prestige was for me—the way I craved the stimulation of my own former career, or simply how I longed for the sound of foghorns over the bay. He never once asked about my deep morning breaths as I sought out any hint of salt in the Midwestern air. Instead we went inward, silently tucking ourselves away from each other, not uttering a single word, pretending for a long time that everything was okay.

It was different back East in our green farmhouse before the pregnancies, before three years of attempting to conceive, before I gave myself over to Jonah, to motherhood, when in those happy early years of our marriage, I would carry Miles's coffee mug into the breezeway and block the exit.

"You're not going anywhere yet, Dr. Bancroft," I'd tease.

Miles would often start the day hiking my skirt over my thighs, and many mornings we'd find ourselves pinned against the pinewood door, stripped naked, both of us wanting each other, as Miles whispered, "What do you predict for us today, weather girl?"

But after the baby and the move, I couldn't quite imagine showing off my legs, or Miles finding the time to help me rediscover the missing parts of myself. I found my loneliness blooming—missing not only that regular touch, but also our former life, who I was before I became a mother, my job, my brain, my research, my body, and who Miles and I used to be together. I started living my life looking backward, seeking out the past and longing for familiarity because nothing in our new life was recognizable to me. I wondered, of course, if Miles was lonely too, though it scared me how most days that thought left me feeling almost nothing.

On that morning of my fortieth birthday, I did not reach for Miles when he left. I did not block him at the door and encourage him to pull me from my clothes, nor did we make promises to each other about the day. Instead, I stayed seated at the table with Jonah, to whom Miles blew a kiss, our mutual love for our son the one thing holding us together when he walked out the door.

Once Miles was gone, I announced in as singsong a voice as I could muster, "Library time!"

Jonah smiled at me with all ten of his teeth and ripped the bib reading "Hung like a five-year-old" from his neck, a gift from my mother, who has never known the lines of what's appropriate, and, to my chagrin, a token Miles continued to salvage from the trash and use, no matter how many times I threw it away.

"Bye-bye time!" Jonah shouted, letting me know he was in agreement with the plan. And after stuffing his wide toddler feet into a pair of snow boots, I logged on to Facebook once more to read Dean's message, wondering how my life might've turned out if I had ended up with him, recollecting all he had once protected me from.

CHAPTER TWO

CORRESPONDENCE

T HE FIRST FEW EMAILS WE EXCHANGED WERE benign. I told Dean where I lived and explained my research in climatology—not the broadcaster kind, but the atmospheric chemistry kind. I didn't mention that I had quit. Then I brushed over a brief account of my seven-year marriage to Miles, recapping it in one sentence before I shifted gears to rave about my son.

Calling him "the true love of my life," I detailed the number of Jonah's molars, his creamy luscious skin dusted in freckles, his corn-silk hair, his curious eyes dark as chocolates, going on in that manic way triggered by a mother's love to describe how Jonah, in his raspy little voice, would recite "Twinkle, twinkle, little owl" in lieu of the original verse, boasting that my boy, unlike any other sixteen-month-old child I knew, could name three constellations: the Big Dipper, the Little Dipper, and Orion. I gibbered on at such length about my son that later that afternoon, when Dean told me he'd never had any children, I was embarrassed.

And, because he asked, I spent most of that morning uploading pictures of my life for Dean. The images were of Jonah and me together, pictures I'd taken myself, my arm extended as we squinted into the sun, smiling up at the lens. I chose the shots carefully, posting only those in which I looked less like an exhausted new mother and more like my former adventurous self. But not wanting to present myself as too out of his reach, I omitted pictures that were of the three of us—Jonah, Miles, and me—feeling guilty only in passing about leaving my husband out.

And, if I am remembering this correctly, it was shortly after I posted those pictures that Dean first popped up on chat and we began a real-time correspondence, volleying compliments and the details of our family lives back and forth.

Dean: Claire, great photos. Motherhood looks good on you.

Claire: Your wife is stunning! How did you meet?

Dean: Oh man. Roll of the dice.

Claire: What do you mean?

Dean: On the beach, not far from where I first saw you, same time of year, November, freezing-ass cold. There was this lunatic out on the water riding waves with a neon parachute bungeed to a surfboard. It was her, kite sailing through the downpour.

Claire: I can't imagine it—in New England in the winter!

Dean: It looked incredibly physical and risky, which I love, so I sat parked at Hawk's Nest Beach between residential showings, waiting, watching her for hours. Eventually, she came to shore, and I walked to the beach where she was peeling off her wet suit and invited her for coffee. Two weeks later we were living together.

Claire: What a story!

Dean: There's a lot more to that story, but I'll just say this for now, Heather's the kind of girl who wakes up and decides to jump out of airplanes, total wildcat, which is also how I remember you.

Claire: Not anymore. These days I'm all tucked in by 9:30 p.m. I've become such a snore.

Dean: You're still in there, I bet. And, well, truth be told, I'd be terrified to start a family with Heather. She's over the edge. A classic unruly redhead.

When I look back on that exchange now, I see how Dean got me thinking about risk and how little of it was left in my life. And maybe hearing him talk about his wife started me thinking in depth about my own marriage, trying to recall a time when Miles had felt that way about me, when I was utterly daring and fun—before we plummeted into something domestic and uninspired, before I left those best parts of myself back there on the coast.

If nothing else, I was intrigued by the fact that Dean had married an extreme version of that madcap girl my husband once found in me. So it was then, I remember, that I lost the first of many afternoons scrolling through Dean's images to scrutinize his life and contemplate the adventures he had with his wife in that Connecticut town where I was born, comparing it to what Dean and I had, once upon a time, and what we might've become had we shared a future together.

That afternoon, as Jonah slept, Dean set the stage for what would unfold between us in the weeks to come, revealing very little about himself beyond the daily grind of his real estate tours and the staging of open houses for our former mutual friends, and instead focusing his correspondence almost exclusively on the intimate details of a past we shared together.

> **Claire,**
>
> **I don't know if I should say this, but last night I thought about your hair. The way it smelled. How you braided it after a swim, sitting in your yellow bikini and cutoffs in the bed of my truck. It was so thick it never seemed to dry. And I remember teaching you how to drive. It was summer, July of '86. You were tan. And drove all of 35 mph in a 65 mph zone on the freaking interstate.**
>
> **And what was that sticky stuff you wore on your lips? The berry kind? I remember tasting you for hours.**
>
> **You were so sweetly shy when I followed you upstairs and sat you on the windowsill to undress you after your dad died. I'll never understand why I started to fade out of your life afterward, or how I allowed myself to kiss you good-bye forever on your birthday that winter. I was a stupid jackass of a kid.**
>
> **Dean**

Reading his emails, I allowed myself to become the girl Dean wrote about, letting everything in Madison fade out—the laundry baskets full of clothes to fold, the toys scattered across the rug, the isolation—and I went back home with him to that long-ago windowsill in my mother's second husband's house on the day of my father's funeral, with the hot sun streaming in, my face wet with tears, Dean unzipping my navy-blue romper, his breath in my ear, his mouth on my neck. And in his reiteration of that afternoon, I unearthed a desire I believed myself no longer capable of and began to sense myself coveting not only him, but also the me that he remembered, yearning for her youth, her spontaneity, her energy, her skin.

Serendipity played its role in how those messages affected me, no doubt, and as the therapist has suggested, I might not have been so vulnerable if Dean hadn't caught me just then, after the move and particularly on my fortieth birthday, that ridiculous marker of middle age, another indication of all that was behind me—my career, my youth, my home, and my marriage, it seemed, following suit.

Although, in his own way, Miles did reach out to me. Perhaps sensing my distraction or the gap grown between us, he made a rare call home from work and told me, "Get ready, babe. We've got to do it up for your birthday!"

"I thought we were going to skip it," I said.

"Tonight," he announced, "I'll be home to take you out." And, for once, he was.

Reluctantly, I shimmied into a black dress, stepped into a pair of heels, and glossed my lips red. I pinned my hair up into a twist and thought about all the ways Miles and I could turn

things around. For a long while, I stared into the mirror, turning to the side and sucking in my stomach, examining the lines
around my eyes and smoothing them out with my fingertips,
fingering my untamable blond curls as I told my reflection,
"You're forty years old. Holy shit."

While I dressed, Miles agreed to put Jonah to bed, and once
his little snores purred into the room, the awkward teenager
across the street came over with a book weighing more than
her frame. "Happy birthday, Mrs. Spruce," she told me and
took the monitor from my hand, curling catlike into a wingback chair.

In the car, my husband played a CD he'd made me for my
birthday the previous year. "I didn't really plan anything special," he said. "I thought we could be spontaneous. I know you
like that kind of thing."

But Miles has never been good at knowing the right kind
of spontaneous, and so we walked from place to place, getting turned away at every establishment we entered because it
was the first week of the winter term, and the University of
Wisconsin's men's basketball team was playing at home, in our
new university town. The whole city was booked with students, their parents, and crowds of middle-aged alumni, decked
out in the university's colors, cheery red and white. Hoards of
alums in Bucky Badger sweatshirts and coats had returned to a
place they held dear, a place that reminded them of their youth,
a place they loved to revisit because a part of their story began
there, while we, in contrast, bumbled down side streets in long
black dusters with our iPhones directing us through a city to
which we remained strangers.

Block after block we peered into restaurants, finding couples our own age holding up pint glasses and stemware, their eyes glossy with drink, their cheeks rosy with nostalgia. And as we checked with the hostess stations, hoping for a seat in each place we passed, we witnessed roars of laughter as friends leaned across tables to embrace each other. All of it made me homesick for our life back East.

After looping Madison's capital square three times, unable to find seating elsewhere, we settled for a Nepalese restaurant on State Street that served mostly takeout but offered a few wobbly tables near the window. We were ridiculously overdressed, and both of us were trying to make the best of things, feeling the pressure of the occasion and the expectations of the first date we'd had in ages.

In an attempt to sound encouraging, I said, "This is cozy," while we huddled over a greasy menu and I pushed my disappointment with the venue into the empty pit of my stomach. Outside, groups of coeds dressed in support of the home team, wearing Badger-red snow hats and red-and-white-striped overalls, huddled against the cold and cheered for what must have been a victory over at the basketball stadium.

While I waited for Miles to place our order, I checked my cell phone to see if there was word from our sitter. Finding none, I scrolled to my Facebook account, where there was a photo from Dean, no note this time—just a scanned snapshot from an old Polaroid camera, a picture of me blowing out the candles on a giant sheet cake with a *Happy 15th Birthday* he had iced in pink across the center of it, before he kissed me that final good-bye.

Considering the flurry of flames cast over the cake, I recalled my high school chemistry lab, my ninth-grade science teacher that year, Mr. Barnet, and how one day after class, when I was supposed to be on my way to second period study hall, I simply couldn't tear myself away from the tornadic flames we had made. Set on a lazy Susan, the conflagrations rose and spun into motion as currents moved through a protective mesh screen, replicating the role of trees in a wildfire and whirling the flames into a vortex. Beholding the beauty of that illuminated twister, I stayed in my seat long after the bell, charmed by its animated whirl.

Mr. Barnet dragged a wobbly metal stool over to sit beside me and said, "Pretty cool stuff, right?"

Almost in a trance, I whispered, "I love it," while the fire cyclone gained momentum.

"Then stay a minute," he told me.

Opening his cabinet and pulling down a plastic container that looked like an egg crate, each compartment holding what appeared to be salt, Mr. Barnet wiped a platinum wire with hydrochloric acid and dipped the looped end of it into the first sample on the tray. He then waved the wand through the fire, the flame changing from orange to sky blue—the fire gone magic.

I laughed with pure pleasure and asked, "How did you do *that*?"

"Arsenic," he said, sliding a heavy volume across the space between us.

The book, *The Chemical History of a Candle*, featured the image of a taper whose single flame seemed to blow across the cover, as if someone were making a wish.

"You should read this," he said. "It was written by the English scientist Michael Faraday in 1860, who once gave a series of Christmas lectures for young people at the Royal Institution of Great Britain in London. Each of his experiments deduces the chemical and physical properties of fire."

All those years later, sitting at a wobbly table in a Nepalese restaurant on my fortieth birthday, I could still recite the title of the first lecture in the book's series: "A Candle: The Flame—Its Sources, Structure, Mobility, Brightness."

And when I spotted Miles returning to our table with a tray full of steaming food, I slipped my phone and the image of my fifteenth birthday cake back into the side pocket of my winter coat.

Miles took his seat and apologized. "Babe, this isn't what I expected. I had no idea the town would be so crowded on a weeknight. I hope this is okay."

I forged a smile for him, not wanting to dishearten him by revealing my own disappointment with the night, with our marriage, or with this new life he had chosen for us.

"It's great," I encouraged and lied the way you do for someone you love, willing myself to feel some simple gratitude for the food he set before me.

At the only other table in the restaurant, a trio of undergraduate boys rated the girls walking past the window on an academic scale of "hotness." The thin boy with reptilian eyes and a fedora was the ringleader. "Okay, so a hot chick would be like a 4.0. An average cute one would be like 3.0 or 3.5, and a chick who is a 2.0 would be what we call fuckable only when drunk."

I wondered where a forty-year-old woman would rank, knowing that in our previous life, Miles and I would have made jest of their conversation, adopting it as our own, one of us winking at the other and proclaiming something like, "I think you're more a 3.5, babe, but for the rest of your curry dish and a quickie, I'll grant you a 4.0 for the night."

Instead, we stared blankly into our entrees, eating salty vermicelli while swatting away a fly that had somehow survived the winter and joined us for my milestone birthday celebration.

I wanted to go home and take off my heels, and while I was speculating about where our laughter had gone, Miles stood up. Regal in his suit and tie, as if we were at a large party in a room full of people, he cleared his throat. "I'd like to make a toast to my beautiful wife."

The three boys beside us grew silent. The asshole kid wearing the fedora clapped.

Noticing their attention fixed upon us, Miles sat back down and leaned in close to me. With his steaming cup of tea held high—to our disappointment, the restaurant served no wine—he lowered his voice.

"Claire, happy birthday. I love you. And despite your desire to leave on every light in the house when you go to bed, and although you *never* make chili con queso as good as mine, and even though you put chicken bones in the garbage disposal, which makes me insane, I love you still. I love that you make everyone you talk to feel like the most important person in the room.

"I love your big, loud laughter, and I love the way you play with Jonah, making spaceships out of blankets and boxes, launching him through the atmosphere in his booster seat. I love your pie crust. I love the way you kiss me. And maybe most importantly, I love the way you dance in your underwear when you're happy. I know you've been out of sorts since the move, babe, and I hope you'll be happy again soon." He touched his mug to mine. "Claire. Happy birthday!"

I sipped from my tea, feeling my bottom lip quiver while I blinked back tears, wishing that motherhood, that being his wife, that the privilege of those things alone could heal what was broken in me.

From his pocket Miles pulled out a gift, my favorite photo of Jonah making a spooky face in his Halloween shark costume. The picture was matted and placed inside a four-by-seven silver frame, engraved with the words "Boo Forever."

I hooted then. My big, loud laughter for Miles, the tears streaking my cheek, and I recognized a tiny bit of myself in the mounted image of Jonah's grin. I understood the way a child locks your love, how Miles and I would, no matter what, always be the two people who loved Jonah more than anyone else ever could.

Miles arranged the gift between us and said, "We have such a sweet boy, don't we? All those years of worrying we'd never get a baby, and we got the best one there is."

He gulped down the rest of his tepid chai and appropriated the mug, tucking it into the pocket of his sports jacket from which he had produced my gift. Noting my usual look of disapproval when he pinched a glass, he blushed. "A little souvenir to remember the night." Then he picked up a spongy slice of green tea cake from our tray, eating most of it in one bite, and brushed the crumbs from his newly mounting belly.

On the long, subzero walk to the car, we held hands, and despite my attempt to embrace the sweetness of Miles's gestures, his unusual attempt to be unrehearsed, the framed photograph, and a beautiful toast in my honor, I felt myself retreat. After all we had endured with the move and me giving up my career for his dream, followed by the heralding of my middle age that made me feel more old than middle, I had hoped the evening would somehow reassure me that I was—and that we as a family would always be—okay.

Out front of our house, Miles asked, "Kiss me?"

So I gave him my cheek and rubbed my hands together, forcing another grin in his direction, while I again slid from the moment into a memory of Dean guiding me across the creek, where we found a sandy stretch alongside the bird sanctuary and explored the uncharted parts of each other, ending the night on our backs, breathlessly regarding the summer constellation Scorpius, with its mythological sting.

When Miles opened the door, the sitter greeted us with, "Wow, you guys are home early!"

From the ten-dollar bills he kept held together with a paper clip, Miles peeled away twenty bucks and handed them to her. "Thank you," he said reaching for the girl's coat, which hung as thick and downy as a sleeping bag from a hook in the front hall.

And while he saw her out, I kicked off my shoes and slipped into Jonah's room. There I coiled up on the rug beside his crib. I closed my eyes and listened to the white noise machine project the crash of waves—the noise I still miss most.

Miles whispered through the door, "Claire, come to bed." But when I didn't respond, he crept in and covered me with the blanket I kept on the back of the rocking chair, tucking it tight around my body to keep out the cold.

Once, Miles would have lifted me from the floor and carried me to bed, coaxing me out of sleepiness and into passion with his lips and breath and warm, deft doctor's hands. But I could no longer even imagine such brazen desire on his part, much less on mine. I wanted to blame its disappearance on our move to the Midwest, whose lake waters, devoid of a changing tide, lacked the kind of dependability that kept me steady.

But I see now that my knock from our equilibrium was no fault of Madison but something that started seven years prior, in the meteorology lab back East when those images of the past returned to me. Unobstructed, looping like a movie reel, they grew more frequent during our futile efforts to make a baby; once we had Jonah they lessened some, but worsened again with the stress of the move, during which I bottomed out completely.

For three years prior to arriving in Madison, after the house was done, I'd made getting pregnant the new project and the central theme of my life. I thought about it at work, at home. I dreamed about babies—human babies, animal babies, myself as a baby.

I took all the assessments: ovulation testing, ovarian function tests, luteal phase testing, luteinizing hormone tests, follicle-stimulating hormone tests, estradiol tests, progesterone tests, prolactin tests, free T3 tests, total testosterone tests, free testosterone tests, DHEAS tests, androstenedione tests, cervical mucus tests, ultrasound tests, hysterosalpingograms, hysteroscopy, laparoscopy, endometrial biopsy.

And I made Miles get tested too.

Again and again I asked him to jerk off into a cup and deliver the specimen for semen analysis testing to the lab at the University of Connecticut Health Center, where he worked. And for me, he did this eleven times in desperate attempts to quell our frustration and disappointment.

"Are you sure?" I would plead. "It doesn't make sense. The results can't keep coming back normal." I wanted answers, scientific findings, to substantiate our failure.

Each time he took a test, Miles responded by handing me the printout from the lab screening and said nothing.

Sperm count: 40 Million
Sperm motility: Grade A .90
Sperm morphology: Regular .60
Pus cells: Absent, Volume 3 mil

To my dismay, we tested normal every time on every screening. Miles and I were both scientists, yet for us science failed to provide a hypothesis that explained exactly why we could not conceive. We were older, yes, but all the statistics were in our favor. Our parts worked, and our hormone levels—despite our "late parental age" of thirty-seven and thirty-eight years old— were, by all technical definitions, exceptional.

Yet with all those thermometers and charts, all those visits to make love in his office and at my lab, with all those quickies in the car, the planned overnights at downtown hotels and little inns by the sea, with all that lingerie I ordered online, we were disappointed every month, finding my period there again on day thirty-three, almost exactly at noon.

Gradually we lost our sense of humor and gained, instead, an awareness of our collective failure. Both of us blamed ourselves, then each of us quietly blamed the other. Finally, following Miles's announcement of "I just can't do this anymore, I feel like a farm animal," we conceived a baby without any scientific interventions on our fourth wedding anniversary.

When I came down the stairs with six smiling pregnancy test sticks, the sum total of two boxes, a bouquet of optimism that I presented to Miles where he sat on the couch writing a grant, he looked up at me, then examined each one.

"I guess there was nothing wrong with us," he announced, pulling me into his arms. For a moment he held my face between his hands, his eyes wide open and glossed with tears. "Finally," he whispered. Then he pulled me onto the couch, the weight of my body creasing his stacks of manila envelopes and medical journals as he climbed on top of me, breathing me in deeply, kissing my wrist, and directing my arms around his neck.

We held each other a long time. I cried from exhaustion and joy. And with most of our clothes on, clinging to each other, we surrendered the blame and made slow, deliberate love. Our jeans kicked off into crumpled piles by our toes, we kissed. Deep kisses. Kissing until our bodies boasted a celebratory rhythm and Miles's research notes slipped off the couch and scattered across the floor.

And for those first fourteen weeks of gestation, Miles read aloud to me each night from *What to Expect When You're Expecting*, whose title he edited with a black Sharpie marker to read instead: *What to ~~Expect~~ Obsess about When You're ~~Expecting~~ Obsessing*.

Nervous, we remained tentative with our humor and our

hope, anticipating the second ultrasound, waiting for the thud of the heartbeat to confirm the good news we would deliver to the world. Each of us raced to that appointment on our lunch breaks from work and waited in the darkened room, our hands folded in our laps, as we fixed our gazes onto the screen.

The sonographer guided the jellied end of the knob over my belly as I studied the black-and-white projection, depicting a clear image of our baby's head on a tiny tadpole body.

The technician said, "Let's see."

On the screen the image was static.

"Shouldn't it be right there?" I said. "The flicker?"

"Just a moment," the technician told me, nodding at my husband as she stepped through the door.

But I already knew from my husband's exhale, the furrow of his brow, his false smile, that there was no more baby.

"It's early," he whispered into the dark. "We haven't told any-body. And this is good news, really, that we even got pregnant."

Something inside of me unhinged. "*Good* news?"

"We can try again." Miles squeezed my hand as the doctor walked in.

I didn't squeeze back.

After that, Miles never mentioned the miscarriage.

I took a cab back to work.

The following day, another cab drove me to and from my D&C at the hospital where Miles held his clinic. There, a surgeon dilated my cervix before putting me under general anesthesia to remove the contents of my uterus, first using vacuum aspiration to take away the lifeless fetus, then a metal rod with a sharp loop to perform the curettage to prevent infection, scraping and scooping my insides that already felt broken.

While I was in the recovery room, Miles did not come to greet me. He said he wanted to be there, but I asked him not to. He didn't push it. Diving into a private sorrow, I chose to endure the loss of our baby alone because seeing Miles's disappointment only made me hurt that much more, believing my body was responsible for failing us and our marriage somehow.

Six months passed before we finally made love again, when following a holiday celebration for Miles's lab staff, we had drunken sex on the rug by the fireplace, where I woke up with my high heels and cocktail dress on, under a quilt Miles tossed over me on his way up to bed. The next morning, while I stood at the coffeemaker rubbing my eyes, he planted a wet one on my check and handed me a pint glass he had pilfered from the bar, filled to the lip with orange juice. "Fun night?" he said, a question to which he tentatively awaited my agreement.

Four months later, when I was too sick to hide it any longer, I announced to Miles that I was pregnant with our son Jonah. I had taken the initial pregnancy test at work, pushing away any glee as I dropped the result stick in the biowaste bin behind the Atmospheric Resources Lab where I conducted my research.

During workdays, when I knew Miles was with patients and too busy to contact me, I scheduled my ob-gyn appointments, along with the first three ultrasounds—one at seven weeks, one at twelve weeks, and one at twenty weeks, more pictures of my tiny baby than younger, more fertile moms ever get.

I didn't want Miles at those screenings because I knew if we lost Jonah, he would never shatter the way I would. So I made the pregnancy all mine. And as I navigated my fears for all nine and a half months of my term, I did so mostly alone, turning inside myself, hiding in the walk-in closet when I needed a good cry.

Jonah was born two weeks past his due date, a big ten pounder, with both of us present. And once we moved beyond the complications of his birth—the cord around his neck, the slice through my middle, both of us battered and bruised—Miles and I went home and clung to each other inside the farmhouse we had restored and finally furnished together. By the time the baby was seven or maybe eight weeks old, a time when I could not yet discern where my son began and I ended, Miles's desire for me became inexhaustible.

It was me, once insatiable and greedy with our love, who grew ambivalent about our marriage, struggling with the idea of sex after childbirth, incapable of recalling how exactly we came to make the sweet baby boy who took everything I had to offer. And as my breasts became a food source, their circumference expanding while my mind withered from sleep deprivation into something as sharp and capable as a bowl of oatmeal, Miles sought me more than he ever had in our shared life.

"Claire," he would whisper. "Let me touch you."

On the rare occasion that I attempted to undress for him, out of a sense of obligation for his patience and relentless desire, I grew modest in the company of that blousy flesh stitched together by a raised purple seam, where my formerly taut belly had been a place of pride. Instead, I wore my postpartum body like a relic of the labor trauma we were all fortunate enough to survive, but for me, my body seemed an impossible source of pleasure.

"Your body is so much curvier, and sexy and full," Miles whispered to me one night, taking a milk-drunk Jonah from my arms and lowering him into the bassinet beside our bed. "And I miss you, Claire. I want to be close to you."

Dizzy with fatigue, I ignored his request and fell onto the mattress with a peanut butter sandwich, wondering if I would ever again read a book, hold a complete thought, fit into my jeans, or be myself in some recognizable form. All day I had fantasized, not about making love to my husband, but about finishing my morning read of a one-page article in the *New York Times*, reporting the arrival of the Leonid meteor shower.

Leonid was at its cyclic crest that night in November, and from the heels of the constellation Leo the blitz of meteors would radiate as midnight struck, just when my new baby would stir for his third round of nursing for the night.

I told Miles: "If I sleep through Leonid, I will have to wait decades to see anything like it. At a peak like this, it will stream forty meteors per hour. It's no Halley's comet, but the sky will be majestic."

Miles pledged, "I won't let you miss this one."

He kissed a smudge of peanut butter from my upper lip and rolled over to set the alarm clock on his bedside table. He stirred restlessly as I read, and a few seconds later he pulled the article out of my grip. Kissing me again, tiny pecks, his uncertain hands fumbling with the buttons on the old flannel shirt that had become my uniform.

"I'm so tired," I said.

"Let me touch you, Claire," he pleaded. "It doesn't have

to be anything more than that." He tugged the shirt over my head. The scruff of his face grazed my back. The warmth of his mouth navigated down my spine. He caressed me for hours like that, one vertebra at a time.

Afterward, while Miles stayed sound asleep, I woke to Jonah's cries before the alarm ever rang. And with my tiny son swaddled tight in a blanket, I went downstairs, took my jacket from the hook, and walked out onto the deck, where I nursed him in a patio chair and Leonid fell over us like magic.

CHAPTER THREE

NOSTALGIA

FOR THE FINAL HOURS OF MY FORTIETH BIRTHDAY, Miles left me alone with Jonah to sleep. Beside him I pulled my knees to my chest beneath the blanket and fell into the memory of Dean feeding me a slice of sheet cake, each of us licking icing from the candles and kissing cake crumbs from the corners of each other's lips.

For so much of my adult life, I had kept those nostalgic memories of Dean archived, because stowed with them remained the grief I experienced as a girl, its expanse tucked away in an empty, haunted place inside of me, like a drafty cellar to which I kept the door closed. But exhausted by a sense of uprootedness, forlorn and longing for that feeling of home, disillusioned by the tedious nature of motherhood and marriage and aging, I permitted myself to reminisce with Dean and unlock the door to that memory, writing him again the next morning.

Dear Dean—

It was a Bonnie Bell Lip Smacker that I wore—Very Cherry. And I still wear it, even though I am, yikes, officially forty! (Great picture BTW.)

And, yes, I remember that windowsill in my mother's husband's house after my dad's funeral. I was wearing a navy blue romper and my pink ballet flats. It had to be 100 degrees in that room. So hot that summer. You told me you were sorry. You told me that my dad loved me, that you loved me. But then shortly after you slowly slipped away. I remember calling your house. Your mom always answered and I hung up. Then, for the first time in months, you surprised me with that giant cake. I remember thinking everything would go back to normal between us after my birthday. But, a week later, the neighbors told me you had gone off to Texas with Eddie Gabes. I realized that the cake was your good-bye. By the time you returned, I had already left for college.

I haven't thought about that in years.

Claire

We were in our church clothes when Dean reached under my romper, my face wet with the tears I tasted on his lips. Writing the email to Dean, I relived it, how it felt—being in the house that had haunted me all those years—the heat of that windowsill we pressed ourselves against, the vaulted walls in the cavernous Victorian house at Quayside that was like the hold of a ship into which my mother moved the wreckage of our lives after my father died.

And now I couldn't stop myself from seeing it, that big, white house emerging from the fog in a daydream that preoccupied my thoughts as I stood at the sink a thousand miles away, slicing an apple for my son.

So, when Dean told me that he was the new titleholder of 101 Quayside, perched in that very room where we had made love, the home office from which he wrote me, I felt the ache I'd always felt inside that house.

Claire—

Pretty tragic we never crossed paths when you were still in Connecticut. And in Mystic of all places, only twenty minutes up the road. We could've been doing this all over drinks. Also, I feel awkward mentioning this to you since you hadn't brought it up when you contacted me, and I'm surprised your mother wouldn't have told you, but I bought 101 Quayside from them a few years back. I saw Kat and Craig at the closing. Your mom looked great. She and I are actually Facebook friends. She reached out to me just once, maybe six months after the real estate market crashed, saying she felt bad, telling me she was certain that over time the house would regain its value. It's weird, right?

And, I should mention, I hadn't sought out the place or anything like that. Another broker told me it was listed. He thought it was a great investment but didn't have the capital and talked me into it. He got the commission, of course.

Anyway, I never intended to live here. We kept it as a corporate rental, you know, an income property. Too much of you inside these walls for me to consider it otherwise. But then things changed, business-wise and personally, so now I'm here on the waterfront.

Really, can you even fathom it? Me, a cranky east-end

son of a bitch, taking up residence with the yuppies? It's temporary. A transition. Soon I'll need to make some dough off the property, which never happened as it was supposed to, due to the market crash.

Anyway, I'm sitting in our window and all I can think about now is that romper and your skin underneath it.

Yours,

Dean

That evening at the kitchen table, Miles sat across from me looking over patient records while I reread Dean's letter over a glass of wine. My husband's glasses crept down the bridge of his nose, and he held the weight of his chin in his hand. His exhaustion and the stress of the job were evident in his posture.

"Can I get you something?" I offered, but Miles shook his head no without looking up, sighing before signing his notes.

Upstairs, Jonah was zipped into his sleep sack, curled onto his side, and through the video monitor, I studied his profile, the aquiline nose and cleft chin a mini replica of his father's, features I loved even more on the face of my boy for whom I would sacrifice everything.

"Is there some way I can help you?" I whispered to Miles. "Maybe organize your files?"

Again he shook his head without looking up from his paperwork, so I turned back to my computer screen and clicked on the list of Dean's Facebook friends. Skimming through the names, I noted our mutual acquaintance, Eddie Gabes, who Dean graduated with, the sweet, unsupervised teenage boy who grew up in a motor lodge, the same dear Eddie who sent me a friend request only hours after Dean and I reconnected.

With it, he attached a message about surviving a recent motorcycle accident that had claimed his right arm from the elbow down, asking for my prayers of support in what would be a very hard journey toward sobriety and wondering if I'd be willing to make a financial contribution on behalf of his recovery. And so I sent a money order for one hundred dollars in secret, never mentioning it to Miles, who would only have pointed out the statistical odds of our donation benefiting Eddie's cause.

Moving past Eddie, through the alphabetical listing of Dean's 422 other friends, I found Jimmy Pistritto, also from our hometown, who, last I heard, had served jail time for robbing a convenience store with a hunting rifle. Jimmy had always scared me, even before he pinned me down on a bed in the motor court where Eddie lived. That darkness at the center of him was something I'd recognized, even then, as having the potential to surge.

And just after Jimmy's name, I found my mother's, Kat Stackpole, toward the bottom of the list. I clicked the profile picture to enlarge it and studied her face smiling up from a book, a pink sunset and sandy beach behind her.

Facebook asked me, "Would you like to send Kat Stackpole a friend request?"

"No thank you," I said aloud and snapped my laptop shut.

I studied a waning last-quarter moon out the window over Miles's shoulder, and it was minutes before I realized I was crying, although I'm still not completely sure why.

This time Miles glanced up. "Claire, what's wrong?"

I topped off my wine. Held out the bottle toward his empty water glass.

"Babe, do you think maybe you're drinking too much?"

"It's only my second," I said defensively, wiping my face on the sleeves of my sweater.

"You seem down, sweetie. I worry that you're depressed. And I'm not sure what to do for you." Miles took off his glasses and set them on the table beside his stack of charts.

To his credit, my husband tried to comfort me. The following morning, sensing that I was lost, that something inside me was slipping, he made a rare appearance at home on a Sunday during a long weekend of cardiology call. Pushing through the door, he was full of apologies.

"Sweetie, I'm so sorry. Health care is changing so much right now, and this job is way more intense than I thought it'd be. I'm trying to juggle all the patient care demands at the hospital with teaching the fellows and my research responsibilities at the university. The whole academic clinician role feels impossible. I'm exhausted. All of this work, and not enough research time, then the pay cut combined with our student loans and the insane loss we took on the house when we sold. It's disheartening. Is Jonah sleeping already?"

"He's been down over an hour," I said flatly. "It's nine thirty. There are leftovers in the refrigerator. Foolishly, I had hoped we might eat as a family."

"Sorry," he said. "You need to let go of that expectation, Claire. It's going to be crazy for a while." Balancing an armful of shoeboxes stuffed with plastic bags, all of them ballooned with air and knotted at the top, he headed upstairs, calling back, "I've got a surprise for you."

Curious, I followed him up to our bedroom and peered into the boxes, examining silver glints of light.

"Fish?" I said.

But Miles had already run back out into the cold to heft a fifty-gallon aquarium from the hatchback of his Volvo, shuffling the bulk of it up the walk while trying to avoid a slip on the ice.

His weighty steps on the stairs signaled me to open our bedroom door, inside of which he steadied the tank on a wooden stand, catty-corner along my bedside. He stood back to admire the gift, his hands on his hips, as he stretched up onto his toes and grinned at me like a kid with cookie.

"Well," he admitted, "it won't sound exactly like the tide rolling in, but it's water. Salt water. And maybe watching the fish will soothe you some. Make you feel more at home, with your own tiny ocean."

"That's sweet," I said, softening, meaning it, wanting to unbutton the resentment I felt about the lonely weekend in a city where I was too new to possess friendships and too unfamiliar with the map to explore in what felt like a never-ending snowstorm.

We sat together in the good kind of quiet.

Still wearing his scrubs and wrinkled white coat, Miles cleaned the glass, tested the brackishness of the water with a hydrometer, installed the filter and heater, and added the coral, the plants, and the sand.

While he worked, I pulled plastic bags full of starfish, tiny sea horses, and two silver angelfish, intricately speckled, from the boxes. Setting them on the bed, I examined the delicate sea creatures inside each clear balloon and told Miles, "This is really nice. Thank you."

He turned to me, all smiles. I remember something in his shoulders easing.

"In fact," I goaded, "they look so lovely I want to eat them."

We both laughed at my reminder of Miles's single complaint about our move—the city's lack of fresh seafood, the reason, he claimed, for his new diet of burgers, pastries, and cheese curds, along with his fifteen-pound weight gain. And with my taunting, he tackled me onto the bed, arms dripping wet to the elbows.

"It's not a perfect situation," he reminded me, straddling my lap, holding me down against the pillows. "But it's an excellent place for clinical work and academics. It's the medical teaching setting I hoped for, with important science happening and Lasker fellows, all these great thinkers, and device innovations. It's the perfect combination, everything I wanted."

He kissed me hard on the cheek and returned to the tank.

"So these critters will need to bob around a while," he instructed, depositing the bags atop the water with the same gentleness I'd seen him use to place Jonah in the crib, with the careful hand I imagined he used to operate on his patients. "When the temp hits 78 Fahrenheit, cut their bags open and let them dive on in." He pulled a tiny thermometer from his pocket and left it on my nightstand.

"Thank you," I told him. "It's pretty."

"I'm still working on procuring a beach."

I leaned into him then, wanting to be close, to be held. Remembering how we were, how we could be.

Miles nuzzled a spot beneath my ear. "I miss you," he said, twirling a strand of my hair around his finger.

Clinging to my husband, I felt my morose mood dissipate. "I miss you too," I said in perfect time with the resounding ping of his pager.

"Probably the fellow." He sighed, crestfallen, searching his pockets to silence the noise. "I know, Claire, I know. I'm frustrated, too. It's just…the ER's a mob scene, really sick patients coming through. My procedures are booking months out, and all the fellows are still in their first few months of training. Walking them through the more complicated clinical cases is part of the deal. And then there are my research deadlines—I'm sorry I dragged you into all this craziness. But it won't always be this busy, honey. And I do believe that in the long run, this move will be good for all of us. The whole family."

I fell limp, my hands slipping from our embrace. This job was everything he wanted, yet it had claimed so much of him that there was little left for Jonah and me.

Miles phoned the hospital call operator and held the line. After listening for a while, he flatly asked a few questions about the patient, then said, "Sounds critical. Let's call anesthesia. Consent the patient and round the team. I'll head over now to scrub in."

After rummaging for his coat and keys, he came back to me, trying to be close. "We'll give it another sixteen months, fulfill the two-year contract, and if it's still not working for you, we can recalibrate." He kissed my forehead. "Okay?"

"Okay," I said. "Sixteen months from right now?"

"Yes." He glanced at his watch. "I'll sleep in the call room at the hospital tonight and try to swing by in the morning maybe, if it's not too crazy. To see the baby."

Downstairs I heard a fork scrape a bite from his dinner plate, then the slam of the door before Miles headed back out of the driveway and into the hospital for the night.

The next morning, when I woke to Jonah's cry, the spot beside me was empty, the sheets cool. Miles was maybe rounding on patients or at the lab hunched over slides, a coffee in hand, gliding through the work, refueled by it even.

But his ambition left me lonely. And motherhood too. Although it had been everything I wanted, it did not fulfill me the way I expected it would—the way science had. I felt so fortunate to be home with Jonah, so in love with him, and yet so completely bored by the routine of domesticity, daunted by the redundancy of household chores, which no matter how Miles tried, left me feeling undervalued and starved for intellectual conversations about things beyond how much toilet paper was left in the hall closet.

The timing of our move had made it hard for me to find work in the middle of the term, so I had chosen to stay home to attempt to be the kind of mom I most admired—the kind of mom I had always wanted for myself—one who found satisfaction in beautifying her home, one who had patience for the tears and the tantrums, one who loved cooking for her children.

When I left my career, I had imagined myself decorating Jonah's room as if it were a Pinterest board, cutting out owls for his walls to mount onto a hand-painted mural, and making all his food from scratch. But no matter how good I was at some of those things, mostly I failed. I was terrible at crafts and had no patience for baking, and often I became derailed because those kinds of things were not second nature to me, and because I felt myself becoming more and more disconnected from that decade of my life pioneering ozone research and identifying the chemical compounds contributing to environmental problems.

The things I had once been so successful at were orbiting out of my reach, and my knowledge of them was quickly becoming too obsolete for even the most lackluster professorship. So even though Jonah was an early talker and a good boy most of the time—although some days as inconsolable as me—I found myself longing for the easy gratification that comes from work. Simply, I pined for it more than I ever dreamed I would, and I felt ashamed about missing it.

I paused to admire the tiny ocean my husband had so sweetly brought home to me the night before. And as I stretched my feet out of bed, I discovered the smaller of the two angelfish stuck to the filter.

Unacclimated, I thought, exactly how I felt.

I studied the fish's eyes fogged dead white.

And as I rose, I wondered what else would be sacrificed for my husband's dreams of academic distinction that I'd been asked to chase.

After I learned that Dean had purchased 101 Quayside—the place that housed the poltergeists of my youth—my preoccupation with Dean grew like a cancer, a fixation Miles noted in the expression on my face.

"Claire, what is going on with you?" he asked, fiddling with his glasses. "I'm worried. You're distracted, like you're somewhere else all the time. You don't laugh. You're not playful like you used to be. I know you miss our life in Mystic. I miss it too. But this is a good place for us, babe."

Getting up from the table where we sat, I silently looped a scarf around my neck and tugged a wool beanie over my head. I moved into the living room and recalled the promises Miles had made when he took the job here, assuring me that it would mean more time spent with Jonah and more time to think about how we might grow our tiny family. I tossed another log on the fire, knowing that despite the best intentions, those promises were ones he could never keep.

With my wine in hand, I set my computer on the end table and dropped into the wingback chair by the hearth. I scooted closer to the blaze and pictured a different life: Dean living at the Quayside, drinking coffee in the third-floor bedroom with his beautiful wife, her long legs and perfect teeth, the sun in her eyes and backlighting her hair in the only photo I've seen of her on Facebook, in which she sits on the hood of a Jeep with her arm around Dean.

Dear Dean—

I haven't talked to my mother in years, so I never heard about your acquisition of the property. And, wow, Quayside is quite the place.

That said, I've always felt haunted there.

You may already know this, but as my mother explained

it to Kara and me, a long time back, the house was origi-nally built for a sea captain, Thomas Moses. According to the historical society, Captain Moses served on the USS *Constellation*, where in 1803 he became master of the brig. Then, in 1810 or thereabout, he bought that block of land along the beach and built the Quayside house for his wife and seven children. But he lived there only one year after the construction was finished because he died at sea during the War of 1812. There used to be a pretty creepy portrait of the old captain above the mantel, until Kara and I moved in with Mom. But it terrified my sister so much that she started to pee in the bed, so my mother sold it.

And, no, I really can't picture you there in that house or across the way at the White Sands Country Club, smoking your menthol cigarettes, having a PBR, and chasing it back with a shot of Jäger. I bet you turn some heads. But then again, you always did, and from your photos here, I see nothing in that department has changed.

It is snowing in the Midwest tonight. It never stops. And I do miss home, not the house you are in as much as the old farmhouse that Miles and I restored in Mystic, and always, my whole life, I've ached to go back and find my dad at his little place on Willard Street, where I first saw you shoveling snow.

Isn't it strange how we grew up in those tiny ranch houses, exactly the same, like they were dropped from a cake tin? Remember how you could hear the foghorns from the back deck? I miss the fog rising off the Sound

when the water is warmer than the air. I think the beach is my favorite this time of year. I'm so lonely for it. In fact, I've never been so lonely in all my life. It doesn't help that my husband is distracted with his new job. I'm actually jealous of the hospital. It's pathetic. I dream about breaking into it to kidnap him. Or the place vanishing all together. I have dark ideas about it. Anyway, the whole transition here is more than we had counted on. So I'm alone mostly, raising my boy and hoping to be scooped up from 3534 Topping Road by some crazy spaceship that'll take us away from this perpetual storm.

**   Much love,**

**   Claire**

The firewood in front of me popped and hissed. I sipped my wine and watched the embers warm to the color of a summer sunset, and then I returned my gaze to the screen, toggling through newly uploaded pictures of Dean.

In the shots he looked the part of an L. L. Bean model, rugged and strong. Unshaven, in his survival gear, he hiked up the backside of Connecticut's highest peak, Bear Mountain, wielding an ice pick. Standing beside a sign that read "Rica Junction, Appalachian Trail," he posed with his hands on his hips in the falling snow. With no stretch of my imagination, he looked better than ever, statuesque even, and in his gaze was all that old mystery about him.

I studied the pictures, zooming in to make out another face I recognized: Jimmy Pistritto, who ran around with Dean during our time together, until he was arrested for theft and sent to Enfield Correctional Institution just before I left town for college. In the snapshot Jimmy's eyes had the same dark leer I remembered, something sinister behind them as he furrowed his brow at the camera and held up a beer.

The rest of the shots were postcard images taken under a blue twilight, in which the Berkshire Taconic landscape was dusted with new snow. And while I was scrolling through scenes of mountains and valleys, the severity of that topography not found in the level terrain of the Midwest, Dean popped up on chat.

Dean: You there?

Claire: I am!

Dean: Just read your email. Captain Moses, huh? Fantastic, also, that you remember my love for shitty beer. PBR, yes please! I'm actually throwing back a tall one right now. Is it bad to admit that I can't stop thinking about you?

I hesitated, unsure how to respond, wondering how much to encourage what he initiated, sensing the momentum of it, understanding then that I could let myself grow dangerous with him again.

Dean: Well, I can't stop thinking about you. About us.

Claire: We had fun.

Dean: You were so beautiful. And smart. But we were so young. I wish I met you later, when I was more grounded. When we knew ourselves better. When I knew what I wanted. Maybe we would have had a shot.

Claire: Are you grounded now?

Dean: Maybe not completely, but I've sure as hell learned a lot.

Claire: Me too.

Dean: Let's have dinner sometime.

Claire: I'm eating dinner now. By the fire.

Dean: What are you wearing? ;)

Claire: Sweater, hat, scarf, and jammies. In my defense, I'm freezing to death. It's colder here than anywhere I've ever been in my life.

Dean: You need a bigger fire and some company. You know, I can see it—you there in the window, all by yourself with your dinner plate, wearing flannel pajama pants. The girl I remember. It makes me sad. I want to snatch you up and take you out for dinner on a proper date, with PDR tall boys for me, and for you, a few gallons of red wine.

Claire: I need all of that.

Dean: I'll head right over.

I giggled like a teenage girl, flattered, eager to pursue the fantasy when Miles stepped in front of me, eating a giant cookie covered in red and green sprinkles.

"What's funny?" my husband asked, licking crumbs from his lips and coming to stand beside me.

My face blushed as if my flirtation was apparent. "Just emailing friends."

My computer sounded as another message from Dean popped up on my screen.

Miles smiled, sat on the arm of my chair, and asked optimistically, "Friends here?"

"Home," I said. "I don't have any friends here." I pulled my computer close to my body, shielding the screen.

He nodded and took another bite of his dessert.

"I made those cookies for Jonah," I told him.

"Can't I have one?"

I shrugged and patted Miles's belly.

"For warmth," he said, sucking it in. "I'll run again when the snow melts. Oh, and, honey, can I ask you one more thing?"

"Yes," I said, half listening, glancing down at my computer, eager to get back to Dean.

"Did you tell the neighbor across the street that we were only here until the end of the year?"

"I guess I did." I paused. "Why?"

"Well, first of all, because it's not at all true, and second, because her husband works in the Department of Medicine."

"So?"

"So we have a two-year obligation, Claire. That's the absolute minimum before we can even begin to discuss other

options. You know that. Anyway, her husband came up to me
in the lab and asked if I was already looking at other jobs. My
reputation is important, babe, especially if we should ever want
to make a change, which right now I don't. I can see this place
being really great for us. Madison is a beautiful city. And, my
colleagues need to know I am committed to the department
and the research at hand."

I sipped from my wineglass. "Sorry," I said.

"And by the way," Miles told me through his final mouthful of cookie crumbs, "you left the oven on. I turned it off. I
smelled something burning. Same thing happened yesterday
after you went to bed. Could you be more careful? Maybe
you're distracted. But just, please, honey, take more care."

"Yup," I said, nodding. Wanting him to leave me alone. "I'll
be more careful."

He leaned in to kiss my forehead and stood. "I'm going to
work on my grant a while. Don't wait up on me."

"Okay. Good night."

Miles shuffled off in his slippers, and as he went, I read the last
bit of Dean's correspondence, queued in our thread.

Claire, don't you wonder what it would be like with us now? As
grown-ups? Hopefully, this isn't saying too much. But I wonder.
In fact, I've wondered about that for a long time.

Since he was no longer on chat after Miles left the room,
I sent Dean a brief email before logging off and heading up
to bed, hesitating momentarily before delivering my own
restrained confession.

Dean—

You <u>can't</u> say too much after all we shared. After all you did for me. And thank you for the compliments. I'll admit, I've wondered too. And I've imagined it some. In any case, I hope you're happy and well.

    Love,

    Claire

Closing my laptop with my feet stretched out toward the hearth, I thought then about fire and its scientific definition—"a high-temperature, self-sustaining chemical reaction, resulting in heat and often casting flames"—quite certain that Dean and I still had that old fire between us, in every sense of the term.

CHAPTER FOUR

FIRE

Mr. Barnet, my ninth-grade science teacher, wore the same green-and-black flannel shirt every day of my freshman year, cuffing his sleeves to reveal a periodic table tattoo on his forearm. I'll never forget his lessons in fire, as they influenced most who I would become that year—and who I would become again so much later in my life.

Mr. Barnet began the first unit on combustion by announcing: "Fire is one thing in nature that is not matter."

I can still hear the force of his chalk striking the blackboard as he wrote in block letters:

Fire = Combustion.
Fire = The visible, tangible side effect of matter <u>changing form</u>.

He turned to face the class, rubbing his goatee.

Someone let out a belch.

Norwell Jackson, the captain of the basketball team, was tipping back in his chair, playing with a Rubik's Cube. Mr. Barnet pegged Norwell in the shoulder with his eraser, a warning.

Then, he turned to me. I was snapping my gum when he

said it, the words I still hear every time I see flames: "Fire is a weapon with unlimited power."

Onto the overhead projector, Mr. Barnet placed an artist's sketch originally printed in an old *Harper's Weekly*, rendering the Great Chicago Fire that we were reading about in history class, the sky dark with smoke, masses of people running from towering flames.

"Here's an example of a fire that burned for two days, from October eighth through October tenth, 1871, after either Catherine and Patrick O'Leary's cow kicked over a kerosene lantern or, more likely in my scientific opinion, fragments from Biela's comet ignited a spark that started a barn fire carried on southwestern winds, reducing the city to ash."

He placed another sketch of an incinerated city onto the overhead. Only the skeletons of the brick buildings remained after the inferno had been extinguished.

"Fire is combustion," Mr. Barnet told us. He then lit a piece of paper with a Bunsen burner and tossed it the air. It burned to dust before ever touching the floor. "Combustion is the chemical process that makes things burn."

In the back row, Norwell Jackson cleared his throat and flicked his Zippo lighter, while Mr. Barnet continued his lecture without skipping a beat. "Fire isn't matter at all. That flame is an oxidation process, not unlike rusting or digestion, but this chemical process differs from those because it releases heat *and* light. It makes fire intense, it makes the big ones unforgettable, and it makes all of it sexy."

I had never heard a teacher use the word "sexy" before. The rest of the class seemed unimpressed, but I was rapt.

His next slide featured the space shuttle's engines, fueled with liquid hydrogen and liquid oxygen. He explained how the reaction between the two chemicals—in what appeared to be a very fiery explosion beneath the orbiter—created a propellant that launched the spacecraft into flight.

With a yardstick, Mr. Barnet slapped the screen where the combustion burned red.

"This element, fire, can destroy an entire house in less than an hour, and a vehicle, if ignited from the inside out, in half that time. Propelling a rocket into space takes only T minus 26.6 seconds."

That January 1986, the month of my fourteenth birthday and the start of my second semester of ninth grade, had been dubbed "the year of astrophysical encounters" by NASA, which had arranged for the space shuttle to launch in time to ride the tail of Halley's comet. Their hope was to study the comet with all the technology gathered in the seventy-five years since its prior visit, while hosting a teacher, Christa McAuliffe, from a New Hampshire town two hours north of our own.

But all that enchantment vanished as the *Challenger* split in two that morning of January 28, a Tuesday, after seventy-three seconds in the air. The explosion seemed not just the symbol of a dream turned to ash, but also became the image I would forever associate with the collapse of my parents' marriage.

Arriving late at school that day, I jumped out of Dean's

truck—racing past the office, dodging the tardy sign-in sheet—and sprinted down the hall to our high school auditorium with my model of the comet in hand. I prayed to Mary, Joseph, and all the saints we learned about in catechism, that I had not missed the countdown and liftoff with our New England heroine on board.

I made it in time and scooted to the edge of my seat as the missile ascended under the combustion of the engines that Mr. Barnet had explained to us. The spacecraft arced through the air, a white tail like the comet's trailing behind it. But shortly after the launch, unexplained dark smoke billowed out beneath the shuttle as the rocket split in two. Our teachers looked at each other, and the broadcasters went silent.

In an instant, the illusion dissolved, and I knew that burning up with the shuttle and our dreams were all the letters we had written to the crew, including Judith Resnik, the second female astronaut in space, and Christa McAuliffe, the teacher who had visited our classroom and to whom we spent much of our first semester drafting and typing up letters.

January 5, 1986

Claire Spruce
290 Willard Street
East Lyme, CT 06333

NASA c/o Christa McAuliffe
Teacher in Space Project
Johnson Space Center, Houston, TX 77297

Dear Mrs. McAuliffe,

In one week you will take off from Kennedy Space Center at 11:38 a.m. and as soon as you go, you will become a hero. In fact, you already are a hero to me. Even though I am only fourteen, I think about my future a lot. I run track and work on yearbook so that I can be the first person in my family to go to college. I was a Girl Scout in elementary and middle school and learned the basics of camping and survival. I can even make a fire with a flint and two sticks. I have patches on my badge to prove it, but I was never good at selling the cookies.

This year my science class will be participating in the Teacher in Space Project and I am very excited to take classes broadcasted from the shuttle. Do you think there is a chance of seeing Halley's comet as it rotates the Earth? We have a telescope at our school, but even with a study hall pass no one is ever allowed to use it. I would love to see pictures of it from where you are.

I was hoping you might send me your picture and autograph so that I can include them in my science project called, "The

Ultimate Field Trip." I am making a model
of Halley's comet to go with it. A couple
more questions: (A) Do you have any kids?
(I think it would be so cool if my mom
went up in space to see the comet!) (B)
Did you always know you wanted to go into
space? (I have known since I was born that
I want to study the atmosphere.)

Good Luck!

Claire Spruce

Grade 9
Lyme High School

Watching the shuttle falling from the sky, I imagined my
letter falling too, part of the ominous confetti sprinkled over
the Atlantic, and sinking into the deep. And in that audience
where I sat with my classmates after the explosion, we waited
quietly, more quiet than we'd ever been in school, and perhaps in our whole lives.

In the auditorium we scanned the walls decorated with red,
white, and blue streamers, but the horns we had blown at
liftoff went unsounded in our laps. From my pocket I pulled
the letter Christa McAuliffe had returned to me and clasped
it to my chest, my rib cage heaving, as I unfolded the creased
paper and read it again, certain already that she was dead.

NASA

Teacher in Space Project

Johnson Space Center, Houston, TX 77297

Claire Spruce

290 Willard Street

East Lyme, CT 06333

January 19, 1986

Dear Claire:

I am delighted that you took the time to
write. When I was fourteen, I really wasn't
sure what I wanted to do, so you are ahead
of me there, but I was always very active
in Girl Scouts, just as you mentioned you
were in elementary school. And, like you,
I have been eagerly awaiting Halley's
visit, as it will be the only chance in
my lifetime to view the comet orbiting
Earth. On our mission we will carry out
the first flight of the shuttle-pointed
tool for astronomy (SPARTAN-203). It is
a Halley's comet experiment-deployable
device that will allow us to observe and
photograph the comet. It will be incorpo-
rated in several of the lessons from space
that I will be teaching in partnership

with your school as part of the Teacher in Space Project and the Shuttle Student Involvement Program (SSIP).

As you might imagine, I am excited about going into space on the Shuttle Challenger and I hope that more young women like you are going to be interested in NASA career opportunities later on in life.

To answer your question, I have two children, a boy and a girl. I miss them dearly, as my training at the Johnson Space Center here in Houston keeps me far from home. But, that said, it has been very exciting for me to take advantage of this opportunity and I look forward to my mission in late January.

Enclosed is the photograph you requested, and thanks again for writing. I will be carrying the letters from your class with me as a token for good luck on our mission.

Sincerely,

S. Christa McAuliffe

The sacrifice of the *Challenger* crew—and for me, the loss of Christa McAuliffe, especially—revealed the profound truth, that we were all changed by watching the orbiter breaking apart and those seven crew members dying in front of us while their spacecraft disintegrated over the Atlantic Ocean. We were no longer the children we had been, and at fourteen years old, we turned inside ourselves.

The girls sitting in the folding chairs in front of me no longer held hands and grinned at each other in excited anticipation. Each person in that room dived solo into grief. No one ate their pizza slices, and our ice cream melted in the plastic bowls in the back of the auditorium as a teary-eyed Mr. Barnet rolled the AV equipment away.

Ushered into our adulthood, we awaited Principal Jensen's voice over the loudspeakers to announce what was already clear—Christa McAuliffe, the thirty-seven-year-old mother of two, who bore a likeness to our own mothers, would not be teaching three classes from outer space. Something had gone terribly wrong.

We were let out of school early, and I waited for my mom to pick me up, trying to understand how I could ever let go of that dream, the moment I had waited for all year. I asked myself if there were any guarantees, any promises that our parents or NASA or even President Reagan could keep. And I clearly remember deciding then that if he asked, I would give myself to Dean.

I don't remember her doing this any other time, but that afternoon of the *Challenger* disaster, my mother left her job as an emergency room nurse at Hartford Hospital early to pick up Kara and me from our schools. Out front of my high school, Kara waved apathetically from the front window of Mom's station wagon, signaling their arrival.

Both my sister's and my mother's eyes were red from crying, yet their duplicate beauty was still intact. Kara's and Mom's full lips quivered; their mouths were downturned. I got in back and we drove in silence. In the rearview mirror, I watched my mother blink away the tears that streaked her eye makeup and soaked her face. Behind me, grocery bags rustled as we made the sharp turns leading up to our driveway.

Parked in front of our house were my Uncle G's plumbing van and my dad's friend Rex's battered Jeep with its notorious bumper sticker: *Draft Beer, Not Boys.*

Inside, the guys played cards—their weekly Tuesday afternoon poker match, something my father had organized with his friends who were also out of work, either by choice like my uncle or because they were walking the picket line like Dad and Rex. Sometimes other neighborhood guys joined them, but most often it was just Dad, Rex, and Uncle G who sat around the table, all of them going through various strings of jobs, unemployed on and off for years. The game gave their calendars some consistency and was one they had played since high school, never missing a week, except for a couple of years after their numbers were called for the Vietnam draft.

My father was the only one who served in that war. Uncle G, my mother's brother—or, as my dad called him, "the Lucky Fuckin' Mick"—had failed his physical examination due to the Ménière's disease he blamed every time he got drunk and fell down. "And Rex dodged the whole mess," Dad explained to us once, "to marry Marian, his first wife, the prettiest of the three, moving with her up to godforsaken Halifax, Canada, to make candles and sell salt cod." But following my father's and Rex's return after those nearly two years away, the three amigos all picked up where they left off and the games resumed at our house.

That January afternoon, in lieu of the poker chips they could not find, the men used my mother's sea glass as their markers. Mom stored her prized collection in giant mason jars sorted by colors—one filled with just the rare blues, another with greens, a jar for whites, one for the browns, and then the most treasured, filled with pinks and broken pieces of antique pottery.

"What the hell are you doing?" Mom asked my father when she stepped in from the cold and up to the table with bags full of groceries. Her mouth was pinched.

My father scratched his beard with his cards. "What the fuck does it look like we're doing?"

Rex eyed my mother, thumbing a gold crucifix nestled in the thicket of chest hair that grew up from his V-neck sweater and blowing cigarette smoke from his nose like a dragon.

Next to him, Uncle G wore a plumber's shirt monogrammed with "Hot Shit" where his name tag should read "Gerald." He had a thick mustache like Magnum P.I. and a Marlboro hanging from his lip.

"Don't get your panties in a tangle," he told my mother, his sister. "We couldn't find where you hid the poker chips so we compromised." He smiled then and flicked his ashes into an empty beer can.

Without a word, Mom leaned over the table. Sweeping her

arm across the surface, she collected the cards, her colored sea glass, and all the dollar bills on the kitchen table into a paper bag holding the week's produce. She looked at my father as she did it. Even in her fury, my mother was beautiful, her Irish skin rouged, her pursed lips seeming the caricature of a kiss.

"Guess that's fold," Rex announced, leaning back in his chair.

Uncle G ran the back of his hand across his forehead. His palms were dirty with the work he'd been doing on our water heater in exchange for a place to crash while he was in between girlfriends. "Kat, you need a drink," he told my mother.

In one pull, Mom guzzled the beer that was sitting in front of my father. "I'm taking a walk. Don't wait on me."

Next to me on the living room couch, Kara colored while I watched my parents. I thought about the note my mother had left for my father that morning, the one I had read after snatching it off Dad's dresser. It remained wadded up in the pocket of my parka, and because I'd taken it, my father spent much of his morning walking the picket line with Rex, oblivious to Mom's impending split.

"You're dismissed," Dad shouted at my mother and pointed to the door. "Take your walk. Weather might cool you off."

I was anticipating my own dismissal after homework was done so I could meet Dean at the creek. While my uncle helped himself to another beer, I opened the *World Book Encyclopedia* to the letter *C*. Under a photograph of an old cave wall with a comet sketched across it, I read the Mongolian legend that dubbed comets "the daughters of the devil, warning of destruction, fire, storm, and frost whenever they approached the Earth."

When I looked up from the book in my lap, my mother was pulling on her green winter boots and tying her scarf. Then she slammed the door behind her.

I wondered if perhaps Christa McAuliffe had suffered from Halley's arrival as the legend predicted. And as my mother disappeared, my panic rose. I feared she too might be placed in some unknown jeopardy out there in the cold with the falling dark, so I grabbed my coat and hat and followed behind her.

"Dad—" I called.

"Just go," he yelled back.

For a year, my mother had been walking to Sea Glass Beach alone when she was angry or quiet or sad. But I could remember a time when she'd walk off with my father, hand in hand. And just a year prior, on the Fourth of July, the four of us had walked beyond the creek and over the seawall together. Everyone was disappointed because thunderstorms rained out the fireworks, but to assuage our disappointment, Dad brought two kites on the trip to surprise us. One was a dragon with a long yellow tail, and the other was a neon butterfly.

Kara and I had moseyed down the beach, but Dad ran with a kite in one hand, gripping my mom's palm in the other. They raced like kids down the sand, as Dad's dragon and Mom's butterfly took flight.

Dad hollered to Kara and me to catch up. "Girls, come on! Let's get them higher!"

Kara had an orange Popsicle stain around her mouth and bent over breathless, her hands on her knees, when we finally reached my father.

Mom held both kites while Dad pulled additional spools of twine from his shorts' pocket. My mother smiled at me, the wind whipping her long, dark hair in her eyes, as the mansions beyond the seawall hovered like disapproving chaperones.

Dad added to the lines and showed us how to let the twine out slowly. "Give barely an inch at a time, or you'll crash and burn."

"You're a damn fool," Mom told my father as he added a third spool. She shook her head, but she laughed loud.

When the thunder cracked, Mom looked at my father, then at us. "Maybe that's enough."

"We're grounded," Dad said. He kicked up a shoe. "Rubber-soled sneakers."

My mother was barefoot.

Lightning struck and the sky darkened to almost purple.

Mom turned toward home, her kite trailing behind her, and hollered into the wind, "Peter? Girls? You coming?"

Kara did cartwheels on the wet sand. Pink shoelaces hung from her ponytails. Her scatter of freckles, the beauty of her high cheekbones, and the heart shape of her face made her my mother's twin.

"Kat, you're no fun anymore," my father shouted back. "You used to be fearless."

Mom stood still a moment. She examined my father. There was a pause. A change washed over her face. Then she let go of her twine completely and we all watched her kite nosedive into the ocean.

But as I tailed my mother after she took down Dad's poker game, she was anything but still. Her anger fueled her speed, and she kept a good forty paces beyond me, shrinking toward the horizon. With her ponytail wagging behind her, she could easily be mistaken for a girl my age.

At the creek, our first marker, I wondered if my mother would run and leap the width of the water. Unsure of the tides and fearing that she might find herself immersed, her down coat billowing as it filled with a current that could easily take her under, I ran to catch up.

But the tide was dead low and my mother marched right across the creek, soaking her green boots. On the sand she broke into a run that lasted until she reached the breakwater, and then she scaled the five-foot rise of the rock wall and dropped over the side.

She was out of my sight for several minutes, the jetty separating us from each other. When I finally crested the climb, I stood atop the granite ledge a moment, wanting my mother to look back, to call my name and wait for me to join her. But she kept jogging ahead, her tied hair swinging behind her like a pendulum.

Beyond the wall, I dropped onto the beach, my momentum growing sluggish against the wind as I chased after her in my heavy moon boots.

Across the creek was a world so different from the one we lived in. There homes were the size of city blocks, and fancy inns rose above manicured walkways to claim ownership of the frost-covered sand. Passing the mansions, I could no longer concentrate on my stride, and I slowed, peering into their lit windows and thinking about how my father admired those kinds of master homes, always claiming that with a little more money our lives would be all ease.

To my shock, there at Quayside, my mother veered off the strand and down a pebbled path, while I made ground on her. Close enough to track her course, I followed her up to a paved drive, to the walkway of a house whose colossal door she opened and entered as casually as if it were her own.

I stopped in my tracks, taking in the house my mother had entered. It was grand and white, erected in the time of whalers, when women walked its watch in petticoats and squinted out over the ocean for a glimpse of familiar ships coming home. As I stood shivering in the dark, a room on the second floor of the three-story house brightened. From my vantage point, I saw a leather sofa next to a large desk covered in papers. Next to the desk was a huge telescope, even more remarkable than the one in Mr. Barnet's science lab, and it pointed out toward the blue. I had trouble believing that my mother could know someone there, yet there was a throb in my belly all the same.

Mom came into view, and I shook my head in disbelief as she shed her white ski parka and hung it on the telescope, as if it were a coat hook. I thought of Christa McAuliffe, her smiling face in the autographed picture, and how my mother had cried and cried when she drove us home from school only hours ago.

In the illuminated window, a slim man with silver hair approached my mother. His robe was the same stark white as her parka, white like the telescope and the clapboards of the house, white like the drifts of snow that collected along the breakwater.

He put his arms around her.

I held my breath.

What I wanted then, what I prayed for, was that my mother would turn toward the window, somehow seeing me there in the impending dark, and that my presence would stop her from doing what would happen next. But in the orange light of the room, she unfastened the man's robe and slipped it from his shoulders. He stood before her naked, something I forever wish I had not seen. Then, she pushed him onto the desk and climbed on top of him with her green boots and jeans still on, while pulling her turtleneck over her head.

"Mom, no!" I shouted.

Gulls shrieked back from breakwater, and anger percolated from where my worry and sadness had been.

Part of me wanted to run inside, to catch her red-handed and say simply, "Come home." And another part of me, the biggest part, wished I had never crossed the breaker to discover her.

Full of adrenaline, I raced home, slipping as I ascended the cold rock jetty, and charged toward the creek. Rushing through the rising tides of the stream, I was soaked waist high. Undone by what I had witnessed, I wished those waters could quell the fire in my heart, but it bloomed into an inferno no ocean would ever halt.

Back in the empty living room of our tiny ranch on Willard Street, I peeled off my wet Levis and wriggled into a dry pair from a laundry basket left on the couch. From the television blaring into the empty room, President Reagan assured a grieving nation that the Teacher in Space Project would persist.

"We'll continue our quest in space," he said. "There will be more shuttle flights and more shuttle crews and, yes, more volunteers, more civilians, more teachers and women in space. Nothing ends here; our hopes and our journeys continue."

On the deck off the back of our house, out beyond the chatter of the media's questions to a deflated-looking President Reagan, I could see the silhouettes of Rex, Uncle G, and my father, who held Kara's hand. The men passed a joint between them, and when I opened the door, I was surprised to find that the discussion was not about my mother's departure, but NASA's inability to determine the cause of the explosion.

My father spoke in a grave tone. "By now, there's not a prayer that anyone on that crew survived. My platoon leader once told us that the brain could only last four minutes without air before the functions broke down. By six minutes it's game over. They're gone."

Rex shook his head, his arms folded across his chest. Despite the chill he wore no coat. "We won't hear anything until the Coast Guard finds the debris."

From where they stood, I could hear foghorns in the distance.

Uncle G dropped the butt on the deck and snuffed it out with the toe of his boot. "NASA's going to keep this bullshit 'no comment' policy when it comes to the astronauts. They might know the whole story now, all those radios and devices on that rocket, but they aren't gonna tell the public shit until they're good and ready. And I promise you this: none of it will be their fault."

"Dad," I interrupted, "I'm going to work on my comet project with my lab partners. Can I be back by ten?" I wanted to ask him about my mother, if he knew when she would return, but I couldn't find the words.

"Great," Dad mumbled, staring as far off as the Milky Way. He pulled the winter cap Mom had knit him for Christmas over his ears. "Walk your sister to the skate pond when you go and I'll pick her up when she's ready."

Kara and I kicked a stone between us as we walked through the neighborhood. Tasseled with blue and pink pompoms, her skates were slung over her shoulder. "I thought your project was done," she said. "Didn't you bring it to school already?"

We both watched our feet.

"This is a different thing," I lied. "Group work. Individual projects were handed in."

Kara stopped dead in her tracks and set her skates on the ground. Her face was the carbon copy of our mother's. Even her expression, the way she pressed her lips together, was the same. "The astronauts, do you think they felt it?" she said.

Ahead of us, the street lamps wore halos.

"Felt what?" I said.

Kara shouted to hear herself from under a pair of fuzzy earmuffs. "The fire. All of us watching them burn to death?" Her voice echoed off the indistinguishable houses lining our street.

"No," I lied again. "I think it happened before they felt a thing." But in my mind I imagined air masks falling from overhead compartments, sirens, the shudder of the cabin, heat from the flames, followed by the resonating clap of the fatal belly flop the capsule made off the coast of Florida. I pictured each of the crew members' faces watching the others from behind their masks as their oxygen winked out, while at home a thankful Barbara Morgan, the runner-up for the mission, ate Doritos and drank Cherry Coke with her kids, watching the whole thing from her couch, grateful to God that it wasn't her, after all, who got to be the Teacher in Space.

I took Kara's mittened hand in mine, and as we turned into the warming hut at Marsh Cove Park, I lied to her one last time to protect her from the sadness in her eyes. "They never even had a second to think about anything other than how happy they were to be chasing Halley's comet across the sky."

"Good," Kara said. She shifted her weight from one foot to the other and waved to her friends.

"Call Daddy to come get you when you're done," I told her and handed her a shiny dime.

Then, as I had done only hours before while tracking my mother, I rounded the bend, where, at the creek's dead-end, I saw the billowing exhaust of Dean's truck. I hadn't expected him to be there before me.

He sat alone in the dark, leaning against the bed of his pickup, the tailgate open, blowing cigarette rings at the night. He was handsome like Simon Le Bon, the lead singer of Duran Duran, my favorite band in those days, but in a tougher, less British way. In his jeans and camouflaged hunting jacket, with his cigarettes and coffee, Dean already seemed somewhat old. I guessed that having four sisters and no dad at home weighed him down with a cargo of responsibility. At seventeen years old, he had a steadier job than my dad, and working hard to make money for his family seemed to be the thing he honored most.

Dean pointed to his watch when he saw me. "You're early," he said. "I'm glad." He walked toward me across the frozen ground and wrapped his arms around my neck, whispering, "I've been thinking about you all day."

We stood like that, holding each other until I shivered.

"It's bitter," he said and escorted me to the passenger side of the pickup.

In the cab, Dean played Dream Academy on the tape deck and began to kiss my face and neck, pulling me out from my layers of clothes. The windows fogged with the heat of our breath. The tape clicked over to the B side. Dean slid one hand inside my jeans. The other tugged his belt from its buckle.

"Wait," I said.

Dean touched my face. "Don't be afraid."

My eyes filled with tears, but I was no longer sure who I was crying for.

"Trust me?" he asked.

I nodded and disappeared inside myself as Dean leaned me across the bench seat. His mouth made its way down my chest.

I wondered where my mother was.

Resting a warm hand on my belly, Dean slid the fabric of my panties to the side.

"Open your legs," he whispered.

When I didn't respond, he did it for me.

I held my breath until his mouth found its way back to my neck and lips.

He pressed his forehead against mine. Our noses touched. His mouth tasted of coffee and smoke, and he buried his hands in my hair. I surrendered then and closed my eyes, envisioning the rocket split in two, my mother's coat hung from the end of the telescope, the man dropping his robe to the floor, Mom's green boots, her turtleneck over her head. And I saw flames for the first time—red, orange, and blue.

Barely touching me, Dean made half-moons with his thumbs on the lobes of my ears and lured me into a spell. With his fingers and tongue, he stirred my need for him until it turned urgent.

He whispered, "I'll be careful."

Against a moment of pain, my mind went blank.

Then the tape ended, the music silenced, and the strange day vanished with it.

In a way that felt safe, like possession or love, Dean took my face in his hands and stared into my eyes. "My girl," he whispered. He smiled reassuringly and smoothed my hair off my forehead, before starting the whole process over again.

Thinking back on it now after all that happened over the past twelve weeks, I believe Dean understood all those years ago that some part of me would forever belong to him, because for me, sex would never again be that forbidden or dangerous or new.

That night of the *Challenger* explosion, as I lay sleepless in my twin bed beside Kara, who snored lightly from beneath her covers, restless images of my mother circled my mind. I could not shake the vision of her hanging her parka from the end of that telescope, the naked man draped in his robe like a king, or Mom's bare back as she pulled her turtleneck over her head.

Unable to sleep, I padded out our front door in my coat and slippers to my mother's station wagon, which we had nicknamed the Dove, parked in the street along the curb. I swear it was beckoning to me to stop her.

It was unlocked, as always, so I climbed inside. Gray upholstery drooped from the ceiling, fabric that flapped in the wind like the wings of a bird whenever we drove the car with the windows down.

The old 1973 Chevy was in constant need of repair. Dad often put it on blocks to work on it himself, but watching him do so caused all of us alarm. My father's body was not as strong as it had been the year before, when he was still working as an engraver at Colt Firearms, and my mother seized every occasion she could find to remind him of this fact.

Something about going on strike had caused his midsection to grow softer, not fat exactly, but rounded at the waistline, more like a woman's belly than a man's, while my mother grew slimmer and slimmer with her Richard Simmons exercise tapes and the pink cans of Tab she took along for her walks to Sea Glass Beach.

The interior of the Dove contained parts that I had learned would be easy to ignite: carpets, seat foam, soft plastic along the dash—the highly flammable materials we had learned about in Mr. Barnet's chemistry unit on combustibles. And the paper cups and newspapers stacked on Mom's passenger's seat made for perfect kindling.

Before I struck the match, I sat inside the car in my pajamas, rummaging through the glove box, where I discovered a picture of Mom and Dad before Kara and I were born. In the snapshot Mom wore an A-line minidress and held their goofy Scottie dog, Holiday, in her lap, while Dad, who looked like a little boy with his crew cut and Army uniform, leaned in for a smooch.

I studied the picture before putting it back, wondering how she could leave my father, whom she had moved in with before they were married, when she was still seventeen. It was unfathomable to me then that my own mother could actually walk into another house, a completely different kind of life, and take off her clothes for that silver-haired man.

But, looking back, I remember Mom talking about different kinds of lives, lives out of our reach, lives she envied, wanting them for herself and our family. Those notions were divulged to all of us when my parents fought, most often over the money we never had, or when my mother came home from a double shift still in her starched, white nursing uniform to find a messy house and my father and his friends watching television or shuffling a deck of cards.

Her message to Dad was always the same: "I worked forty-eight hours straight and I come home to this," punctuating her assault by reminding my father of all his failed promises. "When we got married you said you'd take care of us, Pete.

You promised I'd be able to stay home and raise my kids."
Sometimes Dad would reach for her; other times he would
grow heated, frustrated by his inability to grant her that life.
But no matter how he responded, Mom headed straight out
the door for her walk, and I had discovered where she went
to seek comfort.

Wadding up sections from the *Hartford Courant* on the Dove's
passenger seat, the same newspaper that had announced my
parents' courthouse wedding after my father was called to the
draft in 1969, I balled up every last bit of the Sunday edition
into kindling, the ink marking my hands black.

What I knew from Mr. Barnet was that fire needed two
things to burn: oxygen and fuel. My fuel sources were the
paper and the lighter fluid I'd lifted from Dad's Weber grill
on our front porch, next to the silk daisies he left outside all
year long. Under the grill's dome, he kept both the butane
and a long-handled grill lighter inside a plastic bag. I squirted
the lighter fluid like a water gun, dousing the paper and the
interior. Then, climbing into the backseat, I rolled down the
windows on each side of car so that oxygen could nourish
the flames.

Once the prep was done, I slammed the doors and waited
for someone to stop me.

I imagined my father on the front stoop, calling my name
and asking me, "Just what in the Christ are you doing out
here, Claire?"

But when I turned to the house, it stared back like an unlit
jack-o'-lantern.

"Stop me, long-haired star," I called to Halley's comet.

I thought if nothing else, my summons might wake up my parents or Kara, and they would come outside and we could find a way to make things better for all of us.

But the house stayed dark and the sky did not answer. I did not see the comet that night. I cannot blame it for starting my fire, and I cannot credit it for stopping me.

From above, only Orion winked back, his club in hand, protecting us from Taurus, the bull, in heaven.

I put the letter snatched from my father's dresser into the car with the last of the coupon inserts from the Sunday circulars and triggered the lighter with my thumb. Not wanting my mother's words to be true, I ignited the letter first, then the loose fabric of the car's interior. The heat flamed up against my hands and my face, while the rage welled in my heart. I shut the door and walked swiftly toward the house in slippers soaked by the snow.

There was a hush, a moment of peace as I walked off. Then I heard the whoosh of the fire gulping the oxygen and that furious, glorious rush of flames.

I approached the front door, and reflected back at me from the bay window of our house were flashes. They crested over the car like waves, oranges and blues, reds, a sliver of green. They lapped at the sides of the vehicle and reached over the hood. Witnessing it, a kind of warmth spread through me. It moved from my heart, up my neck, out my arms, down to my frozen toes. The awe caught in my throat. I giggled. I remember covering my mouth with both hands, tiptoeing into the foyer, and shutting the door, pausing to behold that miraculous thing, the same combustion that allows flight, and I counted: "Three, two, one, liftoff."

I crept up the stairs and slipped back into bed next to Kara, shutting my eyes and feigning sleep when she stirred.

There was a minute, maybe two, before the sound of fireworks, followed by an explosion that roused everyone else inside.

My father ran down the hall, shouting to my mother who slept on the couch. "Kat! Jesus Christ, it's your car! It's on fire!"

She yelled back. "Get the kids!"

They scrambled, my mother running up the stairs, my father coming down the hall, colliding at the top of the landing. One of them gasped.

"Girls!" my father hollered.

I sprang from my bed, turning the corner behind Kara to find my parents watching the flames from the window.

And, there, despite all the distance between them and the letter Mom had written, my parents held each other, proving the lesson Mr. Barnet had imparted:

"Fires possess an ultimate, unlimited kind of power."

CHAPTER FIVE

REPOSSESSION

E VEN BEFORE RECONNECTING WITH DEAN, I SOMETIMES
dreamed about the Quayside, that view from the windowsill where he and I last made love, carrying with it a dark
reminder of all that had been poached from my childhood
the minute my mother opened the door and stepped inside
the place. Those consequences of my mother's affair kept
me inside my own marriage, one I became ambivalent about
after the move, and even before, when I started to question
it shortly after the birth of our son.

Miles tried to make things right. I don't blame him, really.
He sensed my slipping from the present a few weeks after
arriving in Madison, believing I was falling into a transi-
tional depression. That's what he told my counselor, that he
thought it was something he could fix if he had more time
to pitch in around the house.

And I wish, of course, that the answers were as basic as
Miles making his own coffee and rinsing his mug when
he finished, or managing the mountain of trash in his office
and clearing away the bowls encrusted with food strewn
across his desk. Those were the chores generally left for
me after he headed for the hospital to perform acts of
God, while I stayed behind to tidy the mess. And sure, I

resented those things at times, but the trouble was deeper, old trouble all mine.

When he came home late one night to find me tearful, a box of faded snapshots of the Quayside scattered across the floor, he said, "Maybe the drive was too much," blaming the nineteen hours in the overstuffed car four months prior and the 1,100 miles we'd crossed with our screaming baby as the shortest days of winter set in.

In some ways, he was right. With each tick of the odometer, I slipped further from our axis, allowing a magnetic field to form between us, replacing the powerful attraction I once felt for Miles with resistance to the change.

Our first night in the rental house, the start of the fall term for Miles's academic responsibilities for the Department of Medicine, began with a fight. We were tired and weary from the nineteen-hour drive, a race through the night to meet the movers, who were already unloading our things when we arrived.

I held Jonah in my arms as I entered the narrow quarters Miles had rented for us, a place he had found during his recruitment and that I had not seen. Inside, it was stark and angular. The stairwells had tight, sharp corners, not a banister to be found. Each wall was paneled in dark wood, aside from the front room made entirely of windows. The bedrooms had cast-iron balconies with no railings, the worst kind of situation for our new walker, Jonah, still unsteady on his feet. And each room hosted a beautiful open-concept fireplace with no glass around the hood to contain the flames.

Although beautiful, the place was not a family house. It

felt, as I walked through it, like a house Miles had chosen for himself, a hasty self-serving choice made for its proximity to the hospital, ignoring Jonah's safety and my own comfort. This disregard was reminiscent of my husband's lack of consideration for my career when he pushed for a relocation I had already expressed apprehension about. The work of motherhood and the priorities of our family seemed to be afterthoughts to Miles, swept up with ambitions, and I was enraged by that.

"Isn't it great?" Miles asked.

I cut open a box of dishes. And lifted them toward the cabinets I'd lined with paper. "You've got to be kidding me." I paused.

Miles grinned ear to ear. "I love it. And it's so close to the lab. Super convenient."

Heat ran through me. My face flushed. And something in me, something I had been holding tight, snapped. I tossed plates and saucers to the ground, where they broke into shards.

From the Pack 'n Play beside me, Jonah erupted into tears.

I screamed at Miles. "Did you think about anyone other than yourself for even one second before you dragged us here?" And what I couldn't tell him in that moment, because I was too angry, was that I was desperately afraid.

I was thirty-two years old when I was first drawn to my husband. My third glass of white wine was empty as Miles and I stood in a mass of people in Boston Red Sox caps watching the playoffs, all eyes holding fast to the flat screens lining the bar, while Jason Varitek stepped to the plate, working his way toward erasing an eighty-six-year curse.

Miles, who was one year my senior, stood out from the crowd in his Cleveland Indians T-shirt, which announced his dedication to the Rust Belt team and the hometown he had left behind. With his serene green eyes and full lips, dressed in the tattered vintage crewneck tee beneath an open dress shirt with monogrammed sleeves, he presented himself as an attractive combination of awkward and refined.

"An Indians fan, *really*?" I said as I moved past him to get a closer view of the game.

He looked right at me and raised his hand in the greeting of Chief Wahoo. Fumbling through his pants pockets, he placed a guitar pick, a fistful of ketchup packets, his Ohio driver's license, and one marmalade jelly packet on the bar, then bought my drink with a wad of wrinkled singles held together by a paper clip.

I held up my glass for a toast. "Go Sox," I said.

"Sometimes I steal things," he told me, "to hang on to the important moments." Then he touched his snifter, a keepsake he would later pocket, to my wineglass.

"To the Sox. To meeting you."

For a split second his fingertips grazed the fleshy center of my palm, and he gave me a nod as if we were in it together.

During the game's eighth inning, Carl Crawford and Aubrey Huff scored two runs, setting the Red Sox up for a 4–9 loss. I hissed along with the crowd before Miles swept me off to the wharf.

We cut through cobblestone alleys toward Mystic's waterfront port, where all the buildings leaned against each other, exhausted by their old age. The willows that lined our path had yellowed with the September frost, and the gaslights set between them drew moths out from the dark. We walked to where the streets ended and the docks began, the tide gently frothing and a low fog rising off the ocean.

Ambling through the village, Miles held my wrist, not my hand, and anyone who saw us would have thought I was being dragged. Yet I submitted willingly to the childishness of the gesture, which endeared me to him immediately.

"Want my hand?" I offered in an almost-shout over a tugboat horn.

"I'm taking your pulse," Miles announced.

Then, through the open doors of the pubs lining Main Street came the collective grumble of a wanton Red Sox nation. And, as if inspired by their groan, Miles pulled me into his coat and we stood looking over the water, our backs to the noise.

He did not kiss me but whispered instead, his lips barely touching my ear, "Nervous girl."

"No, no." I corrected him. "Excited girl."

He let go of my wrist and guided my fingers to his neck, where I felt his pulse racing and the world receding around us. I breathed deeply, smelled the salt in the air, and asked the same question: "Nervous man?"

He whispered, "Maybe."

And in that moment, staring out over the flat waters of the Atlantic, dark and slick as obsidian, I knew somehow that the two of us would run off into the unknown together.

"Beautiful night," I said.

"But no wind," he added. "Otherwise, I'd take you out in my old dory right now. But without a motor, we might be set adrift."

It didn't sound so bad. "Let's swim," I said, buzzed by the wine.

Feeling enchanted by the mild autumn night, I tugged on his arm, moving us further down the wharf, growing eager for the possibility brewing between us. I pointed to a spot above the horizon and below the quarter moon.

"Sea smoke," I told him. "The ocean is warmer than the air. Probably the warmest, calmest waters we'll see until summer."

I pulled off my coat and laid it across the creaking dock, then slid off my sandals and wiggled out of my jeans.

Miles watched me.

"You're insane!" he said, meaning it as a compliment.

And shortly thereafter he was tossing his own coat onto the wharf, shrugging out of his shirt, and pulling his Cleveland Indians T-shirt over his head. "So we're really gonna do this?"

His body was lean and chiseled in those days, the physique of a runner or a swimmer, maybe, some sinewy sort of Iron Man. And in the dark, his smile was bright.

Then I took him by the wrist. And as I heaved Miles toward the end of the plank, wearing only my tank top, bra, and panties, he was heavier than he appeared. Unable to budge him further, I stood on my tippy-toes and shouted: "Ready? One, two, three!"

Headfirst into the water with my best swan dive, my body plummeted through the calm. I held my breath through the momentary shock of the cold and opened my eyes, watching the bubbles and silver light as I crested to the water's surface.

Standing shirtless in just a pair of jeans, Miles watched me bob.

"No way!" he shouted.

I let out a shriek. "It's only cold for a second!"

Miles took several slow paces backward, his head held low like a scolded puppy, and as soon as I believed he had decided against it, he dropped his jeans, stepped from them, then ran as fast as he could, cannonballing into the bay.

A foot away from me, he came up for air.

"You're nuts, you know that?" he called out with such open admiration that it made me laugh too, delighted at myself.

We swam toward each other, treading water and giggling like kids, holding on to one another and finally kissing until Miles's teeth began to chatter.

"Let's get warm," he said, initiating our return.

I hurried up the slick rungs of the wharf first.

Close behind, Miles spotted me, keeping his hand on my hip.

Still giggling and hopping to ward off the chill, we dried our dimpled skin on our coats and shimmed our damp bodies into our jeans. Dressed, we stood for a moment, beholding one another. He grinned. "I like you," he said, and all I could think about was that kiss. I wanted more of it, of him. Then driven by an intense attraction, I took his hand.

"Come home with me," I told him.

Both of us ran, shoes in our hands, winding through the cobblestone streets against the breeze, until we reached the door of my apartment, where I turned the key.

I glanced over my shoulder at Miles.

"You were right," I admitted. "Nervous girl." I wasn't so sure I was prepared for what would unfold, but I wanted it nonetheless.

Miles smiled his wide, bright grin and said confidently, "You should be."

And there we began.

But Miles, I've come learn, is not as vulnerable as me. I'm still the nervous, needier one, and my husband has come to view that wariness as an unattractive insecurity.

Although our relocation was exhausting and hard, it was "just a move," as Miles likes to remind me now. "Not even all the way across the country, just half." And, yes, he is right. People do it all the time, people with much harder lives than our own.

And I should feel thankful that our son pulled through the pneumonia he had the week after we arrived in Wisconsin, where my mother's letter waited, in which she wrote to Jonah: "Moving is tough, my sweet, sweet boy. But what's a little loneliness, my dear," even though I am quite certain she has never allowed herself to be lonely.

Simply, the moment our boxes of packed dishes hit the floor, I couldn't stop the sadness. Maybe it was the adjustment to the lack of lithium in the air. Being too far from the ocean has always messed with my head, which is why for nearly forty years of my life I'd avoided living in the middle, the great oceanless expanse of it, keeping a tight hold on the coast. And it was a bad time for us to be here, arriving in mid-September during the onset of shorter days, soon to be trapped by the coming winter, feeling like foreigners in our own country, and just as I was beginning to feel a part of the world after my clunky initiation into motherhood.

Maybe I didn't want to start over again because I didn't know who to start over as. The former outrageous blond girl I remember was unrecognizable in the murky-haired stranger with puffy eyes who looked back at me from the mirror. Maybe because Dean remembered who I had been, I was compelled by him and those old powers he had over me.

Having grown up with four sisters, and being the youngest and only son born to an Irish Catholic mother, Dean admitted to me that back in high school, his sisters had blessed him with insider information about girls. It was the Fourth of July, we had been dating seven months, and as we sat in the bed of his pickup truck, sharing swigs from a bottle of Miller High Life, he told me, "You know, I used every secret my sisters whispered to each other about boys to my full advantage with you."

I took the bottle from his hands and peeled the label back. We leaned against the cab, counting fireflies. "I don't have those kinds of secrets," I said. "But after I caught my mom in a lie, I set her car on fire."

Dean seemed neither shocked nor amazed. He simply held me as if he understood the motive.

Over his shoulder, I watched Roman candles flaring up into the sky.

"We all have secrets," he said, his face buried in my hair. "I bet when we're old, we'll have a lot more skeletons in the closet. I've got a few fires I'd like to set myself. If I knew where my father lived, his house would go first."

We sat silent for a moment. Maybe it was then that we first considered making a fire together, mutually imagining how the scene would play out. Then Dean jumped from the bed of the truck onto the gravel road and walked toward the creek. He lit a smoke. Something told me not to follow.

Above us I located Scorpius set off by Antares, the sixteenth brightest star in the sky. I considered what other secrets I would have to keep and, like the scorpion battling Orion, I wondered what battles I would fight.

When I turned back toward the water, Dean had stripped out of his jeans, down to his boxer shorts, and was wading into the stream.

I've never told my husband about the fire I set in my mother's car. Dean was the only person who ever knew. Although I'd like to think that Miles and I could tell each other anything, we can't. Or at least I can't. I learned the hard way to keep my secrets after I divulged my mother's infidelity to Miles in the early months of our courtship. That character flaw became something he referenced anytime her name came up, pressing on a wound that would never heal, reminding me of the danger in sharing old confidences.

In a moment of tenderness, I came close to telling Miles

about the car fire only once. It was before Jonah. We had been camping at Maho Bay in the U.S. Virgin Islands, celebrating the completion of his doctoral program in medicine. We were alone on the beach, our skin branded by the sun after a day of snorkeling. Drinking rum from the bottle, we sat with our faces illuminated by a bonfire we had built together.

Miles threw his hand over my shoulder. "What is it about fire?" he wanted to know.

With our eyes open, we made love there on the sand. But Miles's gaze remained on the blaze, and in his eyes I watched the reflection of light flicker. I wanted to tell him then how I got away with it, how I kindled the car with newspapers and struck the match, but I didn't because Miles had always possessed a righteousness, a belief in order and laws typical of the son of a judge. Disclosing my crime would mean opening myself up to questions that, if answered, would reveal a part of myself that made even me uneasy. So I tucked that part of my story deep in the corner pocket of myself.

But I did tell Dean how the fire trucks pulled onto Willard Street just seconds after I slipped back into my bed, faking sleep, before my parents came to get us.

"My father cried," I explained in a whisper. "And he pulled at my mother's shirt so hard, trying to hold her, that we heard the fabric tear as she moved away from him. When the officers came to the door, he finally let go."

"I remember that fire," Dean said. "It was in the *Hartford*

Courant. The article was all about how your dad was out of work, walking the picket line at Colt, and how he was the victim of vandalism. They blamed it on the changes in the neighborhood after Pratt and Whitney moved south. My mom was all worried about her property value." He moved my hair off my shoulders. "It wasn't a bunch of thugs from New London after all. It was you."

"Me," I confessed to Dean. "To punish my mother."

When the cops arrived at the scene, they questioned my parents on the stoop while it snowed and snowed. Kara sat in my lap and we watched them from the living room. It was the last time I saw my mother touch my father, her fingers on his shoulder as the officers drove up. They were both afraid and Dad grabbed her, tried to keep her in his grip, but she pulled away from him, even as he begged her "Please" and "Don't" and "Wait."

Despite the fire, Mom left the next day. She had packed just one bag and set it in the hallway the night before, the same rose-colored suitcase she took on their honeymoon weekend to see the Statue of Liberty, before Dad left for Vietnam. Other than her luggage, everything else stayed behind with us, even Mom's sea glass.

As a girl, I blamed myself for my parents' divorce, always wondering if giving Dad that letter might've made a difference in his behavior, if he might've been softer, more attentive in time to save things. Perhaps, if he'd been given a chance to read it, he would have pleaded with her to reconsider the split. And although it was never my intention, as an adult I've come to understand that by confiscating my mother's note and setting fire to her car with it, I made things far worse for Dad, who was caught completely off guard when she left.

Without her own vehicle, Mom was no longer able to move herself into her lover's house. Instead, that next morning, "the Douche Bag," as my father later named him, fetched her in a Mercedes the color of banana cream pie. Together they backed out of the driveway into the fog while Dad leaned in the door frame, watching, and the yellow crime scene tape billowed along the edges of our front lawn.

Soon after Mom left, I abandoned my ownership of the arson, exiling it so far away from me that it was as if the story belonged to a stranger, something I overheard in a restaurant, maybe. But once Dean resurfaced, that summer returned to me with a fury—that intensity, the loss, the fire, the heat, all of it.

Dear Claire,

Since you've agreed there is nothing that can't be shared between us, I need to tell you a few things. First is that you're right. The house at Quayside is haunted. For me, haunted mostly by you.

Right after we closed on the place, Heather wanted to move in, make it our home. Who wouldn't? The view is goddamn breathtaking. But I couldn't bring myself to live here with her in a place where I felt your presence. So, I nabbed another property on the marsh. Insisted that the Quayside offered more as a rental for the bigwig insurance execs at Aetna than it offered us as a home.

Second thing, it wasn't until Heather and I split, over a

year ago, that I moved in. I just haven't brought myself to update my relationship status on Facebook. Too depressing, which is why I haven't mentioned it yet. The story is real tragic—like they all are, right? Heather jumped ship. A year later she's engaged. But when she left, she went big. Took our cash, her jewelry, had a moving company come when I was at work. Basically, stripped the house of all the antiques and art, all the other shit she had bought, and moved in with her chiropractor. The guy was like twenty-five years old, and supposedly he begged her to have his baby.

My guess is she tried to break it off and he wanted to keep fucking her so he told her what she wanted to hear. The affair had been going on about a year. Of course he conveniently made his play on her thirty-fifth birthday, following a conversation she and I had, in which I told her I wasn't sure that at forty-three years old and knee deep in debt was the best time for me to start a family.

Big mess. Lawyer said not to fight her on the marsh property because it's all in her name, advised I take Quayside and walk. Start over on my own. Whole thing makes me sick. But who knows, maybe one day we'll both be living back on the beach together, the way it should have been all along.

Then again, maybe not. With all the sadness living inside these walls, I can only imagine you felt frightened here as a kid.

And, you could call me, some night. Actually, please call: 1-860-555-8468.

I'm lonely too. Let's not let each other be lonesome anymore.

Yours,

Dean

CHAPTER SIX

DISPLACEMENT

O NCE I ACQUIRED DEAN'S NUMBER, ALL I COULD think about was dialing it, and by the following morning, I had committed the digits to memory. Jonah went down for his morning nap as usual, and I reached for the phone, pressing the eleven digits. But after the first ring, I told myself, "Don't," apprehensive about where the call could lead, and hung up.

In an attempt to keep my mind occupied, I washed the breakfast dishes and let the water run over my hands. I envisioned Long Island Sound, my hand cutting through its cold waters over the side of the weather-beaten Cape Dory sailboat, which had been sold along with the house and most of our belongings.

In Connecticut, before Miles took the job at the University of Wisconsin, I could watch Niantic Bay from my kitchen window, the old wooden docks groaning as the tides went out. But out the window of our rental house, we had only a view of the Target at Hilldale Mall, the department store's bull's-eye emblem marking the spot of everything gone missing.

Interrupting my daydreams of home, the phone rang and the machine picked up just as I found the receiver and answered the call.

"Still there?" I asked over the recording.

But the line fell silent, followed by the drone of a dropped call.

I considered Miles ringing to check in and thank me for delivering his pager; he always managed to leave something behind in his mad dash out the door. But by the time Jonah and I tailed him to the lab that morning, before our 10:00 a.m. story time at the library, my husband was already scrubbed in on a case with a patient.

I tried to call back on both Miles's cell and at the hospital's cardiology lab, but each line went straight to voice mail. Then, before I set the phone back to charge, I impulsively dialed Dean, hanging up after one ring for the second time that morning.

"You're pathetic," I told myself.

Taking a longer morning nap than usual, Jonah slept to midday and I further busied myself with endless chores, pushing away thoughts of Dean by folding baskets of tiny jeans and one-sies, unloading the dishwasher, and leafing through a cookbook to figure out something for dinner. As I sanitized baby bottles and vacuumed Cheerios from under the high chair, I eyed the computer and tried to convince myself, "Let it be."

In the basement, I pulled clean bedding from the dryer, hauled it back up to the playroom, and folded it while it was warm, but once I got to the fitted sheets that make me crazy, I stopped and the phone rang again.

Wishfully, I anticipated Dean pulling my 608 area code exchange off his caller ID and returning a call to me. I recollected the low rasp of his voice and answered.

"Hello?"

There was a pause.

My heart pounded, a flutter rising from my chest into my throat and blushing face.

"Hello?" I said again.

"Can you hear me?" my husband shouted.

"Miles," I said, falling into a chair, disappointed.

"Jesus, honey, I've been trying to reach you all morning." There was panic in his tone. "The lines here keep cutting out."

"What's wrong?" I asked.

"My lab," he shouted. "There was a fire."

Behind him I heard the sirens and the low voices of men asking questions.

"My research," he said despairingly. "Everything could've been lost."

Miles continued to speak into the receiver but I couldn't quite connect his words. I stood up, pacing from room to room, turning off the radio and looking for my shoes.

"You want me to come over there?" I asked, peering out into the endlessly falling snow. "Jonah is still napping, but I could wake him."

"Please. And grab the blue external hard drive off my desk. I want to back up all my work. I want to make sure that nothing else is lost."

"Okay," I said, opening his office door and shuffling through the mess of papers and folders to find the external hard drive. I took a deep breath to steady myself. "The police? Are they with you?"

Miles cleared his throat. "The Madison Fire Department responded to the call at 10:15 this morning. It came from Clyde on the maintenance crew. My research, the files, the data from our experiments, all of it would've been wiped out if the sprinkler systems hadn't kicked on and scared off the perpetrator."

"Jesus. That's right after we stopped by to drop off your pager on our way to the library. We just missed it."

"Do you understand how bad this could have been, Claire? People could have been injured, or worse. My laptop's been here every night. I've just been trying to keep the peace at home—I know how much you hate the time suck of the research, the lab, the job. I didn't want you mad at me. But everything I've done here could have gone up in smoke."

Trying not to scream about how much work he *continued* to bring home regardless, I said, "It's awful. I'm sorry," while my own anxiety rose.

Miles corrected himself. "It's not your fault, honey. I'm just really upset. The point of origin, from what they have so far, was right outside my office door, on the back outer side of the lab. The arsonist came in through the security doors. They used amateur stuff—gasoline, from what they can tell."

I asked, "Do they have any idea who might have done it?"

"No. Not a clue. But I was thinking—do you remember that one resident I told you about, Dalton, the one with the impulse control issues? I found him gambling online during rounds last month. The guy clearly has some screws loose, but I don't think he's a felon. The animal rights activists have always threatened to try to shut the wet lab down. But really, it could have been anyone. It's horrible. I never thought... I just cannot believe something like this could happen."

"Of course not. That's so scary." I pushed Jonah's bedroom door open to wake him and whispered to Miles, "Hang in there. We're on our way."

In my arms Jonah's body was warm with sleep, his eyes groggy. I lifted him from the crib and said, "Daddy needs us."

Inside the School of Medicine, housed in the belly of the university hospital, Miles sat on the floor of the inner stairwell and hugged his knees to his chest, his white coat on the floor beside him, his tie loose and unraveled around his neck. Next to him stood a thin, tidy man in a crisp suit, anxiously drumming his fingers on his lapel, while a barrel-shaped firefighter expounded on the findings.

"No doubt this was an incendiary fire. Arsonist used straight petrol and a rag, basic Molotov cocktail, sign of a rookie. And from what I can make of the alligatoring—the way the wood is charred along the walls inside the lab—it was unsophisticated accelerants all the way around. Lucky for us, the culprit was hasty. Had the perpetrator used the oxygen flow in that back hall, this place holds enough chemicals to go up like a firecracker. Dudes who are big-time arsonists, who plot it out, the professionals making big-gun fires—they go more for your petroleum distillates, benzenes, and xylene isomers to get a flashover and bigger, more destructive flames. Best thing to do now is follow up on any leads from your staff, Dr. Bancroft. You should know that arson is about the hardest crime to link to a person, but we'll do our best."

The lean, angular man in the suit nodded and shook my husband's hand. "I'll be in touch."

While I waited for them to finish a more hushed

conversation, I thought about fire and how it can all be reduced to the basic science of combustion undoing the chemistry that photosynthesis brings together. Even as a teenager, I was fascinated by the simplicity of the reaction that leaves nothing but water behind.

That behavior of the fire triangle—fuel, oxygen, heat— was first explained to me in the classic experiment from *The Chemical History of a Candle, Lecture III: Products—Water from the Combustion*, the one I memorized the summer before college, replicating Faraday's proof in my mother's kitchen by taking a cold drinking glass and placing it over the flame. The glass grew damp, as Faraday explained: "immediately H_2O was produced by the taper in appreciable quantity."

In the corridor of Miles's lab, the firefighter droned on to Miles, but I knew that hydrogen and its changing forms would give the important details of the investigation away. And I recognized how heat removed the hydrogen and oxygen molecules from the walls of the lab to produce water vapors no different from those that source the waters of the Atlantic Ocean, a thousand miles too far away.

Finally, when he saw us awaiting him, Miles rushed over and clutched me tight, Jonah snug between us.

"Love you," he said. "Thanks for coming."

"What else can I do?" I whispered.

He shook his head. "I don't know."

The three of us stood huddled together for a long time. And with Jonah between us, Miles and I shared the kind of touch we hadn't had in months, full of mutual need.

Interrupted by men in latex gloves scurrying through the

double doors, Miles ushered us aside. I inhaled the smell of charred paper and melted plastic and peered nervously through a swinging door, behind which the real damage lay. Officers wound the police tape along the hall, and droves of impotent campus security circled the corridors with walkie-talkies, trying to stay out of the investigators' way.

I handed my husband the jump drive. "Want to get out of here and grab lunch?" I offered. "Take a breather with me and the little guy?"

He shook his head. "You guys head home. I need to go upstairs and round on patients, then I'll need to spend some time sending out emails to all the residents and fellows, see if anyone in the department might've seen anything suspicious."

"Tell me how to help," I pleaded, slipping my hand around his waist.

Miles dismissed my offer. "Just take care of Jonah."

"It could have been a lot worse," I acknowledged.

He nodded and sipped water from a paper cup. "I'll try my best to get home before Jonah goes down." He stroked our son's cheek with the back of his hand. "Okay, buddy?"

Back home, Jonah and I went through the daily routine: first lunch, then clean up and play. We ran to the bank and the dry cleaner, the grocery store and the pharmacy. Strolling store aisles, I was hunting for a gift to cheer Miles, when I stumbled across two stuffed pugs perched side by side on the pharmacy shelves.

I yelped with delight and an elderly woman sucking on mints

and perusing birthday cards glanced up at me with a finger to her lips, hushing me as if I'd woken her from slumber.

Holding the stuffed animals, I remembered Pansy and Sebastian, our former neighbors' dogs, racing fully costumed down our stretch of shore, and I laughed out loud, squeezing the plush replicas to my chest—the ideal present for Miles, to lift his spirits when he needed me again.

Back home, I wrote out a card and arranged the stuffed pugs on the counter, sticking a couple of makeshift bumblebee antennas on one, a flower headband on the other, for my husband to find when he got home. I hoped the gesture would comfort him, an inside joke to remind him that I did understand, and that for him and our new life, I wanted to be necessary.

Dear Miles—

Things could be so much worse. We could be as crazy as Ned and Sheila Whitaker! Hang in there, and hang on to me. I'm here and I love you.

OX

Claire

A few hours later, back at the sink, I peeled potatoes for dinner, while Jonah pushed trains and built cities along the kitchen floor. Stopping every once in a while, he wrapped his arms around my legs or fiddled with my bare toes before demanding my attention for a quick squeeze.

After an early supper, we bundled up for a walk, both of us dressed like Eskimos, and headed down the footpath in the dark. Over the hills, I pulled Jonah in a sled toward the snow-covered golf course.

The swish of my ski pants was the only noise over the still blanket of the fresh snow.

"Look," I told Jonah when we crested the hill. Stopping to lift him from his seat, I pointed to the crescent moon in the dark, sapphire sky.

"There's Orion," I told him. We followed his belt with my gloved index finger and then found the open star cluster Pleiades to the right.

"Seven Sisters," I said and wondered about Kara, my only sibling, counting out the nearly two decades that had passed since we last spoke more than the occasional words required in holiday card greetings. I hoped she was happy at home in Connecticut with her family, a short drive from where we grew up. But I couldn't help wondering if she'd ever been desperate out there in the world, like me.

By bath time, Miles was still not home. Pushing Jonah's boats over the sudsy waters, I tried to recall a night when Miles had knelt there beside me and we bathed Jonah together, during what was, for me, the sweetest part of the night. But my calculations came up empty, and I recognized how separate our lives had become since he took the job. Miles's and my paths were running parallel, with no foreseeable point of intersection.

Toweling off Jonah's sturdy frame, I focused on what was in front of me and kissed all the sweet baby creases on his ankles and wrists, zerberting his belly, pinching his juicy little thighs. Jonah screeched with glee.

I laughed too, even though what I felt beside him, as I so

often do, was the bittersweet pang of motherhood—that joy of watching Jonah grow, paired with the grief of noting his baby-hood zipping past. And there, kneeling beside the tub, aware that I was parenting my boy alone, I was certain that for Miles and me, there would be no future babies unless I could change things somehow. For our family it would likely be just Miles and his work, and Jonah and me.

Once I put my son to bed, I became beset by isolation and called my husband, beckoning him home, hoping to offer some comfort, thinking that maybe today we could support each other and that I could take on a real role in things.

"Hey," I said. "Any more news? Want to come home and take a breather?"

"I'm still backing up files," he told me flatly.

"Don't you need a break after today? I could help you."

"They haven't even initiated the investigation yet." He sighed. "I'm distressed by the whole thing. And I have the grant looming. You turn in. I'll be late."

I did as he suggested and took slow, deliberate steps up toward my bed. Feeling more dismissed than tired, I logged on to Facebook to see who was on chat, sensing the need to sum up the day, but also knowing that most of my mommy friends back East, an hour ahead of me, were fast asleep, making it all the more justifiable for me to instead reach out to Dean.

Dear Dean—

Today was a weird one. This morning my husband's lab was set on fire. We were there just minutes beforehand. Can

you believe it? So scary. They have no idea who is responsible and thankfully no one was hurt, but the whole thing
has left me unsettled.

And what's worse is that Miles doesn't seem to need me,
even now. I had assumed he would—at least for some comfort. But he's still not come home. I guess there's nothing
new there, but it's disheartening all the same. It's like the
hospital and the labs it houses have stolen him from me altogether. I can't feel anything other than hostility for the place.

Anyway, I don't know if any of this even makes sense.
I guess what I'm asking is did you ever feel alone in your
marriage, like you weren't necessary for anything? That's
where I'm at right now.

Be well,

Claire

Later that night, I woke to find Miles in bed beside me, his
snores like the shallow purrs of a cat. His back to me, I moved
against the warmth of his skin and pulled him close. "Finally,"
I whispered, glancing at the clock, the hour well past midnight.

While Miles showered the next morning, I got up and made
the coffee before Jonah woke. And as I discarded the previous day's grounds, I discovered the card I had written to my
husband unopened, next to the stuffed pugs, toppled over on
the counter.

"How did you sleep?" I asked him coolly when he joined
me downstairs.

Miles leafed frantically through his duffel bag. "Slept fine," he
muttered, searching the countertops until I held out his keys.

He kissed my cheek and took the mug I offered from my hand. "I've got to meet the investigator before a case, so I'm going to scoot. That whole mess is eating me alive."

Jonah called, "Mama," from upstairs, and as I headed up to get him, I said, "Did you like your surprise?"

"Surprise?" he asked.

"The card on the counter," I said. "And those pugs."

He looked at me blankly.

I pointed. "Remember Pansy and Sebastian? I thought those little guys might make you smile."

"God, I'm sorry. I'm so wiped out, I never even noticed. Very sweet, thank you."

Miles took a sip of coffee and headed toward the hallway mirror to check his nostrils and straighten his tie, again leaving the unopened card behind as he raced off.

I walked up the stairs, wondering why I bothered, and pulled my iPhone from my back pocket, reading a short Facebook message from Dean, the post timed just after midnight.

Dear Claire—

That's horrible, such crazy shit. You guys okay? Maybe you should just get out of there for a few days, come home. Come see your friends, your family, stuff your face with shellfish, and meet me for a beer. You need to see the ocean. It'll do you some good. And maybe your husband would miss you?

    You deserve to be happy too. You really do.

    And you are right, marriage shouldn't be so lonely. I

know mine was. You start to realize that it's a hell of a lot
less lonely to be on your own.

Anyway, I'm here for you.

Yours,

Dean

While Jonah ate his cereal and stuck his fingers in his milk, I read the message a second time, then set my phone bearing the message on the counter. As I went on with the day, I moved through the routine but fantasized about Jonah and me bundled up in snow gear walking our old stretch of beach, while Pansy and Sebastian came dashing past, chasing tennis balls and wearing matching cable-knit sweaters. It hit me that maybe Dean was right, that maybe I wasn't just homesick. Maybe my ambitious, distracted husband really didn't need my comfort. In fact, it seemed he needed nothing from me at all.

Two days after the lab fire, the investigations still incomplete, the day began with the yellow whirl of light on top of the snowplow illuminating my bedroom. I dressed quickly that morning, made the pancakes, and as the truck scraped snow from our street, I mused over those long-ago plow rides with Dean, the sea out before us as he cleared the far end of Willard Street, removing the snow from my dad's driveway and dropping it from the seawall into the creek.

I cut Jonah's pancakes into small bites and wondered if Miles came home last night, or if he left before dawn, seeing no trace of his mug by the sink where he usually set it.

I finished my coffee and poured Jonah a small dish of syrup. He clapped his hands together in a cheer. "Dip!" he hailed.

I placed his breakfast on his high-chair tray and kissed his cheek. He swatted me away.

The doorbell rang.

I grabbed my purse and dug around inside for my wallet, making a check out to Sage Anderson, the old man who cleared our lane, and entering the amount of payment in the register, sickened by how much we had already paid for snow removal that winter.

The bell chimed again.

But when I left Jonah to pay Sage and thank him for his help, I could barely catch my breath. Twenty-five years and 1,100 miles from where I'd last seen him, Dean D'Alessio stood on my icy front stoop.

"Claire," he said softly.

CHAPTER SEVEN

DESIRE

DEAN'S FEATURES WERE EVEN MORE STRIKING THAN I remembered, his eyes that unmistakable blue, the corners of his squint notched by time. His body had that same tall, brawny build, and his demeanor was as easy as if he were invited.

He smiled. "After reading your message yesterday, I couldn't take it anymore, so I grabbed the first flight out this morning."

"It's you," I said in the tiniest whisper.

He thrust his hands deep into his pockets. "I hope this is okay, me showing up like this. I just... I had to see you."

I tried to regain my composure and scanned the yard for signs of my husband. Anxiously chewing my thumbnail, I took a step back, distrustful of my own excitement.

He said, "You're even prettier than I remember."

I looked down at the yoga pants I had worn the last three days and pushed my dark-framed glasses on top of my head. "I'm a mess," I said, pulling the clip from my hair and letting it tumble to my shoulders, my attempt to make the best of the wreckage.

And as Dean and I stood there beholding each other for the first time in twenty-five years, Sage Anderson slammed the door of his F-150 pickup and walked up the footpath to my house with the predictable yellow snow removal invoice in his hand.

He hollered, "Mind if I interrupt?"

"Good morning, Sage," I said and handed him the check already made out in his name.

"Cold one," he told us.

Dean confirmed. "Sure is."

The men shook on the weather.

Dean and I watched Sage limp back to his truck. Then we took a long moment to examine each other.

Inside, Jonah cried, "Mama?"

I tugged at a strand of my hair, conflicted, wanting to invite him in.

"The baby's in his high chair," I said. "And my husband said he might try to stop home. I just can't—"

Dean rubbed his thumb under my chin, and the intimacy of the gesture softened my defenses.

"We'll figure it out," he said.

Jonah called out, "Mama! Uh-oh!" Then began to cry.

"Go," Dean told me. "We'll find another time. I had to come. You sounded so upset."

I watched him pat his coat pockets, searching for smokes. His shoulders were broad, and he'd maintained the weathered fitness of a man who worked outdoors.

We looked at each other again with some old recognition, and he wrapped his arms around me. Lifting me off the ground, the mass of him swallowed me up. I almost wept with the generosity of the embrace, sensing the tug of what was behind it—my body remembering. I hugged him back. We held each other too long, I suppose. But his touch was like going home, the comfort of the familiar, and toggled to it was the accustomed grief of what had been lost back there.

"It's so goddamn good to see you," he whispered.

Reluctantly, I let go and Dean jogged down my steps and across the street, and got into a silver SUV that sat idling there. Calling my name from the open window, he said, "I'll be in touch."

"See you later," I called back and shut the door, but I was already nervous about the follow-up encounter, understanding the danger in what Dean had come to pursue and how willing I was to follow through.

"Mama!" Jonah called through tears. I shut the door, glancing at my reflection in the hallway mirror on my way to the kitchen. Not a lick of makeup on my face, and I had not showered in days. "You're disgraceful," I uttered and raced to my boy, my heart still pounding as I went.

A gooey well of syrup pooled out of Jonah's reach, and as I mopped it off the table with a sponge, I understood that with all the online flirtation and the retelling of what we once felt in the cab of his pickup, narrating to each other the explicit details of what we wanted more of, Dean and I had dragged our shared history too far out of the long-ago and into a current place and time, where, if I let it, it would grow reckless.

I carried Jonah into the living room, wrapped him up in a blanket, and pulled him close to me. Grabbing the remote, I turned on *Sesame Street* and peered out the window.

Dean was gone.

But still, I trembled with panic, and also delight and an

eagerness that had become foreign to me. As I attempted to reassess the meaning of his arrival, I peeled a tangerine for Jonah and decided to write Dean an apology for sending him off so abruptly. I'd tell him I was just caught off guard and explain that I already regretted not asking him in for a cup of coffee.

Logged on to the computer to message Dean, my second shock that morning was discovering a friend request from my mother, her familiar profile image backlit by a pink sunset. It was a simple plea:

Claire, honey!

I see we share some mutual friends. :) Let's connect! I want to see pictures of you and your boys, the new place too. How are things out there? I've heard nothing since receiving a change-of-address card from Miles. I hope Jonah is still getting my letters.

Love,
Mom

I clicked Ignore. Annoyed by my mother's casual attempt to track me on Facebook, I paused, as I recall it, for just a moment and contemplated a response to her before I deleted her request entirely, too distracted by the next message in the queue, from Dean, who had already beaten me to the punch.

Claire—

Sorry for the surprise. That wasn't fair. But I believed you

**when you said you wanted a spaceship to come rescue
you. I know you're lonely. And I don't have a rocket, exactly, but when you catch a minute, give a holler. I'll be at
the hotel, waiting to catch up.**

Dean

While I typed up my response to him, Dean popped up on
chat.

Dean: Amazing to see you this morning, Claire.

Claire: I was just sitting down to write you. I'm shocked!

Dean: I'm sorry it was unannounced. You sounded so sad in
your message. Plus I wanted to get out of town for a few days,
anyway. Needed a break. And hoped to cheer you, so I brought
you some things—your ninth-grade report card, for one, and
also your mother's ring, the one your father gave her, the one
you couldn't bear to keep. I wore it on a chain way past our
time, and then I set it away. I could never bring myself to chuck
any of it. I have your track T-shirt too.

Claire: Mom's ring? I forgot about that thing. And the report
card? How were my grades in ninth grade, anyway?

Dean: Do you really need to ask? A+ in science, of course. Back
then I'm pretty sure you loved Mr. Barnet even more than you
loved me.

Claire: OMG, Mr. Barnet! I loved no one more than I loved you. That said he DID let me play with fire in school. He also had a telescope and like a thousand books on Halley's comet.

Dean: You were obsessed with that comet. Blamed everything on it—the Challenger. Your parents' divorce. The fires you set. I think the next Halley's comet comes in 2062, something like that. You'll be turning ninety and I'll be ninety-three. If I'm lucky like my grandpa, I'll still have all my hair.

Claire: The next year of the comet is 2061. I will be a spry eighty-nine. Where are we meeting? Seems by then, it might be more appropriate for us to have a drink. I feel bad about running you off today.

Dean: We will meet where we always meet—the creek. I remember being there with you when you told me about igniting your mom's car. You said it made you forget to be sad for a while, that fire was like water—it washed things away.

Claire: Baby's fussing. I better scoot! Let's talk soon. I'll try and figure out a good time to meet.

Dean: Are there still things that make your heart pound?

Afraid to answer, I logged off and left him with an automated message: *Claire Spruce is no longer available for chat.*

That night Miles worked late, and after Jonah went to bed, I took a bath and tried to disregard the impression of Dean's thumb on my chin, that dangerous reminder of his touch. I shaved my legs as my son's toy schooner floated by. I blew on the sails as I'd taught Jonah to do and thought about our last summer day sailing across Long Island Sound. It was September. Jonah was a newborn, nearly a year and a half ago, almost to the day, which was the last time I felt assured in our love, our marriage, and our shared life.

In the cabin below, Jonah had fallen asleep swaddled in a blanket despite the humidity. Together, Miles and I pulled in the genny and folded up the sails. I tied them, as I always did, sitting on the bow, looking at the toenail sliver of a moon rising over the horizon. Hearing Miles toss the anchor, I turned around.

He smiled at me and held a finger to his lips, a signal not to wake the baby, while he tiptoed toward me. Once he reached my side, he slid the strap of my sundress off my shoulder and rubbed his thumb down the nape of my neck. Leaning himself up against the mast, he pulled me close. His lips were salty, and under a sky the color of apricots, he hummed in my ear as he fumbled beneath my sundress. We took our time with each other in what felt like a new forever.

With our sleeping infant and all that new love pouring from us, Miles wanted me, despite my unfamiliar postpartum body. And I not only felt more desired by him than I had since the beginning of our relationship, when he courted me with lilies, but also respected by him in a way I had never experienced before becoming the mother of his son. I was the champion of

a complicated childbirth, a woman who was far tougher physically than he had ever predicted.

Yet after the move, that wantonness dampened. Maybe my
resentment about leaving home or the job that took Miles away
caused things to change. But no matter the reasons, that flicker
of desire didn't return to me until Dean's reappearance. And
following our unanticipated encounter on my doorstep, I had
to remind myself that I did not want to end up like my mother,
entertaining an affair and leaving my husband behind to weld
together some renovated version of a family life. So soaking
in the tub that evening, I pledged to reignite some of that old
need I assumed Miles and I still had stowed away somewhere
for each other.

After toweling off, I executed a plan for romance by making
a late dinner of steak and potatoes with rosemary, and wore
red lipstick with no other makeup, Miles's favorite kind of
sexy. I pulled on a black sweater dress, and in the kitchen, I lit
every candle I could find. After dinner was in the oven, I sat
on the center of the island circled by candlelight, with a glass
of red wine. Out the back windows, I watched the glimmer of
snowbanks under the porch lights and waited for my husband
to come home.

"Hey," he said, stomping the slush off his feet when he finally
entered at half past nine. He looked around the kitchen, then
back at me. "Everything okay in here? Is the power out?"

"No," I said. "Candlelight supper. Thought we could have
some wine."

Miles flicked on the lights with an apologetic glance and sorted
through the mail. "I'd love that, but I've still got a ton of reading

to do. Crazy day in clinic and I haven't even signed off on all my patient records and procedure notes yet. Then there's the investigation, and the grant deadline is next week. Rain check?"

On my tiptoes, I reached up for my husband and wrapped my arms around him, pulling his belly tight against me. I pushed unwanted thoughts of Dean from my mind. "Take a break," I said. "You need to eat dinner anyway."

I kissed his cheek; he absently wiped my lipstick off.

I poured him a glass of red wine and topped off my own. Switching the lights back off, I tried to stay enthusiastic about the expectations I had set for the rest of the evening and my decision to attempt to salvage things between us.

"Honey, I really have to finish up my dictations and decipher what's most pressing before my clinic in the morning. Would you be terribly disappointed if I ate in the office so I can wrap things up?"

My temperature rose, then plummeted to a defeated simmer. I told him, "Sure. Eat in your office."

"Really?" he asked, noting my flat tone.

"I was trying to connect," I explained.

He squeezed my hand on his way out. "Another night, I promise. I can give you my full attention."

"Go." I pointed to his office door and polished off my drink.

"You sure you're okay?" he asked. "I appreciate dinner."

"Yup, I'm fine," I said, but of course I wasn't.

From his office, Miles called out, "Delicious, thank you!"

Alone in the kitchen, after a few bites from a supper I was no longer excited about, I sat Indian-style on the island with a plate in my lap. My efforts seemed foolish, as I watched the candles soften into waxy puddles. Flames flickered near the end of their wicks, and I thought about brightness, how the survival and intensity of a fire is solely dependent upon the oxygen supplied to it.

I recalled the experiment performed in *The Chemical History of a Candle: Lecture II—The Brightness of the Flame*, proving Michael Faraday's theory that the outcome of combustion is always water, the atoms of hydrogen changing form, all of it carefully noted and highlighted in the margins of that old book still packed up in the attic. That lecture yielded one of my favorite quotes about the splendor and intensity of the chemistry sustained inside a single flame.

"Is it not beautiful to think that such a process is going on, and that such a dirty thing as charcoal can become so incandescent? You see it comes to this—that all bright flames contain these solid particles; all things that burn and produce solid particles, either during the time they are burning, as in the candle, or immediately after being burnt, as in the case of the gunpowder and iron filings—all these things give us this glorious and beautiful light."

In the kitchen, my own candles reached the end of their wicks, dimming the room to near darkness. I opened my laptop, my escape from the separateness between Miles and me, knowing Dean was only a few miles away, eager to meet.

Claire,

Any chance you could slip out tonight for a drink? Or maybe lunch tomorrow is easier? You could bring your little guy.

I'd love to meet him. I'm at the Concourse on the lake, but could go anyplace. And you're welcome here anytime. Room 1014. What works best for you? I've come a long way, and all I want is a little time with you.

   Yours,

   Dean

I fantasized about grabbing the keys, driving downtown to his hotel, and knocking on the door, Dean delighted to find me there. Instead, I walked to the fireplace and opened the flue. The cold rushed in. I told myself I would let Miles work for an hour, and then I would try to tempt him with dessert by the hearth. I tossed the junk mail and an unopened letter from my mother addressed to *Mr. Jonah Bancroft and Mrs. Claire Spruce* into the fire, and in its soft light, I read a newspaper article from the Sunday *New York Times* describing a geomagnetic storm whose radioactive particles, traveling about 1,400 miles a second, were predicted to reach the Earth's surface by Monday morning.

Watching the mail carbonize, I wondered how we might keep Jonah unscathed as he made his way into a world shrouded by a deeply wounded atmosphere. Checking the video monitor, I watched my vulnerable boy curled there under his night-light, while the white noise machine played the sound of waves crashing on some far-off automated beach. I filled my champagne flute and set one aside for Miles while I waited.

At midnight, I woke up alone next to the hearth, shivering beside the fire, which had smoldered black to ash. I checked the monitor in my hand and then tiptoed down the hall and peeked into the office. Miles looked frozen blue in the light cast from his computer screen.

"Come to bed," I said.

"Yes." He nodded without looking up. "Twenty minutes."

Upstairs I washed my face and dried it on a beach towel monogrammed with our initials. As I did so, I sensed a panicky sort of defeat.

Turning down the bed, I wondered if this was how my mother felt with my father. She wanted him to want her, right up until the end, and even in the letter I'd swiped all those years ago, her only real complaint was that she was forlorn.

Just as I dozed off, Miles came upstairs and crawled in beside me.

I strained for his attention one last time, rolling over to kiss the back of his neck. I pulled his naked body against my warmth, a final attempt to reach him despite his exhaustion, a silent plea for him to rise to the occasion of me needing him.

He rolled toward me. On my back he drew tiny circles with his thumbs. He whispered in my ear, "You left the oven on again."

"Oh, God—sorry," I whispered, rubbing his shoulder.

He moved a pillow under my head and let out a long breath.

We had moved toward each other, holding one another for warmth, our bodies awakening—remembering—our legs entwined, when his pager went off, the sound of it like an alarm.

Miles jumped out from the covers, picked his white coat off the floor, and searched the pockets for the number.

In the corner of our bedroom by the window he stood naked, his silhouette protuberant at the middle, and arched his back into his hands. The phone pinched between his shoulder and ear, he advised a resident. He whispered something about an echocardiogram, then pulled on a pair of scrubs, confirming, "It's a tough call. I better head in to see the guy."

I wanted to wait for Miles, to hold my body in that place where we were interrupted, but he'd be gone much of the night, I imagined. The job had become more than either of us thought we were taking on. And it wasn't just the hours that Miles was away that were daunting, but how much he was missing even when he was home. As I retreated, I wondered if maybe my mother needed to leave my father for her own survival.

Near dawn, when Miles returned from the call, he crawled into bed without undressing and squeezed my hand.

"I'm lonely," I said out loud.

Barricaded under a pile of pillows, my doubt grown impermeable, I wanted Miles to say something back—"Me too" or even "Shut up!"—but within minutes, he was snoring.

I considered shaking him awake to explain step by step how I needed him to touch me, to comfort me, to help me find some reminder of who we were, the way Dean returned that feeling of familiarity to me with the simple tip of his thumb under my chin. Instead, I shut my eyes and lay sleepless, seething with hopelessness, and when I did finally doze off, I was back home, dreaming about comets and their luminous tails.

CHAPTER EIGHT

LUCY IN THE SKY WITH DIAMONDS

THE SPRING FOLLOWING MY MOTHER'S DEPARTURE, Halley's comet began its approach toward the sun, what would be its first potentially visible pass by Earth in a seventy-six-year voyage around our nearest star. One evening that April, in anticipation, my father woke Kara and me to watch the comet with him, after Channel 3 Evening News anchor Gayle King announced that the comet might soon be visible in the night sky.

Dad weaved in between our twin beds with a drink in his hand. "Wake up, ladies," he said, ice cubes rattling in his glass.

Kara and I sleepily trudged downstairs, following our father out onto the back deck with windbreakers over our jammies. Together we stood huddled against the chill, looking up into the western skies.

The peepers were early that year. Their chorus sang as they waited with us for a glimpse of those five-billion-year-old dust grains shedding behind the comet and creating what we'd hoped to see, a lustrous tail.

However, I knew even before he woke us up, according to the information Mr. Barnet had given our science class, that it was two days and three hours too early to see the comet from any northeastern vantage point. I did not share this with my father in my half sleep because he already felt like he was wrong about so much. "Thanks for thinking of us, Daddy," I said instead, squeezing his hand and hoping he felt appreciated, at least by his daughters.

My father mussed my hair and pulled Kara in tight for a hug. "Sure wish we had a telescope," he said as he covered us all in blankets.

My father loved Kara and me, and his love was never anything I doubted. In fact, his affection for us was so big that I knew to keep my blooming romance with Dean top secret. I somehow understood, even then, that my father could not handle his daughter loving an actual man, someone whom he would deem too old for me, especially after Mom had been lost to him already. Dad saw all teenage boys as a threat to his control, so the only man who was permitted at the center of our lives would be him, for a long, long time.

Although Kara was still too young for this to matter, Dad sensed I was distracted by something and he was wise enough to know what. "You better not have a boyfriend," he warned, when he found me with the phone cord stretched across the kitchen into the pantry, as I talked to Dean in a whisper before bed.

"Gross," I reassured him, my hand over the receiver.

"Good." Dad smiled. He ripped the cord from the wall. "You can talk to your girlfriends at school in the morning."

After Mom left, my father counted on me to do all the things she was responsible for: the laundry, the lunches, the shoveling, and in spring the prep for the vegetable garden. To lose any part of my allegiance threatened the makeshift stability we'd cobbled together in my mother's absence.

Looking back now, I understand the double role I took on that summer. I was not only a girl in her first relationship, but also the collector of my father's broken love—gathering all the frayed pieces of it, trying to help him make something out of those tattered threads.

And that April night Dad wove those threads tight as he summoned the comet for us with a song. In his best a cappella, he warbled, "Lucy in the sky with diamonds, Lucy in the sky with diamonds, Lucy in the sky with diamonds, ah, ah."

While he and I repeated the chorus over and over again, Kara played jacks on the deck under the porch light.

"All right, already," she finally told us. "I think that's enough."

We then sat with just the peepers for what felt like an eternity, until Dad asked with a sigh, "So, have you girls heard from your mother?"

My sister did not respond to the question and kept her eyes on the jacks. I watched her hands catching and releasing that small ball. Neither of us knew if he really wanted an answer, and if he did, we both guessed it was better to lie. Kara shook her head, and I shook mine.

But we had heard from her, yes.

After working an overnight shift as a floor nurse at Hartford Hospital, she came to us in her white nurse's uniform. She had visited me first at the high school athletic fields where I ran the track after school. She stayed only long enough to tell me, "You look good out there, Claire. So graceful," shouting the words over the fence during the baton relay.

When our coach blew the whistle for the timekeeper, I leaped across the finish line to greet her. Mom handed me a snack in a Tupperware container, like she always had, and headed down the block to Kara's middle school basketball practice to do the same—after which, I presumed, she would head off to visit her boyfriend in the mansion at the end of the Quayside, although the details of her whereabouts were always left unclear.

After she left that first morning, Kara had asked our father, "Is Mom staying with Grammy?"

He answered abruptly, "No. She's with a friend from work."

And although I was fairly certain where she was and what she was up to, I continued to keep that knowledge a secret, understanding that Mom's betrayal could have horrible consequences for my father.

But that April night without her, under a cool breeze, with our faces turned toward the western part of the sky, I pretended that Mom was searching for the comet with us. I imagined her closing one eye to peer through the end of the giant telescope from the bedroom window in that house overlooking the sea. And I felt better believing we remained connected by the occasion of the comet, all of us searching the stratosphere in unison, like a family.

I missed my mother—the smell of her perfume in the morning as she readied for work, the way she tapped her spoon on the rim of her coffee cup three times before her first sip, her tattered pink slippers at the foot of the bed. I often went into her bathroom and touched the bottles of makeup and nail clippers she had left behind. She wasn't there, but the reminders of her were everywhere.

The comet never came that April night, though our father poured himself two more drinks and kept us up until dawn, promising it would appear.

"Another few minutes," he told Kara, shaking her shoulders to keep her awake as she leaned against him, her head bobbing as she fought off sleep.

"Girls!" he encouraged us. "We can't miss this opportunity."

But Kara and I snuggled up under sleeping bags and blankets on the lawn furniture and fell asleep.

The next morning, while we munched on muffins in the breakfast nook, Dad announced, "Girls, I need your help with something. You're both staying home from school today."

He poured his coffee into a plastic mug and drove us past the bus stop where Dean had made a habit of meeting me. I knew he would wonder where I was, but there was no way to sneak off to call him and explain.

With the radio low, we drove beyond the marsh, through the town's center and out by the freeway to the parking lot of the Stop & Shop, where we napped in the car with our father until the doors opened.

Groggy from the late night, we followed him inside, snaking up and down the aisles until we reached the rows of feminine hygiene products and shampoo bottles.

Dad scanned the shelves.

"What are we getting?" I asked.

"Hair dye," he said, annoyed that he couldn't find it.

"This?" Kara said, pointing to a box featuring a beaming Carol Alt with a dark, shiny mane of hair.

"That's it," Dad said. He chose Miss Clairol, chestnut brown, semi-permanent #700. "Will this work?" He pointed to his hair, looking to me for confirmation.

I laughed, but his stare told me he wasn't kidding.

I picked up a few other boxes and examined the colors, opting for dark chestnut amber #800.

"Dark chestnut amber is a better match," I said.

"Daddy, can I get a candy?" Kara whined as we walked toward the checkout.

I kicked her in the shin to shut her up.

Taking a wad of crinkled singles and a five-dollar bill from his pants pocket, Dad handed his money and the hair dye to me.

"Meet me at the car after you pay," he said. "Kara can have whatever she wants."

In line, my sister and I scanned the Fun Dip candy, Big League Chew bubble gum, and Laffy Taffy. Next to the sweets was a *Time Magazine* showing a picture of Chernobyl's nuclear power plant disaster and the ash-covered crops of the Soviet Union. I imagined the kids in Russia under a red flag, waiting in lines at empty supermarkets with only one kind of bread and no candy at all, as guards rationed their food supplies. I reminded myself that we were lucky, even if our mother was gone and our father was losing his mind.

A cashier with electric-blue eye shadow and a doughy face smiled at Kara, who piled a mound of candy in front of her.

Dad sat in the parking lot with the windows down on his loaner car—he was driving the old Toyota that had belonged to Uncle G, who had kept it as backup for when his plumbing van broke down. Tinny sounds from the radio caught my attention as we approached, the broadcaster letting out a howl, recapping how the New York Mets hit the ball right out of the park the night before. The voice, excited and loud, predicted the blue and orange to take the championship for the 1986 World Series.

"Anyone but New York," Dad said when we climbed in. "Buckner's got to save our Red Sox."

The three of us sat there sharing Laffy Taffy and listening while the station excerpted the hollers of the crowd, followed by the smack of the ball on the bat, a world of baseball for us to disappear inside for a while.

"We should go to Fenway," said Dad. He turned the key. "I'll take you girls someday. No place like it. The bleachers, hot dogs. That old Citgo sign. I took your mother when I came home from the service. It was our first trip after I got back to the States, before you guys were born. We stayed in Kenmore Square. I should have taken her more often. She loved it, even in the cheap seats."

I didn't know how to respond, so I said, "What's with the hair dye?"

"Mom wanted me to take better care of myself. She kept telling me I let myself go." My father slapped his belly. "But I'm gonna start exercising again and get rid of the gray. See if I can get her attention." He nodded to himself. "Everything is gonna be okay, girls. I'll win her back."

Kara and I exchanged glances. We said nothing.

Dad went on. "She's coming by the house later today to collect a few of her things. When I see her, I need to look my best, see if we can talk. But we can't dye it there. I don't want to leave a mess. She hates that."

From the backseat Kara blurted out, "So Mom left us because you got fat and old?"

"Kara!" I yelled.

"Just asking," she said.

Dad flipped on his blinker and turned into Ferry Landing State Park.

"Basically," he explained to Kara, "marriage is like your betta fish. You've got to take good care of it, or it will die. We haven't always taken such good care of ours."

Out before us along the Connecticut River were picnic tables and camping spaces next to public showers and a giant sink to wash camp dishes. "Let's do it here," Dad said, pointing to the facilities. "We just need water and some time."

Because it was an unseasonably warm morning, the park was mobbed with men reading newspapers and stay-at-home moms playing tetherball with small children. We parked in the grass beside a couple drinking from a thermos and holding hands.

"Lovebirds," Dad said under his breath, showing little regard for them as he tromped almost directly across their blanket and waved us on.

"If I remember right, there oughta be a bench and a public bathroom down here, out of the way a bit. Your mom and I camped here once, after drinking and fishing all day. Years ago. Right after we graduated high school."

Dad led us along the river path, beyond the main parking lot to where the grass was high and the fields were full of daffodils.

And while we hiked behind our father, I was guilty of longing to be alone with Dean, to feel his hands under my bra and inside my panties. I felt ashamed for thinking that way in the presence of my father, but I couldn't push the thoughts from my mind.

We reached a clearing with picnic tables scattered along the river's edge. Beside them were beer cans strewn over charred logs from a late-night fire pit.

Out of breath, Dad parked himself on the bench. In his hands he held his Miss Clairol Dark Chestnut Amber #800, thrusting it into the air like a trophy. "Let's get this done," he said.

We tore the box open and I pulled on the clear plastic gloves provided, while Dad shook up the color.

"Take your shirt off, Daddy," I said. "It will stain."

I stood behind my father while Kara held the instructions and snapped her gum. She read to us. "Step 1: Gently massage nutrient-rich color shampoo into hair. Keep off skin."

As instructed, I applied dye the consistency of Hershey's syrup to my father's thinning hair. Overhead the sun cast a golden glow across the meadow while a breeze carried toward us the shrill screams of children playing on the swings, and from the river's edge came the grumbles of small engines turning over as men launched fishing boats from the public landing.

Dad set his digital watch for the required fifteen minutes needed to fix the color. As he waited, he walked the park shirtless, his belly distended and white, and picked dandelions with clear plastic wrap over his head.

Watching him walking through the field with his head down reminded me of a fight my parents had a few months prior. Mom had been angry about bills that had gone unpaid and my father's unemployment. And while she went on yelling and screaming at him, Dad never stopped her. He simply listened, his head hung low, rubbing her back while she pounded the table and shook her head and cried into her hands.

When she finally stood in disgust, tossing the bills across the kitchen and shouting, "I'm taking a shower," Dad went outside and pulled a fistful of dandelions from our lawn. He tied them with twine into a bouquet that he left next to a cardboard heart he cut from an empty cereal box, upon which he wrote: *We'll figure it out. I love you.*

In that meadow along the river at Ferry Park, harvesting a similar spray, he looped the flowers' stems together, placing a dandelion necklace around Kara's neck and a dandelion crown upon her head.

As he called my name, Dad's voice cracked, another necklace in his hand for me.

I wanted to hug him but his sadness frightened me. I could see his pain, but he had worn it so outwardly since my mother left that I had forgotten about it and accepted his despair as typical, simply the way he was.

He circled the flowers around my neck.

I wanted to tell him that everything was going to be okay but I wasn't so sure, so I patted his back and announced, "Time to rinse."

Behind the tables where we sat was a public restroom with cement floors and toilets barely a step above Port-a-Potties. Dad followed behind me and stopped at the sink. I filled his Styrofoam coffee cup with the slow trickle of faucet water, touching my father gently, the way you would caress a kitten, as I rinsed the dye from his hair. Once the water ran clear, I ushered Dad out of the bathroom to wring his hair out in the sun.

"I'm going to get my life back," my father told me. His head was bent over the picnic table as I dried his head with his T-shirt. He slumped forward, his shoulders heaving.

Beyond us, Kara practiced handstands in the tall grass, and in that moment I came close to telling my father that I had set Mom's car on fire to punish her for what she had done to him. I thought it might comfort him to know I was on his side, and I knew it might free me from the horrible burden of carrying a secret. But instead I put my hand over Dad's shoulder and kept quiet.

"I have to look my best," he whispered, gaining his composure as Kara, a dandelion princess carrying imaginary petticoats plucked between her fingers, walked back toward us.

I pulled the comb from Dad's back pocket and raked it through his hair.

"Better?" he asked my sister, turning his head from side to side.

"Better," she told him, though his hair was as black as Darth Vader's mask.

In the car, Dad tilted the rearview mirror to examine my work. "Is it too dark?"

"No," I lied. "It will be lighter when it dries."

We left the park and turned back toward home, passing old tobacco sheds and fallow strawberry fields posting signs: *Pick Your Own*. We drove through the west end of town, alongside estates with lawns like golf courses, before we reached the Quayside Beach Association and the massive white waterfront homes there, so unlike our own, including 101 Quayside, the white mansion topped with a green tin roof, where I had discovered my mother's infidelity.

Behind it was a barn whitewashed by time, and on its pitch, an old weather vane. Shriveled white balloons from a party gone by were tied to the mailbox, and the historical marker on the lawn read, "*Captain Thomas Moses House—1810*." An old collie ran down the lane toward us as we passed. Seeing the place made my heart race, and I could feel my face flush as I looked for signs of my mother.

Dad looked at me then and said, "Imagine what it would be like to live in a place like that."

"I can't," I told him, which was only partly true.

CHAPTER NINE

NIGHT CALLS

MILES DID NOT WAKE UP WHEN THE PHONE CALLS started.

I fumbled in the dark, reaching over him and finding the receiver on the second ring. Answering in a whisper, I peeked at the video monitor to see if Jonah had stirred.

"Hello?" I said, voice full of sleep.

"Claire?"

"Yes?"

"It's Dean. Sorry to wake you. I hadn't heard back, and I'm here just a short time, so I was thinking maybe I can come back in the morning, after your husband leaves. Maybe we could talk over coffee?"

Miles rolled onto his side, then turned on his reading light. "Who is it?" he wanted to know.

Unnerved, I pushed the button on the cordless phone to end the call. "Wrong number," I said, panicked. I held the receiver to my chest, and almost instantly it rang again.

Miles tugged the phone from my grip. "It's late," he said into the receiver. "Who are you trying to reach?"

Fearful that Dean would ask for me, I closed my eyes and wondered how I might explain the call to my husband, curious how much he would care.

When I opened them, Miles was staring at me.

"They hung up," he said and left the phone off the hook on his side of the bed.

Before work, Miles waited on the threshold. He waved to Jonah. "Be good," he said to him, but looked directly at me. His eyes were the color of a lake, dark and bottomless. He was handsome in his suit and tie, his manner serene and steady, but the furrow of his brow betrayed the forced enthusiasm in his tone. "It'll get better, Claire. And I'm sorry about eating dinner in the office last night, about having to work so late. Take a nap if you can. You look tired.

"Good news is that I've collected solid evidence to give the inspector today. The resident I told you about, Dalton Robertson, was definitely in the lab the morning of the fire before he headed upstairs to the wards to round on patients. I have witnesses willing to make formal statements who saw him in the corridor by the cardiology lab moments before the sprinklers went off. The fire chief is meeting me first thing this morning to discuss next steps."

"What a relief," I admitted, a little annoyed by how much of the investigation Miles had taken on himself. It was yet another burden, and an unnecessary one, that took him away from us.

"Shoe!" Jonah screamed, a sneaker in hand, an offering to his dad.

Miles grabbed his keys from the hook, double-checked the contents of his lab bag, and then lifted his head up to the hall-way mirror to inspect his nostrils.

As if it were an old family recipe, I could recite my husband's morning routine, my mind narrating each step like a voice-over in the opening scene of a movie. With Miles's predictability there was seldom any deviation from routine. He shut the door behind him and checked the lock twice after he left.

National Public Radio played at a whisper from the old transistor on top of our refrigerator. *The Writer's Almanac* featured a poem by Wesley McNair, "Goodbye to the Old Life," and although I didn't weep right then and there, I felt it coming.

Outside, the garage door grumbled open.

I lifted Jonah from his booster seat and held him tight. Rocking him in my arms longer than he liked, I listened to my husband gun his Volvo over the snowbank and around the bend. Once he was out of view from the front windows, I put the baby down and checked my Facebook account, eager to hear from Dean.

Claire,

I called too late last night. Sorry for that. I know what we share is complicated, but I swear I'm here with nothing other than your best interests in mind, and I truly believe that you and I could be a big help to each other right now.

Please call once you catch a breather.

My clock here is ticking.

1-860-555-8468.

Yours,

Dean

His persistence flattered me and I wrote him back as honestly as I could, so that for both of us, there would be no more surprises.

Dean—

I am sorry too that I haven't been able to promptly respond to your messages and phone calls to figure out a time for us to meet. To be honest, it is hard, nearly impossible, for me to say no to seeing you. But I also think it is a very dangerous and poor choice for me to be alone with you. We have so much history, and I have been so unhappy, and because of that I just can't have you here in my house. On the rare occasion Miles came home, it would be awkward for all of us.

Love,

Claire

I went about my day then, second-guessing my response, rearranging the living room furniture, and building Lego towers with my son until it was time to put him down. I loaded the dishwasher and streamed the morning news reports from Moffett Field, California, where atmospheric specialist and NASA correspondent Gillian McGowan, one of my dearest friends from graduate school, reported that the Kepler mission had discovered eleven new planetary systems hosting twenty-six confirmed planets.

Just over a month ago, Gillie came from California through Madison to lecture at UW's School of Atmospheric and

Oceanic Sciences with Dr. Doug Hudgins, a NASA scientist we both idolized during our training.

Gillie emailed me about her arrival and we met at a local teahouse, where she divulged the new Kepler discoveries to me over steaming cups of chai, while Jonah sat in my lap scribbling over the chipper expression of Thomas the Tank Engine.

"Don't you miss the research?" Gillie asked me abruptly. She tucked her chestnut hair behind her ear and used her cloth napkin to rub a spot where my son's markers had stained the table.

"Well," I said, kissing the back of Jonah's head, "this little guy keeps me on my toes, and Miles is gone so much that I feel like one of us should be home." I sipped from my tea, suddenly feeling defensive about giving up the work. "Plus, to be honest, Gillie, the research was feeling a little static for me toward the end."

She smiled gently and collected the broken crayons Jonah tossed across the table. "You're so good at being a mom. Frankly, I'd die of boredom if I were home with Caleb and Lila all day. And you were such a dedicated researcher, Claire. Now I bet you would find the field so much more exciting." She handed me a fistful of colors. "Though it might be tough at this point to catch up on all the new data, to become, you know, current. Things have moved so fast. I mean, before this Kepler mission, when you were still working in the lab, there were, what, maybe four hundred known exoplanets?"

"Five hundred," I said, digging in my diaper bag, searching for a sleeve of stickers to entertain Jonah, who'd already had enough. "It was five hundred total known exoplanets across the entire sky."

"God, that seems ages ago. Since you left, Kepler has discovered something like twenty-three hundred more planet candidates, with sixty new planets confirmed."

"Incredible," I said, peeling a *Dora the Explorer* sticker from its backing. "The lab must be buzzing. And you're working with *the* Dr. Hudgins—and at NASA! That's amazing for you, Gillie."

I could sense her attempt to contain her excitement, to protect me from injury, but her eyes shone and she bubbled over, unable to stop herself. "Everyone at the lab is electrified, and the demand for atmospheric investigators is huge, especially with all the global warming and climate changes. It's all the stuff you were doing years ago, but now people want answers, and the industry is committed to solutions. For the first time ever, there's actually money to be made."

Gillie went on enthusiastically and I tried to ignore the jealousy welling up in my throat, understanding the implications of those 2,360 new discoveries.

Jonah pressed Dora's compadre, Diego, to my face. "Sticker!" he declared.

Smiling at my boy, I persuaded myself that motherhood remained enough for me, while estimating that these new findings, having appeared since I first wrote about Kepler five years ago, now rendered my work and my years of training nearly, if not completely, obsolete. I couldn't imagine what I could even offer to the field anymore. And in that moment, I regarded all of my previous research as a lot of hard work and time gone to waste.

Back when I first started working on global-warming investigations during graduate school, my goal had been the same as

Gillie's—to one day work for NASA as an atmospheric specialist in meteorology. My motivation for ozone research and its
effect on the Earth's atmosphere was driven by my fascination
with chemistry, the carbon dioxide produced by combustion
and the sky. But after I fell in love with Miles, his internships
and medical fellowships grounded us in the Northeast and
limited the available opportunities for me, and thus my career
plans grew vague.

Then later, after having my first groundbreaking success at
the University of Connecticut with a paper published in the
esteemed journal *Science*—my article titled "The Sensitivity of
Polar Ozone Depletion"—I believed I was moving closer to
that goal until, with an enormous pregnant belly and a fistful of
blue Mylar balloons, I took Miles's hand after my baby shower
send-off party. I told myself not to cry and held my chin up,
forcing a grin as I hung my lab coat on a hook.

But as my husband hoisted me into our truck, I hadn't completely understood that I would abandon my own future pros-
pects in serious climate-change investigation to chase Miles's
dreams of academic distinction in clinical cardiac medicine.
Driving out of the faculty parking lot, leaning my head against
the passenger window and watching my lab shrink away in the
side-view mirror, I nursed my new ambition to become a loyal
mother to my son, one who would never waver in that role the
way my mother had with Kara and me.

But doing mindless chores while streaming Gillie's account
of Kepler's findings, I couldn't squelch the yearning to be back
in the lab, working with astronomers and astrophysicists fueled
with the same enthusiasm as they hovered over digital images of

the sky, calculating the transit timing variations of new planets orbiting uncharted stars and formulating explanations of how those systems affect Earth and our surrounding atmosphere.

I pulled up the NASA website and studied Kepler's fifty-four planet candidates in the habitable zone, a region where liquid water could exist on a planet's surface. Many of those candidates hosted moons with confirmed liquid, five of which were near Earth-sized, orbiting parent stars. For a moment I experienced that familiar flutter in my chest, the exhilaration I've always received from discovery, but that halted when the doorbell rang.

Heart thumping, I headed for the door, a big part of me hoping it was a return visit from Dean. But when I peeked between the blinds, I caught only a glimpse of the UPS man, who jogged down our drive and left his trail of footprints in the snow.

Once the brown delivery truck pulled away, I fetched the box made out to Mrs. Claire Spruce with *EXPRESS* written in red letters. Carrying it inside, I rummaged through the kitchen drawers for a steak knife to slice through the wrapping.

As Dean promised, inside I found my old track T-shirt with our high school mascot, a Connecticut Yankee, plastered across the front. Pinned to the fabric was a faded Polaroid snapshot, in which I was tanned and barefoot, wearing the logo. A silver medal from a summer race hung around my neck. Flexing a bicep, I smiled for the camera, while Dean's arm rested over my shoulder, a smoke pinched between his index finger and thumb. In the foreground, American flags and streamers waved from the porches of identical houses, Willard Street's preparation for the Independence Day parade.

Boxed up with the T-shirt was a sealed envelope inked: DO NOT BEND. Inside it, my ninth-grade report card and a laminated newsprint image of the Quayside Beach Association sign cast in the bright light of flames, beside it the burning wreckage of the barn at 101 Quayside Lane, the property Dean had bought from my mother. With the image was a yellowed article cut from the *Hartford Courant*, dated July 6, 1986. The headline read: *Second Arson at Lyme Beaches: Police Investigate Connections between Recent Fires after Local Layoffs*.

Turning over the laminated image to return it to the envelope, I found a small note taped to the back composed in the same block letters that addressed the box.

Claire,

My reasons for coming here were not just to see you, that one glance already worth the trip. But I also needed to get away. Things have been tough lately, and somehow I feel that you're the only person I can trust. Anyway, I'm leaving tomorrow night. Before I go, I want to meet in person and give you back your mother's wedding band. Figured it was too valuable to trust with the Pony Express.

1-860-555-8468.

Yours,

Dean

I headed upstairs to hide the contents of the package under a stack of old sweaters. Then said aloud, "Aren't we too old for this?"

Yet I couldn't help but wonder what exactly Dean needed from me, and instantly I was lured back into that dangerous thrill of being with a man who lives by his own moral code. Both intimidated by and attracted to that enigmatic thing living inside Dean, I responded hastily with a message, because he drew out the very impulsive thing living inside me.

Dean—

Jonah has swimming lessons this morning over at the YWCA, so I'm thinking maybe tomorrow if I can get a sitter for the morning, we could meet for coffee? I'm not sure, though. It's short notice. But I'm touched that you still trust me so deeply after all these years. We got away with a lot, you and me, and just so you know, our secrets are the ones I still keep. They have been and always will remain between only you and me.

Fondly,

Claire

Before we headed out for the morning, I fed Jonah and then dug in the front closet for his snowsuit. While we layered up, stomping our feet into snow boots, the telephone calls came again one after another. I paused, glancing at the number on the caller ID, a tightness rising in my chest, a complicated breed of anticipation. Each time a private caller held the line but left no voice mail. I phoned Miles, worried there might be other troubles at the lab, but he answered neither of his extensions at the hospital and failed to respond to any text messages.

Pulling out of the driveway, headed to Mommy and Me swim class, I examined the cars parked along the snowbank on our street and scouted for signs of Dean's silver SUV, thinking about the Polaroid he sent, the image taken the day after my father died.

"Stop it," I ordered myself.

"Stop it!" Jonah mimicked.

He yanked off his hat and tossed his mittens onto the floor.

In the pool at the YWCA, Jonah and I swam away from the steps, and as we became buoyant, I immersed myself in the present. We bounced through the water making motorboat sounds, and my mind drifted. I thought about which dress to wear to a party I was to attend with Miles that night, honoring my husband's students, the MD–PhD candidates at the university. "Try and make the best of things here," I convinced myself.

Along the edge of the pool, the instructor asked us to line up our toddlers. I admired my son's gorgeous, plump belly and his simple energy as he stomped his feet in the puddles along the perimeter of the pool. I was lucky to have this time with my boy, and as he stood there waiting to leap, I felt overwhelmed with adoration.

The audience of mothers and one stay-at-home dad counted as a group: "One, two, three—"

I couldn't contain myself as our babies leaped into our arms. To Jonah, I hollered, "I love you, Ducky!"

"Splash!" he responded and slapped his hands on the surface of the water.

In the shallow end of the pool, we held tight to one another.

I whispered in his ear, "Mama knows how good her life is, Jonah."

We bobbed behind the other parents while I explained myself to my son.

"Mommy is sorry she hasn't been happy here, Ducky. She will do better. That's a promise. Daddy and I are so lucky we can afford for me to be home with you. We have so much. We live in a beautiful, safe place, and we have our health. But I'm just lonely, Ducky. Mommy is sorry for being so lonely."

"Sorry," Jonah repeated. He patted my face and kissed my cheek. "My mommy," he said, and as we reached the concrete steps, he took my hand. Together, my best little buddy and I, we walked up the stairs to the locker room, where we bundled up before we headed out into the cold.

Against a wind that whipped through our coats and sweaters, we walked like astronauts in spacesuits. The gusts were more brutal than the snow squalls trailing behind them, and as we made our way to the car, the predicted flurries began their frenzied descent.

I dug in my pocket for keys, and when I looked toward my station wagon, I saw a silhouette at my driver's side door. I attempted to recall the last chance occasion Miles had joined us for lunch, and seeing him, I grew excited, hoping the fire and the closing of the investigation had put things in perspective for my husband, and brought him back to us.

"Miles!" I shouted.

Like us, he was bundled from head to toe, and through the windstorm I waved to my husband like some girl on a parade float. He waved back triumphantly with both hands, and my earlier worries concerning his missed calls settled down.

"Dada!" Jonah said.

A foot from the car, Jonah reached for him, and as we ran toward his outstretched arms, I noticed a long, blond strand of hair blowing out from under his cap. The man was not my husband; it was Dean.

Picking up Jonah, disconcerted that he would find us there, I walked back toward the doors of the YWCA.

"Claire!" he called.

I scooted between vehicles veiled in white, Jonah's head bobbing as I carried him. He whimpered, "Mommy's car?"

Dean's boots squeaked behind us on the packed snow. "Where are you going, Claire?" he called. "I just want to talk."

I looked around for the possibility of my husband. Flakes stuck to my lashes; the lot was motionless and, besides the three of us, unoccupied.

"I'm sorry, Dean. I just—" I paused, glancing around again. He was leaving soon, and I thought, what harm could it do, agreeing to it. "Okay, yes, let's talk, then. We could take a drive while Jonah naps in the car."

Maybe noting the tension in my grip, Jonah started to cry as we marched against the wind back to my Subaru.

Dean followed at our heels.

"Cheesy crackers?" I offered, trying to comfort Jonah, strapping him into his car seat.

Jonah sniffled. "Milk?"

I cleaned the clear stream of snot running from his nose, then handed the milk to him.

"Adorable kid," Dean said, nonchalantly taking a seat up front, careful not to rush me, but falling in line with my haste to leave and my baseless paranoia that today would be the fluke instance that Miles would surprise us for lunch.

I buckled up, shifted into reverse, and we fishtailed out of the lot.

"I appreciate you taking the time," said Dean. "I know you didn't exactly invite me here."

Driving past the university, I said, "That's my husband's clinic." I pointed out the brick hospital building, the medical campus a sort of compound.

"Looks like a fortress," Dean said.

I vented. "More like a prison. They barely let him out. He puts in fourteen-hour days, sometimes more than eighty-hour weeks, like Rapunzel locked in the tower. Then there's call, every third night and every other weekend. He's totally distracted, obsessed with publishing, with discovery, the way I used to be. He's always talking about medical device innovations, new catheters this, new pacers that."

Glimpsing my husband's car in the hospital lot, I relaxed, stopped talking so fast, and settled into the hush of the falling snow. We drove beyond the university medical center and the emergency vehicles racing past, out along the lake through neighborhoods not my own.

The boulevard became desolate.

And after some time, Dean broke the quiet and told me gently, "You're still so beautiful." He reached to touch a strand of my hair, as if he couldn't help it, then rested his hand lightly on my knee, leaving it there when I didn't protest.

I stared straight ahead, failing to push back the enticement he triggered.

Winding through town, past the capital, talk radio played at a murmur and Jonah fell off to sleep as I knew he would, exhausted by our swim.

"So here's the story," Dean said finally. "You ready?"

And with the question, I was catapulted back into the old thrill of being in it with him, together. "Ready," I said.

He cleared his throat. "My trouble is that the Quayside house is underwater, way underwater. I don't know what I'm doing anymore. It's been a really hard few years," he said, inhaling deeply through his nose. "The property is only appraising at $420,000. I paid $950,000 when I bought it, and the taxes alone are $37,000 a year. I do okay, but I don't do *that* okay. If I sell it now in this fallen market, I'll lose my business. I'll lose everything.

"And I know it's crazy to barge into your life like this, but I'm desperate. I just needed to get away from everything. I didn't know where to turn. I needed to see you. It's probably wrong for me to be here, but sometimes all I can picture is us, walking the beach again. Claire, come east for a few days with me, please. It'll be my belated birthday gift to you. I'll take care of everything."

I thought about his money troubles, how he couldn't possibly afford to do such a thing, how there was no way I could just leave Miles and Jonah like that and go. "Dean, I can't. For so many reasons."

"Why not? There're a million reasons to go. Bring your little boy. Come home, come see the ocean. Visit your sister. Eat scallops. Think about it a bit," Dean insisted gently, his hand massaging my knee. "The inn is super kid-friendly. They have those Pack 'n Play things. You guys could dig some clams like we did as kids. I've got everything you'd ever need."

I looped the last stretch along the lake, then turned back toward town, slowing as we reached the parking lot of the YMCA, not saying a word more.

Dean took his hand off my leg to silence the buzz of his cell phone, but I still sensed the heat of his touch, even after it was gone.

CHAPTER TEN

CONTACT

WHEN HE GOT HOME, I TOLD MILES THAT I didn't feel well, that I couldn't go to the party.

"You're not one to miss a party," he said. He put his hand to my forehead. "You're feeling pretty bad?"

I pressed my head against his palm, wishing Miles could somehow enchant me, the way I felt driving beside Dean, and I hated myself for all of it.

"Sorry," I said. "I was looking forward to meeting everyone."

Miles moved his hand to my cheek, and I let my head fall against his chest.

He said, "You don't feel warm."

"Stomach," I whispered.

But in reality, I was drained. And as much as I wanted to stop myself, I couldn't keep my mind from turning over Dean's invitation, the pull of the ocean, the familiar things there. And despite the immediacy of my refusal, it hadn't sounded convincing, even to me, when on the drive back toward the YWCA, Dean had smiled at the silence between us as if he were recalling some fond memory.

While I was linking the cuffs of Miles's sleeves and straightening out his bow tie, that silence was all I could think about.

Beside us, Jonah steered a tiny train across Miles's dress shoe and over the hardwood floor of the bedroom, the television behind him declaring an Amber Alert for a little girl missing somewhere outside Milwaukee.

Miles and I looked at each other, acknowledging the same parental fear. My husband shook his head gravely, making it a point to touch my shoulder before he turned off the TV and kneeled down next to our boy. "If you go anywhere tonight with Jonah," he told me, "promise me you'll be vigilant. You've been preoccupied, and I worry about you guys too, you know, about something happening here when I'm gone."

As he said this, I imagined rummaging through the baby book to choose a photo for media outlets if our son was ever taken from us. It's the fear I fought throughout my pregnancy—a constant worry that my child might go missing. Maybe it was anxiety grown out of my own youth, when as kids, during the days following my parents' separation, we spent our few hours with our mother collecting provisions for the school week, always lagging in the dairy section among the milk cartons that created a billboard of missing children.

There, Mom pulled Kara and me into a huddle, saying, "Check and see if you recognize any of them." We watched her turn all the faces toward the aisle as she retold the story of Gretchen Carlota, the little girl who was stolen from Hartford Hospital during Mom's shift, shortly after Mom moved in with her boyfriend.

"We were so understaffed and I was so distracted," she explained again and again, "and one night some sicko went into the little girl's room and walked her right out the door." She squeezed us tight. "I'd die without you girls," she said, yet she had chosen to leave us all the same.

Miles ushered me to bed. "Go up to rest. I'll put Jonah down before I leave and bring you up some chamomile."

I watched my husband in his tuxedo play on the floor with our son. Together they counted the small trains Jonah attempted to link together.

What are you thinking, I asked myself. I didn't want to lose the father I saw in Miles, and even more so, I don't want to lose Jonah the way my mother lost me.

In fact, the last time I really believed my mother was mine, she was sitting on the floor beside me, just as Miles was with Jonah that evening. But with Mom and me, it was on the overcast morning of April 11, 1986, Dean's eighteenth birthday. That evening an unseen Halley's comet would make its closest pass of the Earth amid overcast skies. Mom no longer lived with us, but she had come to my father's house to pick me up for our freshman class trip to Mystic Seaport.

She had volunteered to chaperone in an effort to spend more time with me and arrived early, before I was dressed, with a tray of coffees, one for herself, one for my dad, and one for Uncle G, her brother, who had become a fixture in our house after Mom's departure. She did her best to be kind to my father when their paths crossed, even though her gestures were often perceived as charity acts by Dad, who took the steaming cups from her and, as we watched, poured them down the sink.

Mom did not react, but tiptoed upstairs ahead of me to peek in on Kara who was still asleep in her bed. From behind her, I admired Mom's low ponytail that fell down her back over her

short-sleeved angora sweater, paired with pin-striped Gloria
Vanderbilt jeans, the back pockets of which were dusted with
little rhinestones. She looked skinny to me, and in those days
she seemed to grow younger by the day, dressing less like the
moms on our cul-de-sac in their sweatshirts and corduroys, and
more like the college girls that Uncle G and Dad whistled at
from the porch.

In my parents' old bedroom, Mom sat Indian-style on the
braided rug while I changed outfits once, twice, then a third
time in front of the full-length mirror. Mom sipped her decaf,
watching me examine myself over each shoulder, and asked
finally: "Besides the field trip, what are you dressing for?"

Her direct questioning always disarmed me. There was
no judgment in her voice, no attempt to uncover a secret
(although she was often intuitive about when to probe), and her
inquiries were presented practically, as if she were speaking to
an adult. Because of this, she was always the parent with whom
I was most likely to divulge the truth.

"It's my boyfriend's birthday," I blurted. "So I was going to
skip the bus ride home and have him pick me up for a concert
in New London. I told Dad the trip goes late."

Mom responded as candidly as she'd asked. "Then wear the
black jeans."

She pulled them from a pile of crumpled clothes and smoothed
them out before us, matching them with different tops, as we
knelt on floor together in the way I imagined a real mother and
daughter would—for the last time I can really remember.

And before sending Miles off to his party alone, I lingered in
the doorway. I watched my boys link the caboose to their line

of passenger cars, and I considered, for the first time, a confession, revealing the truth to Miles about the Facebook flirtations, about Dean's coming here and his invitation to fly me home, and taking responsibility for all of it. I consider what it would mean to disclose this truth to Miles, to ask for his forgiveness and move forward.

But because I had left too much of my history untold, so many details of my past life hidden from him, and with things so shaky between us, I guessed that the truth might come with its own threats, offering little protection and too much to wager. So I headed straight to bed without reaching for him at all.

At midnight, the second evening in a row, the house phone rang. And even though I was home alone, I didn't answer it, believing that Dean was calling for an answer.

It rang again at one. Then two. Then three.

Miles was still not in bed following the last call. He had left for the dinner party hours earlier, and although the event itself would never go that late, I had foreseen my husband talking about databases and patents and hospital policies, and drinking scotch from a flask in the lab with the post-docs until sunrise. I also knew that if he indulged in more than a single cocktail, he would never risk driving home, but would instead curl up on the couch in his office to sleep for the night. I checked my cell phone just in case he'd tried to contact me and found no text messages, which was his preferred mode of communication. Slightly worried, I tossed and turned.

At four a.m. I woke abruptly on my own and called Miles's cell phone.

It rang from the floor beside the bed where he must've left it in the pocket of his white coat.

By six in the morning, I woke again. Panicked and pacing the rooms of our house, I opened Miles's office door, where I found my husband still in his tuxedo jacket and asleep at his computer. EKGs and files from the fire investigation were scattered on the floor. A sense of relief and frustration washed over me, my worry wasted on what I should have already known— Miles was working, and this time right here at home.

While I stood in front of him, the landline rang for the fourth and final time. I picked up the phone on his desk and said nothing.

The caller held the line.

Miles didn't stir.

"Dean?" I whispered. "I want to go home with you."

That morning, when I emerged from the house to head out for milk, Miles's car was long gone. I opened the door of my Subaru with my son perched on my hip and strapped him inside.

Jonah pointed.

I startled.

Against the bumper of my car, his back to us, Dean smoked a cigarette and sipped from a thermos.

I slammed the door. "You scared me," I shouted.

He turned, calm, Romanesque in stature, and smiled.

I envisioned Vulcanus, the god of benevolent and hindering flames, and in that sober light of morning I became uncertain of my decision and disgusted with myself. "You know—" I began.

"Claire," Dean interrupted, sensing my hesitation, "I'm not trying to complicate your life. You wanted to be rescued, remember?" He lowered his voice and moved closer. "It'll do you good," he reassured me. His eyes watered from the cold, and he wiped them on the unfastened sleeves of his coat.

Something about his gesture prompted a recollection of the clean-shaven boy I remembered—Dean genuflecting in the aisle at my father's funeral, weeping into his hands before making the sign of the cross. How he touched my waist and shuffled us into the pew, where he stood between Kara and me, his arms draped over our shoulders, pulling us in tight, a gesture I had seen him do with his own sisters when they were brokenhearted over boys.

His grip never softened during the opening hymn, "Be Not Afraid," sung by Uncle G, who wore Dad's only tie. The casket was draped with an American flag in front of the altar, and in the pew in front of us, my mother clasped her husband's hand so tightly that her knuckles went white. And during Uncle G's shuddering through the last lines of the song, I cried into the sleeve of Dean's linen sport coat, which was held in place by two silver safety pins where the sleeve buttons had gone missing.

Nuzzling his face into my hair, then looking up toward the ceiling, Dean said, "I'm sorry, Mr. Spruce. I promise to always look after Claire."

Then, in front of Father Motta, in front of my mother and her husband and all the guys from Dad's heyday, before all the cousins and aunties and uncles and neighbors who had come to grieve with us in disbelief, Dean escorted Kara and me from the church into the black stretch limo that chauffeured us to the cemetery blooming with tiger lilies, delphinium, and irises, among which a dark hole had been hollowed into the ground.

At the reception that followed, Dean nodded solemnly to my mother and lifted my sister up off her feet for one last hug before he took my luggage upstairs to the guest bedroom in Craig Stackpole's house. Standing beside the window, overlooking the spot where it happened, the charred wreckage of the barn like a dark wound in the dry grass, we made love through my weeping. The salt of my tears was in our mouths, my sobs soaking the strands of hair around my face.

With the pinned-together cuff of his linen coat sleeve, Dean wiped my face, as he loved me in the guest bedroom, one that would later become my bedroom until I left for good. He told me simply, "I'm sorry for everything."

Jonah banged on the car window, jarring me from the reverie, while my old protector snuffed out his cigarette in the driveway.

There was no reason for me to believe that Dean was wrong.

He said, "A few days alone might be good for Miles too. Plus, I'm desperate. You're desperate too. I can see it. You can't lie to me."

He was right. I couldn't. And clearly he had come to protect me, to keep his promise to my dad, this time safeguarding me from loneliness.

Thankful for it, I reluctantly resolved myself to the trip. "I'll come. I could use the break to think. But I'll need some time to figure out the details before I go."

Dean rested his thermos on the hood of his car and bent toward me, our faces close enough to kiss. He drew a document from his inner jacket pocket and placed it in my hand.

"I've given you time," he said softly. "You've emailed me for weeks, and I'm here because you asked for help. Flight itinerary is in the envelope. You take off Monday, and there's an additional ticket for the little guy."

We stared at each other, and as we did, I surrendered to the teenaged boy who'd held me up as they lowered my father's body into the ground and the grown man who had come all this way to reclaim the memory of the girl I used to be.

He added, "I've arranged for everything."

Worried about the money and about how he could afford to do such a thing, I said, "That's too generous a gift. And what am I supposed I tell Miles?"

"The truth. Tell him you're homesick, that it'll do you good to get out of here for a few days. Moving is stressful. And your husband is never home anyway. Who knows, maybe it will do you both some good."

I scrabbled for some vestige of an excuse to refuse an

invitation I so badly wanted to take and told Dean, "I'll need to discuss it with my husband first," rationalizing to myself that all Miles's professional stressors only seemed to propel him further out of my orbit.

Dean nodded. "It will be good for you."

Then, feeling it was complicated by my part in what had brought Dean there, I folded the envelope into my coat pocket, and my throat tightened with the deep-rooted affection and attraction I have always felt for him.

Dean's fingertips grazed my cheek.

Miles will barely know we're gone, I reasoned, and almost believed it myself.

Miles accepted the idea of a visit back home so easily that it almost hurt to think he could let us leave his side with such little fuss.

"I think I want to go home for a little while," I told him. "I've got a voucher, so it won't cost us anything. I just want to see the ocean, smell the air, and catch up with some friends. I thought I'd take Jonah with me. Maybe even see my mom while we're out there. It's been a really long time."

"If it will make you feel better, honey, you should go. I'm tied up with this whole mess at the lab anyway, and there are deadlines looming. Plus, I've got patients booking six months out. Maybe it'll be a good time for you to get away." He paused to consider. "It makes sense really. And the fire chief still believes the arsonist may have targeted me personally. He's not

convinced Dalton had anything to do with it. Who knows?"
He shook his head. "Anyway, I'd sleep better knowing you
two were far from all the unknowns."

Later that week, in between packing and cooking meals to
leave behind for my husband, I received a text from Miles at
midday, asking if he could spend some time with us before
we went.

> C—I signed my pager over to one of the fellows. I'd like to arrange
> to get off early to be with you and Jonah this evening.—M

But when he finally walked in, dinner had long been served,
the dishes were done, and Jonah was in his pajamas. Straddling
the large suitcase I'd wrestled to the floor, packed with wool
socks and sweaters, our mittens and hats, and my best-fitting
pair of jeans, I forced the zipper over a bursting seam.

Miles tossed his keys on the counter, saying, "I'm later than I
thought I'd be." *So what else is new*, I wanted to say. He examined my face for the complaint I didn't make, then glanced
down at the gigantic suitcase.

"Thought it was a short trip," he said, gently moving my
hands away from the zipper. After rearranging our bulky shoes
and rolling Jonah's clothes into tubes, he tossed out a few
stuffed bunnies. "Those guys," he announced, "can keep me
company." Then he zipped the bag shut with ease.

"Thanks," I said.

Miles nodded. "I know you're mad. I'm sorry, honey. I tried to be here sooner."

Hearing his daddy's voice, Jonah raced stiff-legged, a tiny Frankenstein, and crashed into Miles, wrapping his arms tight around his father's knees.

"My dada!" he screamed.

I left the last of the packing for later and headed into the kitchen, lifting the lid of the Crock-Pot to stir the stew.

"Smells amazing," Miles said, coming up behind me with Jonah in his arms.

I set a spoon down on the counter. "Figured I'd make something you could live off a while," I told him, filling him a giant, steaming bowl.

Patting my back, Miles said, "I really am sorry. I got caught up with a patient. A case came as I was leaving, and it wasn't something I felt the new resident could handle. But I'm here now. Should we open a bottle of wine to have with dinner?"

"You should," I said, still annoyed. "We ate." I poured Miles a glass from the bottle I was already into. "But please, stop telling me you're on your way home only to show up two or three hours later. I'd rather assume you can't make it in time for supper than end up disappointed."

Slurping broth from his bowl, Miles followed Jonah into the playroom.

We sat on opposite ends of the couch while our toddler dumped wooden blocks from a plastic bin onto the hardwood floor, and the distinct quiet between my husband and me—that reserve like a wall between us—reminded me of my parents' silence before their split.

"Let's build a tower!" Miles cheered in an attempt to redeem the night and my mood. He placed his dinner aside and kneeled on the ground to stack the blocks three feet high.

Jonah, wild with laughter, knocked the tower to the ground.

"Mommy, we need you," Miles said. "Come help us."

"You don't need me," I hissed.

He paused. "You're right to be frustrated, Claire. I understand. Take the next few days to go home and relax. When you come back, I promise I'll try harder to keep my schedule a bit lighter." He searched my face. "And maybe I can do a better job about setting expectations. Okay?"

Tugging me beyond the rubble to his Matchbox cars, Jonah called, "Come, Mama! Come!"

For my son, I softened and knelt beside my husband, while Jonah, the link holding us together, rested one hand on Miles and the other on me. Together, we sat close driving imaginary race cars and rocket ships, sending bunny and owl to the moon, until the clock chimed eight and Miles carried Jonah up to bed.

In the kitchen, I puttered until my husband returned, rubbing up behind me while I rinsed suds out of the baby bottles. Slipping his hands into the front pockets of my jeans, he asked, "Come watch a movie with me?"

"Early flight tomorrow. I'll never survive an entire movie."

He moved my hair off my shoulder. "One sitcom? You pick. I'm done making decisions for today. I just want to be close to you."

Curled up on the couch, I chose the first episode of a miniseries we had both already seen, and before we even got past the opening credits, Miles fell sound asleep, the plush pugs under his head for a pillow.

Once his snoring started, I eased out from under the throw
and tucked him in tight. Turning the television off, I set the
baby monitor beside him, and, anxious about the trip and
what might happen when I arrived home, I headed outside
for a walk.

Four blocks downhill from our Madison address, I passed
snowbanks the size of hedges. I breathed in the cold, longing
for the mucky smell of the coast, the winter rows of sailboats
cocooned tightly under shrink wrap, and the salt marshes back
east whose waters freeze slick enough to skate between the
reeds, just once or twice before the snow comes.

Out in front of the Heiden Haus, the neighborhood warming hut for the pond was fenced with Plexiglas and cast under
lights. Big Wisconsin boys looped the rink and their blades
hissed by, while they shouted to one another for the puck, the
defenders approaching the forwards to obstruct a drop pass.

I loved that blunt sound of hockey, the noise of skates
over ice and bodies colliding up against the glass, so I ducked
inside the warming hut to watch the players, remembering my
father's love for the game, the Hartford Whalers on our TV all
winter and into spring, Dad's fist pounding the table through
the Adams Division games, always disappointed by the lack of
a Stanley Cup.

Sitting there in Madison, I recollected my hometown hockey
pond in Connecticut at the far end of Marsh Cove, where Kara
and I learned to skate. With my teeth chattering and Dean's

winter coat spread across my lap, I followed the tilt of his body—LIUT, the name of the Whalers' superstar goalkeeper, lettered across his back—as he shifted his weight from knee to knee, tending the net.

Watching the players in scarlet University of Wisconsin hockey jerseys over their pads, I was the only spectator in the hut, and their voices grew rowdier when a mammoth forward broke up the center. He and the goalie shuffled, a sort of dance, then the giant slapped the puck into the corner pocket for score.

His teammates erupted into song and roared with delight: "Whoomp, there it is! Whoomp, there it is!"

And as they sang, the titan hurled his stick into the night to lead a celebratory lap around the rink. His minions circled behind him, chanting the remainder of the chorus: "Whoomp chak a laka chak a laka chak a laka chak a!"

I chuckled at the boys from where I remained invisible in the dark, some part of myself stirring as I coveted their youth and wondered what kind of teenager Jonah would grow up to be.

The opposing goalie, racing counterclockwise, greeted the massive offender and his parade to present them with a gleaming silver flask. The opponents skated together to form a circle around which they passed the vessel for a clandestine drink. After each boy had taken his swig, they moved back to the center of the rink, finding their positions. Subdued laughter rose from the ice and the boys faced off.

Standing outside of it all, looking toward home, I stepped out from the hut and stumbled over an enormous pair of snow boots in the footpath.

Inside the right shoe, I recognized the blue packaging on a box of American Spirit cigarettes, paired with a yellow lighter. Next to it, the left mate housed a can of aerosol foot spray and a pair of wool socks. I stepped two paces past the suggestion, then turned back, some old danger blooming in me as I seized the cigarette lighter and aerosol can, dropping each into a deep pocket of my peacoat.

I held my breath quiet, welling with rebellion, and veered in the direction opposite home, jogging past the snow-covered basketball courts, hurrying beyond the buried baseball field, and reaching the local elementary school, where I followed the footpath alongside the building. Attempting to dampen the unruliness that surged through me, I slipped between two rusted Dumpsters, whispering, "Don't."

But hidden and bent low between the bins, I did. Taking the spray can in my left hand, I pressed my index finger to the trigger. The aerosol's silver mist cast into the dark, and the mischief I undertook bubbled up into an irrepressible giggle. I spun the wheel of the lighter under my right thumb, but I got only a spark.

I looked around and flicked it again to no avail.

Peering past the field to the pond beyond it, I saw that the boys continued to skate.

Determined, I shook the lighter, striking it once more, and the flint ignited into a single, glorious flame.

I considered the fire and brought it closer to the spray.

Mist touched flare. A flash threw heat, a luminous cloud of oranges and blues.

Happiness stirred inside me, a breed of delight. I admit that I couldn't stop. I threw a second burst of fire from my handmade torch. It gusted between the Dumpsters, where recyclables and cardboard boxes were stacked high.

Whoomp, there it is, I thought, that instantaneous rush of a blaze.

The conflagration warbled; heat carried on the breeze like a weather front.

I tossed the can back at the rush of flames and ran, flashes of heat and light lapping after me like tongues. Sprinting, the yellow lighter still clenched in my fist, I raced away from the school, around the building, back along the paved footpath, and into the darkness. At the edge of the schoolyard, breathless, I slowed to a stroll, returning to myself as I ambled past the frosted baseball fields, beyond the basketball courts, and back toward the now-empty ice rink.

Behind me something burst.

Nearing the warming hut, I heard laughter from the boys resonating off the Plexiglas, and, like an echo's callback, sirens sounded.

Whirling lights, red and blue, intersected my course.

My heart leaped.

You're just a forty-year-old mom out for a walk, I reminded myself. I kept my steps steady and deliberate.

Two officers stepped from a cruiser, flashlights in hand. The first cop, virtually a child himself, called to the boys with a blare horn.

"Gentleman, I'll need everyone's identification."

I slowed my pace and glanced at the blaze beyond the rink. It flayed forward and shrank back.

A second squad car whipped into the elementary school parking lot, and its headlights searched out over the snowfields. I kept moving, my hands in my pockets, where the lighter was clenched in my fist.

With the blare horn clipped to his waist belt, the young officer led a boy in handcuffs to his police car. Behind me were the squeaks of footsteps on the frozen snow. Then an elongated double of my frame was cast into a shadow by a penlight.

"Excuse me, ma'am?" the second officer called out.

I turned, my heart fluttering like a hummingbird. The cop dropped the light from my eyes.

"Officer Murphy," he said, jogging closer. "You live in the neighborhood?"

I shrank my shoulders up to my neck to pinch out the cold. My pulse was a noise I was certain he could hear.

"Yes. Moved in a few months ago, up over the sledding hill. Near the golf course on Topping Road."

I gestured with my chin, released the hidden yellow lighter from my pocketed grip, and offered him my hand.

"Claire Spruce," I said.

He pulled a notepad from his breast pocket and jotted a note.

"Won't keep you long, Ms. Spruce. Just a few questions."

Behind us a boy shouted. "That's *bullshit*. Search whatever the hell you want."

Officer Murphy thumbed his hand back toward the noise.

"Got some underage drinking and pyromania. Was wondering if you witnessed any hoopla by the rink or near the elementary school."

I tugged my hat over my ears and made it a question. "Playing hockey?" It sounded like a guess. I shrugged and added, "Maybe forty or so minutes ago, when I headed by on a walk, they were just skating and singing. A quiet night, otherwise."

"Hockey," he confirmed, nodding at my inanity, tucking

his notepad back into his jacket pocket. His walkie-talkie squawked. "Thank you, ma'am. That's all I need for tonight."

I nodded and moved unhurriedly along the path he illuminated ahead of me.

Up the hill and back into the dark near home, I considered the teenaged boy in the backseat of the cruiser, the envelope from Dean hidden in my closet, Jonah asleep in his crib, the trip we were about to take, and Miles, never stirring as I slipped out, still snoring now on the couch.

I pulled the lighter from my pocket and fingered its trigger with my thumb. As a forty-year-old, stay-at-home mom, I couldn't be further off anyone's radar. Any of that old danger beating inside me was invisible to nearly everyone.

PART 2

"Somewhere out in the back of your mind
Comes your real life and the life that you know."
— Stevie Nicks, "Rooms on Fire"

CHAPTER ELEVEN

HOMECOMING

MILES DROVE JONAH AND ME TO THE AIRPORT FOR our departure, and as we pulled up to the curb, he looked over the seat at our boy, then back at me.

"Claire…I know I agreed to this, but to be completely honest, I started worrying last night that a trip might not be such a good idea. Are you sure you want to go? You seem so spacey lately. The oven was on again when I got up this morning, and I had to blow out a candle in the living room. That stuff makes me nervous about you traveling alone with the baby."

I took a deep breath. "We better head out," I said. "And please don't worry. I'm fine, really."

A couple parked in front of us unloaded their luggage and shared a long, passionate good-bye. Slipping his hands into the back pockets of the woman's jeans, the man snatched her back close to him every time she attempted to leave.

Inspired by them, I supposed, Miles pulled me across the console jammed with empty juice boxes and Matchbox cars and brushed a kiss over my forehead. He whispered, "And if you see your mom while you're home, don't get into it with her, okay? Keep things light."

Of course, she had no idea I was headed east, though I'd let Miles believe a meeting between us could take place, even though I'd only spoken to my mother a handful of times in the last two decades. The first phone conversation was when I graduated from college. The second was when I got into graduate school, and the third was to announce my wedding, to which she was not invited because she refused to attend without Craig. The fourth call was to tell her I was pregnant with Jonah.

In that stretch of twenty-some-odd years, I saw my mother once, during my extended hospital stay after the birth of my son. And the only contact I'd initiated with her since was in the mass mailing forwarding our new contact information in Madison to everyone in our address book, in case she needed to reach us in some kind of emergency.

Occasionally after that, Mom sent gifts to Jonah. The enclosed letters were often addressed solely to him, occasionally to us both, always written on the same monogrammed stationery pressed with her and her husband's initials.

The last time I saw my mother, she looked well preserved, her eyebrows penciled in to set off her steel-colored eyes, and she wore a sundress that hugged her slim figure. Her giant silver bangle bracelets clanged together like cymbals as she entered the hospital room in a burst of noise after my thirty-three hours of active labor, followed by what ended in an emergency C-section that saved both Jonah and me from the unimaginable.

Mom thrust a bottle of champagne in my lap and left a perfect blot of coral lipstick on Miles's face, then, hanging over my shoulder, she rubbed her thumb along Jonah's brow, murmuring: "He looks like your father, don't you think? He has your father's fair skin and his cleft chin."

For me, the comment took from that moment, reminding me

of our collective loss at a time when I needed to be protective of my new joy. Heatedly, and retrospectively I think wrongly, I sent her away without letting her hold her grandson. Since then our correspondence has been limited to letters in which she tells Jonah where "Mimi" (which is how she refers to herself) has been traveling with Craig (whom she calls "Pop-pop") and what types of restaurants they are enjoying in Fort Lauderdale by the Sea, where her husband bought a condo on the four-teenth floor of a giant, pink skyscraper.

When the letters from my mother arrive, if compelled to open them at all, I skim them quickly and throw them away, her loopy scrawl always a sad reminder of the long-ago note she wrote to my father, marking the change of everything.

When I boarded the plane to Connecticut, I already knew I would not see my mother or her husband. Their sale of the Quayside to Dean was something I had not shared with my husband, who believed they were living mostly in Connecticut until Craig could formally retire from the financial sector, at which point they would move to the condo in Florida to golf and sail away their golden years together. Miles never asked much about my family, so when he hefted our baggage from the car and told me not to get into things with my mother, should I see her, I said simply, "I won't. I promise."

An airport security officer whistled his horn and instructed us to "move it along," signaling to Miles that he could not park at the curb.

Relieved to hurry along the good-byes, I said, "See you soon," and pushed against the January gale to curbside check-in.

"How soon?" Miles shouted over the noise of a shuttle.

"Four days—unless we decide to never come back," I said, trying to tease.

Miles pulled Jonah from his car seat and hugged him tight. "You have to come back," he told me. "We're in this together."

I dragged our bags behind me, while the frigid wind whipped my hair into my eyes.

Holding him close, patting Jonah's bottom, Miles said, "I miss you already, bud." Then, to the bulky security officer who blew a whistle as he circled our car, my husband called, "One more second, sir," holding up his index finger, racing us toward the check-in counter.

Together, we three stormed the line and I dug the necessary documents and ID from my coat pocket. There, I discovered the yellow lighter tucked among the paperwork and quickly slipped it into our checked bags before the airline attendant tossed them onto the conveyor belt.

"Park and come inside," I told my husband, meaning it. "Wait with us. We can grab coffee. Talk, maybe?"

He squeezed my shoulder, and his concerned face looked back at the officer who stood at the rear of our vehicle. "I feel guilty just leaving you guys here, and I do want to talk...but they need me in the ER. There's a patient on life flight headed in now." He rubbed his chin and pulled me in for a hug one last time. "I better run," he said. "Safe flight, okay? We'll talk more when you get home. Love you."

He walked to the car, and a part of me believed I should

chase after him. I wanted us to hold each other like we had outside his vandalized lab, to stand inside a moment together so I could explain how I was about to violate his trust and have him stop me before I went any further. I wanted to apologize for being so distracted, so absent from him, and to tell Miles I was so sorry for his losses—the data and the research—and to admit that I too was remorseful for my part in the distance between us.

Hoping he might return to Jonah and me for that imagined embrace, I called, "Miles." He turned back to us, raised his hand in a Chief Wahoo wave, and then dropped into the front seat of his car.

"Bye-bye, Daddy," I whispered into Jonah's ear.

"Bye-bye!" Jonah said.

I set Jonah down and he toddled ahead of me, dragging his robot backpack behind him through the sliding terminal doors. Following my son, I glanced over my shoulder to the roadway, scrutinizing the taillights of Miles's Volvo. His blinker signaled. He turned out into traffic, and inside me was a pang.

Landing at Bradley International Airport is like arriving at a Chili's restaurant with airplane access. The airport is small with just two snack kiosks, a Dunkin' Donuts, and a merchandise stand selling Hartford Whalers hockey T-shirts, even though the team left Connecticut fifteen years ago.

Having declined Dean's offer to greet us, I walked the short distance to baggage claim with Jonah and out the door into the grim fog that often accompanies a New England winter. Out along the tarmac, I watched flaggers direct a tiny Airbus backing from the gate. And there, despite all of it, I shivered with the jubilant sensation of a homecoming.

"Jonah!" I squealed. "We're here."

We picked up the rental car Dean had arranged and headed down Interstate 91 South to the Bee and Thistle Inn, where a two-bedroom suite awaited us. Maneuvering that familiar stretch of road, I shed layers of my current self and steered us into a memory. Dizzy with pleasure the day I got my license, I had driven my first car along that very stretch—over the Baldwin Bridge, off Exit 22, and onto Route 9, the corridor of my youth.

Near the Shoreline Service Center, I slowed as we approached the corner where my father first taught me how to pump gas into Mom's station wagon and check the oil on the old Dove, long before I set it on fire or could drive myself. A few hundred yards later, I saw the tattered green awning of his old watering hole, Cherry Stones, from which Mom and I would fetch him after too many hours passed, while Kara slept in the back the way Jonah dozed off behind me in the backseat of the rental car.

I got a wobble in my belly going back to the East Coast. It was the combination of joy mixed with the dread that comes from realizing that time never holds still and that the old haunts are not always as charming as nostalgia claims.

Passing the turnoff to my childhood development, I saw a yellow sign reminding drivers to slow for pedestrians. The stick-figure person on the roadway marker had been spray-painted with a giant blue cock and balls. And beyond the sign, the houses I envied as a kid look tired and overgrown.

Moving from East Lyme to the haughtier west side of town, where my inn awaited me on its scenic ocean lot, I regarded the tidelands, where brown sea grasses swayed and the naked sumac trees stood watch over the winter that froze everything into slow motion.

At the Bee and Thistle, I did as Dean asked and registered for the room under the name Mary Tooke, the wife of Edmund Halley, discoverer of our comet and a pet name Dean once called me. "Room's under your nickname," Dean wrote in his envelope of printed instructions. "And I paid for all of it in cash in case your husband asks questions."

Up a creaky staircase I carried the skeleton key to a two-bedroom suite draped with too many doilies and lace curtains. The place had the musty smell of a beach property, and a newly lit fire roared for us in the hearth. A Pack 'n Play was set up already, the sheets laid smooth, so I put a sleeping Jonah down, hoping he would continue his snooze while I headed into my adjoining room for a shower, wondering exactly what it was I expected to find there.

Washing my hair, I thought about the last time I was in a hotel without Miles, nearly five years prior, before I quit my meteorology program. At an inn similar to this one near the Idaho State University campus, I'd spent a week attending a women's science convention, during which Barbara Morgan spoke to five hundred female students and faculty members at the Rendezvous Complex planetarium on the twelfth anniversary of Christa McAuliffe's death.

Barbara Morgan, runner-up for the Teacher in Space Project and later a mission specialist for NASA, had become a full-time astronaut at age fifty-five. Her hair was streaked with silver when she walked to the podium to deliver her lecture, and she took her time to adjust the microphone and pour herself a tall glass of water. Projected onto an enormous screen behind her was a slide show of the Milky Way taken from the Hubble space telescope. Looking back at the image, she cleared her throat.

"Although we've been researching for years, we've learned very little about this universe and our own atmosphere," Morgan told us. "It's exciting to realize how much there is left to know about the sky."

The projection transformed from an assembly of stars to an earlier image of Barbara Morgan, at age thirty-two, seated beside Christa McAuliffe, both of them in spacesuits holding helmets in their hands.

To me, it seemed unfair that she would still be cast in McAuliffe's shadow over a decade later, despite her own merits as an astronaut and scientist.

As she took a moment of silence to acknowledge Christa McAuliffe, my admiration for Barbara Morgan was replaced with tenderness, seeing that even with all her accomplishments, the astronaut would forever be wedded to the ghost of my childhood hero, never moving beyond second place.

"It's very loud, very shaky, and you're pressed back in your seat," Professor Morgan said as she explained her first mission. "It's difficult to breathe. But I'm not scared by it anymore. In fact, I'm usually relieved that we're finally launching after that three-and-a-half-hour wait."

She scanned the audience.

"Ladies, imagine the speed at which the launch happens by

closing your eyes, picking a destination five miles away, and envisioning being there in just one second. It's 0 to 17,500 miles per hour in only eight and a half minutes. The movement is faster than a blazing fire."

The Bee and Thistle's floorboards creaked when I tiptoed from the bathroom to the bedroom, toweling off my hair. Turning the corner to check on Jonah in the connecting room, I startled.

Dean stood quietly in the doorway.

"Jesus," I said. "You need to stop doing that."

Wearing a button-down shirt and khaki pants, he held out a bouquet of orange tiger lilies, my favorite flower.

"Shhh." He held a finger to his lips. "Baby's asleep." He pushed the blossoms into my arms. The cellophane wrapping crinkled.

Too awkward to speak, I smiled, sniffed the flowers, and carefully set them on a wingback chair by the fireplace.

Dean wrapped his arms around me. He kissed my neck once, under my ear. The gesture was intimate; the hug lasted longer than a hello. Then he kissed my lips, just a peck, and I pulled away, confused by all my unanchored emotions.

"I have the other key," he whispered, setting it on my bedside table where he had poured us each a drink. He handed me a wineglass, took one for himself, and said, "Welcome home."

I took a sip.

Dean sat on the bed and patted the spot beside him.

"Come," he said. "Let's talk."

CHAPTER TWELVE

STRATEGY

I BEGAN PORING OVER THE IMAGES OF DEAN ON Facebook because I wanted to learn what had become of him in the world, not because I wanted to sleep with him. Initially, I just wanted to scroll through the pictures of his wife and compare myself to her. I was curious. I wanted to see their babies—which I was sad to learn he never had—and I wanted to understand the kind of life Dean ended up with, to see if it was different from the life he might've had with me.

And because I had overheard the hushed voices of mothers in Jonah's music class and older women speaking in whispers in the locker room of the YWCA where I swam, I knew that there was a nation of women out there hunched over iPads and laptops in the evenings, searching for the boys they first gave themselves to, while their husbands worked into the night or watched the Golf Channel silently beside them in comfortable living rooms. Women like me who avoided the dangers that fed our girlhood desires, and who were finally free of worry but full of longing for that kind of passion and our youth, both of which were fleeting if they had not vanished from our lives completely.

But I never planned for those what-if fantasies to move from the virtual world to my bedside at the Bee and Thistle Inn, where Dean and I perched apprehensively on the edge of a brass bed and touched our stemmed glasses together in present time.

"Claire," Dean said as if we were on a date, "to your return."

The St. Christopher medal around his neck was the same one he wore at age seventeen, and strung next to it was the gold wedding band my father gave my mother in 1969, the day after he was drafted for Vietnam. After she left us, my mother set the ring on my bureau next to my ballerina jewelry box with a note she had scrawled quickly, the ink smeared by her hand: *Claire, a keepsake that you may want someday. Love, Mommy.* It fit my index finger, and before sliding it on, I looked inside the band and read the inscription, *K&P Forever*, a reminder for me that nothing promised to us was certain.

Shortly after my parents' divorce was finalized, I could no longer bear to wear the gold band. So after we made love on the beach one night, I plucked it off my finger and offered it to Dean with a different kind of vow.

"Let's never be like our parents," I said.

"Easy promise to keep." Then he threaded my mother's wedding band through the gold links of his chain.

As we sipped our wine, Dean noticed my eyes on the band. "I've worn it a long time," he said and unhooked the chain. "Give me your hand."

I did as he said, and he pressed each one of my knuckles against his lips. I closed my eyes, permitting his touch, knowing full well that it was wrong.

When his mouth reached my pinky finger, he turned my hand over and imprinted the band against the fleshy part of my palm.

I closed my fingers around it.

Dean was near enough to detect the heat of him, the pressure of his thigh against mine. My entwined emotions of desire and hesitation unnerved me, even though I'd allowed him to make the hotel reservations, his intentions made clear. And although I had not invited him to the room, his ambitions were the same ones I had entertained myself.

There, with him at my side, my allegiance grew confused. I breathed him in, that smell of his like summer rain on hot pavement, something clean and earthy, familiar and enticing. It had been a long time since I yearned for a man this way, and I knew that if I didn't move from my place next to him on the bed, Dean would kiss me again, and what would unfold from that moment would be something I couldn't stop.

With my mother's ring branding a mark in the center of my fist, I reminded myself of what I didn't want to be. It was a choice I made because of Jonah, to uphold the expectations I'd set for myself as a mother. I stood up, slid the gold band onto my left hand, stacking it beside my own wedding ring, and shook my head woefully at Dean.

"Let me dry my hair," I told him and stepped away.

He sighed.

I moved toward the sink and watched Dean's reflection in the mirror, wondering what it would be like to make love with him here as adults, while Jonah slept in the adjoining room.

Dean gulped back his glass of wine and poured another. He called after me, "I'll keep an ear out for the little guy. Take your time."

In the mirror I watched as his reflection pulled a slip of paper from his shirt pocket. He eyed it closely and furrowed his brow.

Closing the bathroom door, I leaned up against it and took a deep breath, trying to shed the hope that Dean would follow behind me. I envisioned us there in the dark, Dean's hands under my clothes, the scruff of his beard against my skin, the weight of him guiding us to the edge of the tub, where he would sit and draw me into his lap. I recalled his body, its topography like an old country road driven a thousand times, knowing full well where I would stop off to spend some time.

Dean was the opposite of whom I had chosen, Miles, the cautious physician and scholar, the only child of a wealthy Iron Belt family of judicious intellectuals. When I met my husband in Mystic, that fluke night with the whole of New England roaring over baseball, I didn't know what it meant to be both toggled to and overshadowed by someone else's success, someone who was far brighter and more interesting than I would ever be, and a real scientist, not some fortune-teller of the weather, as I'd come to be. I was spoiled too quickly by the security of my husband's job, because when I met him, I'd been afraid of how I might make my way in the world alone if my research fell flat, and so I chose the safety he offered.

With Dean, the connection was different, drawn from a history impaled right through the broken center of me.

Granting a wish that would never relieve my despair, Dean had doused Craig Stackpole's barn with gasoline and set the place on fire after my father's body was found there. Volunteering for the job when I was too grief-stricken and wild with rage, too impulsive and heartbroken not to be caught burning it down myself, he acted the part of Roman high priest, performing a sacred last rite. In my father's honor, Dean struck the match for me. It was July 5, 1986, the day after my father's death and the day following my mother's marriage to the banker living at 101 Quayside Lane.

In a ceremony held at the Saybrook Fish House, in a wealthy town just east of our own, my mother and Craig made their nuptials with an officiating judge and four mutual friends, before taking off on a harbor cruise.

Craig had no children, and therefore neither Kara nor I were invited to join the Fourth of July reception, but he promised my mother that after they were wed he would treat us like his own dear daughters.

"It's a grown-up affair," Mom said when she broke news of the engagement to me following a track meet my last week of school. She was wearing a fancy shawl and large hoop earrings. She reeked of perfume, something overwhelming and musky, and I longed for the citrus-sweet simplicity of her former Jean Naté.

She went on, "You and Kara can celebrate with us later in the fall when Craig takes us all to Aruba for Thanksgiving. And, really, you'll want to be home with your dad the night of the wedding." She looked down at her shoes, then back at me with eyes full of tears. "I have a feeling your father will need his girls."

When the Fourth of July came, Dad asked Kara and me to pack a cooler, and we picnicked close to Craig's property on the docks of the Quayside Beach Association. From our vantage point, we looked on as a photographer arrived to snap photos of Mom's soon-to-be husband, "the Douche Bag," where he awaited his bride in front of the house in a seersucker suit.

Hitching herself to his arm, Mom appeared in a white sundress, the skirt long and bohemian, just barely spilling onto the sand. She wore no veil and had twisted her hair into a knot ornamented with black-eyed Susans. They strolled away from our perch on the dock and moved down the beach toward the breaking water, their arms hooked, as the wedding photographer chased beside them trying to capture their laughter. In contrast to their joy, my father howled like a wounded animal as he watched, and I knew then it was the sound of something in him dying.

Dad took deep breaths and collected himself, and we drove away from the Quayside. With all the windows down and the radio blaring Steve Winwood's "Higher Love," he sped along Route 9, taking Kara and me to Marty's Clam Shack for the chocolate cones we ate in silence.

Kara chomped the last bite of her dessert and said finally, "Daddy, are you ever gonna feel better?"

Dad smiled for my sister and slapped the table. "Yes, yes. I promise, baby. I'm going to move on and feel better." He pulled a nip from his pocket and poured it into his plastic cup of soda. "I just need a little time," he said. "A little time alone."

As he spoke, I reached out and put my hand on top of his, but I couldn't bring myself to believe him.

That evening, when we got home, Dad took out his cribbage board in preparation for the night's card game and told us to hurry down to the beach. The sun had set and the bugs were eating us alive. The three of us scurried to light citronella candles on the back deck. And what I most remember was how my father collected Kara and me, backing the two of us up against his giant belly where he held us tight, spraying our arms and legs with Deep Woods Off.

"I love you," he said. "Remember, be good and I love you."

When I peeked at him over my shoulder, tears soaked his face.

"You girls go," he told us, catching my worried glance. "I need some time before Rex and Uncle G get here to play cards and hustle me out of your inheritance." He pulled a beer from a bucket of ice, holding it up high as if making a toast. "Tonight, ladies, bed by midnight and don't wake me when you come in." He nodded to himself at what I took to be an acknowledgment of a generous curfew.

Kara ran down the beach ahead of me to meet her Brownie troop. She would spend the night at a makeshift table selling fruit punch and baked goods along the boardwalk to folks who came from neighboring towns to watch the fireworks.

I left more reluctantly.

"Daddy, you okay?" I said.

He shooed me off and took a long pull off his beer. "Honey," he insisted, "go."

And so I did.

But later, while the late-night news recapped Liberty Weekend in America by showing clips of President Reagan rededicating the Statue of Liberty in a blaze of light, marking its centennial as a beacon of hope in New York Harbor, I tiptoed up the front steps under a waning crescent moon, thirty minutes after our generous holiday curfew had passed.

I trod gingerly so as not to wake him, but I learned later that I could have crashed my way through the house and into every piece of furniture, for all it mattered. My father was inside Craig Stackpole's barn at 101 Quayside Lane, slumped against a vanilla-colored Mercedes, wearing one of Mom's old T-shirts, the gold cross that always hung around his neck, and a pair of Hawaiian swim trunks. Blood bubbled from his mouth and down his neck, and the back of his skull was splattered across my mother's new husband's luxury car. A Colt .45 handgun lay on the floor beside him. On the workbench a few yards away was the note:

Kat—

You're never coming home and I just can't live without you. I'm sorry for all of it. I love you. I love our girls. Promise you'll do better by them than I can.

K&P Forever.

—Peter

When the police drove up to our house early the following morning with the news, Kara was practicing her back handsprings in our front yard. She told me later that Mom rode in the front seat with her face in her hands, while Craig Stackpole sat in the back of the patrol car, directly behind her. I was still in bed when I heard Kara's scream. It was shrill and I thought she was hurt. I jumped up and ran down the stairs to find her.

Out the screen door, I saw my sister and my mother crumpled together on the lawn. Kara was kicking her feet and screaming while my mother tried to hold her. A foot away, the officer and Craig Stackpole stood watch.

As soon as I saw Kara, I knew he was gone, but I ran up to my father's room anyway. The bed was made. I felt my tongue swell, my panic snaking from my belly to my throat, as I slipped down the stairs in my stocking feet and bolted for the back deck, where I found several empty bottles and the candles burned down into flat waxy pools. The Boston Red Sox sweatshirt Dad had been wearing was tossed over the back of a chaise lounge.

Paralyzed with grief, Kara and I held each other in my twin bed that evening, my sister wearing Daddy's sweatshirt to bed, the hood pulled up over her head as she wrapped her arms around my neck. In that moment she seemed more like a toddler, the baby in my father's lap who requested *The Tawny Scrawny Lion* five times in a row before Dad pulled up the rails on her twin bed and tucked her in for the night.

Kara and I had shared a room since she turned two, and I knew her bedtime patterns as well as my own—the way she rubbed her feet together to ready herself for sleep, the giant sigh she made before closing her eyes. There was a stretch of time when my sister was three, maybe four, when she woke in the evening and crawled in beside me, dragging her battered bunny across the space between our beds.

But since then, we had not held each other through the night until our father died. The night of his death—and for nearly a month after, while our mother stayed in Dad's house with us—Kara and I slept entwined until my mother later forced us all to move in with Craig, after which my sister got her own room and I never held her again.

The first night after his death, down the hall from us on Willard Street, my mother slept in our father's bed, and most of the night I could hear the muffled sound of her weeping. Craig slept downstairs, alone on the couch, after surrendering to a lost battle earlier that evening when they had begged us to go "home," as Mom called it, to the Quayside, but neither Kara nor I had budged from our room.

And that first night while we lay awake in his house, wondering what we could have done to prevent my father's death, Dean burned down the barn where my father shot himself because I asked him to.

Hollowed by heartache, I called Dean that night to break the news. "I'm going to burn that fucking place down. I swear I will," I told him, my voice trembling.

"You don't have to," he whispered. "I'll do it for you."

"When?" I said.

In the distance a foghorn yowled.

Dean cleared his throat.

"For you, I'll do it right fucking now."

Nearly five years ago, in 2007, before the economy tanked completely and home values plummeted, Dean bought what remained of Craig's oceanfront property from the banker and my mother. He had started snatching up local waterfront properties, which back then seemed to quadruple in value every couple of years. He thought if he bought the place and held on to it, he would make a killing.

In one of our early Facebook correspondences, when I wrote to him about my sadness over selling our home in Mystic, how we lost everything we had invested in it, and how we had to borrow money to bring to the closing to pay out the buyers when we sold, he responded with the details of the Quayside acquisition:

> Claire—
> Buying real estate is emotional business. I do it all the time, and it was still hard for me to buy the place from your mom and Craig. I remembered the tragedy there, thought about your old man walking out back of that house, already dying. And because I had those feelings about it, I guess I wondered if I couldn't honor his death again in some other way once I owned it.
> There was a bidding war on every property along the beach in those days, everyone thinking waterfront could never lose. People offering forty or fifty thousand over asking prices. I did the same and overpaid.
> But the day we closed on the Quayside, I started building out back. A stone wall from the last bits of foundation where the barn sat, and all I could think about was you.
> Eventually, that stone wall fenced in a garden—lilacs, honeysuckle, daisies, mums, all perennial. Same stuff your dad grew on Willard Street. It was for him, you know? And you too.

What I'm saying is real estate isn't always about the investment.

Yours,

Dean

I returned from the bathroom, the floorboards of the inn groaning as I stepped across them to the bed where Dean waited. Attempting to maintain some distance between us this time, I sat.

Dean handed me my wine, and I listened to see if sleeping Jonah had stirred. But the adjoining suite remained hushed. The only sound between us was the crackle from the hearth, warming the draft from the room.

I sipped from the glass, pressed my lips together, and nodded, while Dean's blue eyes seared right through my reservations. We stared at each other, both of us tentative about the complex intersection of our present and the past, and I felt myself surrender.

Dean squeezed my hand.

"Come look at this," he said, pulling me up from the bed.

He led me across the room and pushed aside the heavy drapes to reveal a window seat.

We sat close and watched the sunset. There, out over the Sound, stratus clouds reflected pink and orange light, stretching across the horizon like saltwater taffy.

Dean put his arm around me. I kept my eyes on the distance, but even so, the measure of our breathing became a slow combustion.

"The Atlantic," he whispered. "For you."

Charged, we turned toward each other.

Dean leaned closer, all tenderness.

We kissed.

The first match was lit.

And just like the fires of our youth, the kiss bloomed, our lips parting as we grew fully aflame. Kissing harder, reaching for each other, we lulled and surged, our skin gone sweaty and damp. Dean climbed on top of me, and the kisses reeled us backward through time.

Pressed up against the windowpane, I heard Dean's voice, a rumble in my ear, say, "All these years."

He slipped a hand under my sweater and rested it at the small of my waist. Our kisses softened. Delicate pecks on ears and necks. Dean's mouth explored my collarbone.

I tilted my head back against the window, the glass cool on my cheek, while his palms, uneven with callouses, roamed my shoulders and chest. His fingertips strayed inside the lace trim of my bra, then further—down my ribs, over the fabric of my jeans, and beneath.

I closed my eyes. And remembered.

Dean whispered, "Look at me."

We stood, our bodies pressed into a single silhouette, undressing.

"We should stop," I whispered.

"I need you," Dean said.

And it was done.

We sat holding each other on the window seat, and Dean's hand stroked the inside of my thigh. "Being here with you," he told me, "is so perfect. I was an idiot to ever let you go."

Chilled by a draft from the window beside us, I pulled my sweater over my shoulders and stared into his eyes, their blue that of an infinite sky.

"But you searched for me," I told him. "And I needed to be found."

"We've always been there for each other when it really mattered," Dean asked. "Haven't we?"

In the last of the twilight, a thick fog rose from water.

"We have," I sighed, my emotions roiling.

He held tight to my hand and bent forward to kiss my forehead.

I closed my eyes, and a wash of disgrace moved over me. I thought about Miles and panicked, comprehending the weight of what I'd done and how I had permitted myself to become my mother, the one person I never wanted to be.

Dean pulled me back. "You know, Claire, that I'm drowning."

"Drowning?" I said.

"That house," he said. "Sometimes I feel like it's killing me. It's weird. Just like your dad."

I studied his face and tried to understand exactly what he was telling me.

"Mama!" Jonah screamed, his cry from the adjoining room all alarm, that fear of waking in an unfamiliar place. "Mama!" he shouted again.

Dean rubbed his thumb over my bottom lip. "We need to find a way."

I moved aside to dress and struggled to collect myself.

"Come, Mama," Jonah cried. "Come!"

Conflicted by own guilt and desire, I went to my son. And as I hoisted him from his blankets, he tucked his bunny under one arm and rested his head on my shoulder. "My mama," he said.

We swayed while he roused, a slow dance that soothed his whimpers. And when I laid him down for a diaper change, Jonah pulled off his socks and sighed. He made an immediate request. "Yummies?" he said, then added another. "Dada?" An anxious flutter fanned in my chest.

I snapped his pants and poured his milk, then rummaged through our carry-on for his lunch box. We returned to the connecting room, and I noted how the pillows were rearranged and the wineglasses set away.

Fully dressed, Dean sat in a wingback chair. "Morning, sleepyhead," he told Jonah. Then he smiled at me. "Little man has got himself one pretty mommy."

I sat on the bed against a stack of pillows and quietly spooned Jonah his applesauce.

In a veiled hush, all three of us faced the window, heeding the early nightfall. And while Jonah quietly ate his supper, I replayed the warmth of Dean's breath on my skin, the firm grip of his hand on my waist, the force of his body pulling me back against it, unable to shake the entanglement of my remorse and the desire for more.

"Claire," Dean interrupted. His voice sounded strange. "Do you think maybe we should just…finish it off?"

A shiver ran through me. "Finish what off?"

"The Quayside," he said.

I tore Jonah's peanut butter sandwich in two and handed him half. "I'm not sure what you mean."

"Like I said—I'm out at sea on this. That house is pulling me under. For the longest time I couldn't see any way out." His speech was frenzied. "But then I started thinking, what if there was an accident? A fire? The insurance on it is $950,000. I'd be able to pay off the mortgage, keep the business, and move on. No one would get hurt. And then, who knows? Maybe you and the little guy, you could come home for good. Where you belong. You could start over. With me."

He searched my face for approval.

I trembled, thinking about what he was saying—what it would mean not only to stage a fire, but also the prospect of leaving Miles, the complexity of dividing up our things, and what all of it would do to Jonah, who loved his daddy so much. I faltered for a response, unable to get my bearings. Then, I thought about fire itself—that sensation of striking a match to, of all places, that house of horrors that tormented me the most.

I whispered, "We'd never get away with it."

"That's what I keep telling myself, but then I think, maybe we would," Dean said. "Of course, it would have to look like an accident. And wouldn't your dad have loved it, seeing that fucker gone?"

"He would," I agreed, knowing with certainty that my father would've loved nothing more than to watch Craig Stackpole's house burn and collapse upon itself. In fact, if he were alive, maybe he would have torched the place himself.

Dean reached under the lamp shade to switch on the light and illuminate the dark. "It's not like we've never done it before."

CHAPTER THIRTEEN

BASIC SCIENCE

THAT NIGHT I LET JONAH SLEEP IN MY HOTEL BED, holding him close, waking in the morning to his small hand driving a Matchbox car down my arm and across my belly where my shirt had risen up.

"Road," he said, tracing a finger across the purple raised scar on my low belly, the incision the obstetrician cut to save us both, a wound that still seemed raw.

My cell phone rang, and as I felt for it on the bedside table, I knocked down one of the two empty wineglasses. I replayed Dean's toast, his mouth, his hands, his touch, all the ways he had welcomed me home.

"Mama's phone!" Jonah cheered when it sounded again.

In the soft yellow light of morning, with his tussled blond hair, the footy pajamas Jonah wore made him appear more baby than boy. I caressed his face, feeling that all-consuming love I never understood until his birth.

The phone buzzed a third time. The call was from my husband, one I didn't want to take, but I picked it up anyway, leaden with remorse and obligation.

"How are you?" I said into the receiver.

"Okay, I guess. Miss you guys." Miles sighed. "I've done all I can with the investigation, not sure what will happen. But it's been handed over to the authorities, and now I'm focusing on my clinic and research."

"That's good," I said. "We'll be home in a few days."

I handed the phone to Jonah and told him, "Say hi to Daddy."

"Cookies?" my son asked, pressing the phone to his ear.

He pointed to a box of animal crackers poking out of the diaper bag, the special treat Miles gave him on our way to the airport. Miles said something that made Jonah squeal with delight before he dropped the phone on my pillow and returned to his tiny cars.

I took the phone back. "So, have they started to rebuild the lab yet?" I asked.

Miles cleared his throat. "Yes. Repairs should finish in eight weeks or so. And we've finally gotten enough support in the division to suspend Dalton indefinitely, even if we can't directly link him to the fire quite yet. His volatile behaviors have exacerbated to the point of safety concerns on the wards since accusations about his part in the arson were made, so that's about to settle out. How's it been there, seeing your mom? I'm worried. You okay?"

"We're fine."

There was concern in Miles's voice. "I know I haven't been very attentive, Claire. Are *we* okay?"

I skirted his question and told him, "Mom and I are getting along okay." The lying turned my stomach.

"You're all staying with your sister, then?"

"Hotel," I said.

"I see." Miles paused. "I thought you told me you were staying with Kara?"

"Change of plans," I bumbled. "Call me tonight, after work.

I'll clarify our return details and have a better sense of our plans later on."

"Hurry back. I'll be at the airport whenever you land," Miles assured me.

Outside my room there was a knock at the door.

"I better run," I said, kicking off the covers.

"Knock-knock," Jonah hollered.

"I love you," Miles said. "Kiss my boy."

"I will. Talk soon."

Waving Dean in, I bore the guilt of a traitor, everything I considered my mother to be, and I hated myself for letting things go this far, so far that I could no longer turn them around.

Dean carried a duffel bag and a tray holding two Dunkin' Donuts cups. He handed me a scalding coffee and placed a bag of donut holes on the bed next to Jonah.

Jonah furrowed his brow. "Cake?" he said, his voice a question.

"Yummy," Dean encouraged. "All for you, buddy."

Jonah dumped the donuts onto the bed. "Uh-oh!"

"Have you thought about it, Claire?" Dean said, leaning in to kiss my forehead and easing himself onto the bed beside me. His stare was pleading. "That house will take me under."

"I know," I whispered.

I rested a hand on Dean's knee and a buzz ran through me, along with the comprehension that his request was a favor owed, the reciprocal act come due for the long-ago risk he took for me.

"A fire," he said. "Getting rid of the Quayside. It can save you too, erase all that happened there."

Dean leaned over the side of the bed, unzipped the duffel

bag he carried in, and pulled scrolled blueprints from a tube. Succumbing to my old desire to please him, I took the sketches from Dean's hand and his fingertips ran across my palm. In the space of a breath, our joint arson was no longer a singularity hinted at, something we circled around and forestalled, but a decision extorted by a place that tormented us both.

I glanced at drawings and questioned Dean: "Why exactly do you need me?"

He nodded and sipped from his coffee. "Owner is always the first suspect. And you, mother with a small child, living a thousand miles away, would never even be considered." He caught my eye. "And because I know you. Some place deep inside, you've always wanted to burn that house down yourself. If there's a fire, it should be yours."

And I'll admit it. I wanted to do it. I wanted to char it into dust, that place that stole my father from me. "But you'd be there to help?"

Dean tucked my hair behind my ear. "How I see it is this. I'll plan a breakfast with Fergus Shannon from the urban planning board, and you'd go to the house. I'll need an alibi later when questions are asked."

"So I'd go alone, then?"

Dean leaned against me, delicately slipping his hand under my T-shirt. "Yeah. Has to be you alone. And I don't think it'd be smart to take you over there beforehand. I don't want anyone to see anything or *anyone* unusual. We'll use the sketches to jar your memory, but you know the place. Nothing structural has changed inside. It'll be fast. In and out."

"What about Jonah?" I said.

"Can't you bring him?"

"Bring my *son* to burn your house down?"

Dean scratched his head. "Well, what choice do we have?"

Admiring my precious boy's creamy skin and pursed lips, as he sat on the edge of the bed with jelly from a doughnut hole on his chin, I thought about how scared I have always been of losing Jonah, how if he were ever taken from me, my will to live would be gone. And for the first time since I stepped onto the plane, I was aware of how much was at stake, how much danger I had put us in. How, really, with one slipup there with Dean, I stood to lose everything.

"What if we can't get out?" I said. "What if something goes wrong? I can't put him in harm's way like that."

"Could you leave him here?" Dean asked. "Take care of it while he is sleeping? Or set up some toys and he can play in the crib?"

Listening to Dean, it became clear to me that I was talking to someone who had never had children, someone who had never known that kind of fear and love, those interlaced emotions of parenthood. To acknowledge this difference between us was to feel my desire for him wither and retract. The spell I was under dimmed in the temperance of the morning discussion, while Dean casually examined the plans to refine the logistics of the arson.

But the idea of the flames, the cleansing that category of fire could bring me, didn't release its hold. I wanted that house to burn just as much as, hours ago, I had wanted Dean. I could see the ruins so clearly. I could smell the clean licks of flames and the ash.

"Jonah's safety comes first," I said, struggling to maintain perspective.

"Of course," Dean told me, but I could see he was less worried than I was, and I realized that there was no way that I could make him understand my level of concern, that feeling of absolute dread I got in imagining the well-being of my child being compromised.

Dean was already moving on. "Too bad your parents—I mean, your mom—had the electrical redone before they sold. High-end stuff. Otherwise we could just overload a socket. It would have been a no-brainer."

"Yup. Too bad." His flippancy both annoyed and shocked me, and for a moment I buckled beneath the full weight of the risk I was about to take, before the image of a blackened shell of a house emblazoned itself on my mind. I had burned my mother's car when I was a child, and no one had even thought to question me then. And not even forty-eight hours ago, a Madison police officer had practically looked through me, incapable of even considering that I could hold either the spark or substance of a flame within myself.

No one had ever understood that but Dean.

Dean went on. "Whatever we do, it can't be tagged as vandalism. It has to be an accident, a fault with the structure, or some human error. A cooking fire is fine, but they tend not to do enough damage. I don't want a rebuild. I want a demolition job, nothing left—ashes to ashes, dust to dust. A scrape or a teardown. A clean slate.

"And you...you've been fascinated by fire since high school, always reciting random facts about flames. A firebug even when I met you. Fiddling with cigarette lighters, burning napkins and candy wrappers. And you studied science in college, right? So shouldn't we just blaze that motherfucker right outta here?"

"Combustion is not what I studied, exactly," I said, pulling Jonah into my lap. "But I do know the chemistry, the atmospherics, the way a contained fire undergoes a cycle of growth." I warmed to the subject. "The house will act like a hearth, inside of which the fire will move from a kind of full engagement toward smoldering. So, if you want to take out the structure quickly—to have the blaze be devastating—we need the heat to amass in an explosion.

"We want the warmth radiating from the gases to exceed the ignition temperature of all the exposed surfaces, causing everything to erupt at once. It's called a flashover. And to make that happen we need petroleum distillates for accelerants. Place them near the gas lines." I sipped my coffee and wiped powdered sugar from Jonah's chin. "Where is the pilot light, exactly?"

Dean was pleased by this question. He smiled and ran a finger along the sketch. "Here's where the lines come up from the basement, through the kitchen, up the side wall to the second story, and into the master suite. The lines feed the second-floor fireplace, the gas insert Heather added when we did the renovation. Before the bitch left."

"Got it," I said. "Where's the range?"

"There are two ovens—the range top and stove are along that back wall, but there's also a convection oven built into the center of the island. Right in there." Dean tapped a finger on the spot.

I handed Jonah his milk and turned to Dean. "Ever deep-fry anything?"

"A turkey," he said.

"Still have the grease?"

"No, unfortunately not," he said.

"We'll want some," I told him.

Dean gave me a quick squeeze. I leaned into his reach.

"There's an arrangement that determines whether a fire burns as a surface fire or something deeper," I explained. "We want that something deeper. No matter what you're burning, no matter how you're burning it, no matter the fuel, oxygen causes combustion to accelerate. So you'll want to crack the windows open, a few on every floor, but not so much that the flammable gases sneak out. Maybe a half an inch, and we'll be golden."

"Woman," Dean said, stealing a quick kiss, "I love the way you think."

At the Home Depot in Norwich, far enough from East Lyme that Dean believed we were off the radar, I pushed Jonah in a cart the color of construction cones, and we searched for aerosols propelled by hydrocarbon-based fuels.

Dean walked ahead of us. I told him, "What we need is an accelerant with kerosene, butane, or even turpentine. In liquid form. Mist is best. A fogger, one of those bug-bomb things, rather than a spray. I need to be able to push the button and step away."

We continued along seemingly endless aisles of lamp shades and paint cans and portable heaters.

Jonah fussed. "Mama, yummies!"

My diaper bag full of snacks was forgotten in the car.

"Be patient, baby," I pleaded. "We'll get your yummies in a minute. We're almost done."

We turned past the garden shop stocked with fading poinsettias and clearance shelves of discounted plastic Santa Clauses. Then, down a city block of insecticides, Dean finally waited for us, taking my hand. "Ever wonder if it could have been us? If we could have been a family?" he said. "I could take care of you guys after this."

"No," Jonah screamed. "No! That one." He pointed to a giant plastic reindeer on the leftover Christmas display behind us and screamed. "Mama, that one!"

"He's about to melt down," I said. "I better go feed him something."

Jonah pulled a box of weed control from the middle of a display. Spray bottles of Roundup and Miracle-Gro tumbled onto the floor, creating a roadblock for our cart. Jonah's cry was silent, but then turned into the shrill screech only a toddler can make. He shuddered and sniveled as I pulled him from the seat and held him against my chest.

Dean cleared our path.

"It's okay," I whispered. "That was scary."

Jonah kicked and shrieked; he slapped my face. Dean got jumpy and paced the aisle ahead. From down the lane he held up a bright yellow can. "Is this the stuff?"

I swayed Jonah side to side. "Bring it here so I can see the ingredients."

Dean sprinted back and held the can up to my face. "Bud," he told my son, "let's relax a little."

I read the warning. It noted that the product contained "ignitable liquids, butane, and other petroleum distillates considered highly flammable."

"Go away," Jonah screamed. He swatted at Dean.

I brought him to eye level with me. "Do you want a time-out?"

"Yes," Jonah shouted.

I put Jonah down, and he threw himself to the ground, kicking and squealing, "No, no, no time-out!"

I told Dean, "That's the stuff." He pulled the last seven bottles off the shelf and put them into our basket.

Jonah was panting, his face streaked with tears. "I want Dada," he cried.

"We need way more than that," I told Dean and picked up my son, holding him under my arm like a football. I took my purse and the keys Dean held out to me.

An elderly man in a tool belt and orange suspenders walked toward us, belly first, his thumbs hooked into his belt loops. He had a handlebar mustache. "Folks, how can I help?"

"It's about fucking time," Dean said. "We need more of these." He held up a fogger.

I turned and left Dean to negotiate, Jonah tucked under my arm as I speed-walked out. When the cold air hit his face, he stopped fussing. He took deep heaving breaths, and I turned him upright. He wrapped his arms around my neck. "Where the man go?" he wanted to know.

Trudging through the lot, I required the same heaving breaths as my son, counting to ten to calm myself. In the car, Jonah continued to scream at the top of his lungs and I fished through the diaper bag for a snack. As I searched, my phone rang. The number was one I didn't recognize, a 954 area code, my iPhone declaring that the incoming call was from Fort Lauderdale.

Mom, I thought first, then recalled the litany of friends who spent winter weeks in Florida with their kids. I declined the call.

Pulling fruit from the bag, Jonah grinned at me. My muscles slackened with his cheer.

"Banana," he told me and pulled back the peel all by himself, shimmying side to side with pride.

Waiting, we sang two rounds of "Twinkle, Twinkle, Little Star" followed by several rounds of "Mrs. O'Leary's Cow."

I paused to check my voice mail and found none.

Then, chanting along with Jonah, I thought about poor Catherine O'Leary, the infamous scapegoat for the Great Chicago Fire, a fire that swallowed acres of downtown real estate over two days, while the real culprit, combustible sediment from Biela's comet, went unnamed.

I contemplated the residue Halley's pass had left over my life and worried about the kind of embers yet to fall.

Jonah hummed something akin to the rhythm, and then I crooned the final verse in an attempt to push away my fear:

One night ago,
When we were all in bed,
Old Mrs. Leary left the lantern in the shed.
And when the cow kicked it over,
She winked her eye and said,
"It'll be a hot time in the old town, tonight!"

And as I belted out the last three words—"FIRE, FIRE, FIRE"—I heard Dean's approach, his cart rattling with three cardboard boxes full of flammable canisters, all haphazardly balanced on top of each other.

CHAPTER FOURTEEN

ACCELERANTS

TWO WEEKS BEFORE HIS DEATH, MY FATHER CAUGHT ME IN a lie, and after that night, I vowed to never tell another.

The story I told him was that there was a party for my track team, a sleepover, where I would spend the night with the girls and our captain, Lauren Lombardino, who lived in the apartment complex in the center of town.

My father did not allow sleepovers, but I begged and pleaded. "It's the last party of the year," I said. "Mom would let me go."

Dad paused. He shook his head in disagreement but said, "I want you home first thing in the morning, to meet Kara."

Dad had started working again, after our mother left, tending bar one night during the week and opening the same popular Sound View Beach Cantina for brunch on the weekends.

"Your mom and the Douche Bag will drop her off at nine. I have to open the bar." He warned, "Be sure you're here to meet her."

I nodded, tossing my black jelly bracelets, my pin-striped leggings, my high-top Reeboks, my Madonna T-shirt, and my clock radio into a backpack. My father stood next to me, inventorying everything that went into my bag.

When I turned to kiss him good-bye, he asked, "Why the alarm clock? Won't her parents be home to wake you up?"

I felt the flush rise up my neck and rouge my cheeks. "Just want to be sure I get home in time."

My father simply nodded and left the room. His shift that evening started in an hour, and as he walked down the steps, he hollered, "Whatever you're up to, Claire, make damn well sure that your sister doesn't come home to an empty house."

The real plan was to celebrate school being out. Dean had rented us a motel room for the occasion. We had never had an overnight together, and it was what we talked about most when he kissed me against his truck before dropping me off a few blocks from home at the end of the dark cul-de-sac, where we said most of our good-byes.

After my father headed to work and Kara left with our mother, I ran toward Dean as he pulled into the turnaround at the end of our street.

"Hey," I said as I climbed into the cab.

Together we drove Route 9, turning down the strip at Sound View dangerously near the cantina where my father was bartending, two beaches down from Willard, where there were arcades, Vecchitto's Italian Ice, carousel rides, and the famous Brantmore Hotel (which served all-you-can-eat spaghetti and meatballs and featured a transvestite dancer as part of the live entertainment), beyond which a slew of biker bars had reduced that stretch of beach into an ashtray full of cigarette butts stained with lipstick and little plastic cocktail straws.

The most famous of the bars was called The Cage, in front of which we set our blanket under a cloudy evening sky, listening to the cover band play an acoustic version of Bon Jovi's

"Runaway." We waited there for Dean's buddy, Jimmy, to join us with beers.

All day I had known that I would reveal the story of my mother's affair to Dean that night. It was a burden I could not carry alone, and I thought that since both his mother and father had been unfaithful to one another, he might be able to offer me some comfort. While happy hour kicked into full swing, Dean leaned into an air-guitar solo as I looked out at the lights of Long Island, a place that in my mind was far more exotic and cultured than Connecticut, where all the houses were trimmed with white pillars, and the fathers left in suits to go work in the city.

"So," I said to Dean, never imagining that two weeks from that night my father would be dead, "my mom is dating this creepy old guy. And I know she was cheating with him before she left us—I actually saw it with my own eyes. Now she claims she's going to marry him. But no one knows about the cheating part, how long it's gone on, except for me. Kara even seems happy about the whole thing."

Dean dove down onto the blanket beside me, furrowing his brow as his head bounced in time with the music. "Don't tell your dad about the cheating. Or Kara. Ever. It will only make your dad more angry and crazy. And Kara is just too young to get it."

The drinkers on the patio at The Cage hooted and hollered. Others called out requests to the band.

I asked Dean, "Don't you think it's horrible?"

"Yes." He sighed and pulled me on top of him. "Wanna take a walk?"

Moving away from the noise, down past Sound View onto a quiet residential beach with a long jetty, the waves lapped our ankles and we strolled the beach.

"My dad fooled around on my mom when we were all really little," Dean said after a while. "Left her with his five kids and never gave any one of us a nickel's worth of child support. That's why I got a job soon as I could. Quit school to earn my keep. I watched my mom cry for years."

There was something matter-of-fact in his tone, something resilient that I lacked.

"That's bad," I said. "Could you ever forgive him? I feel like I won't ever forgive my mother. And I don't know how to help my dad. He's really down."

"My mom would take my father back in a heartbeat, but we have no idea where he lives. He's not someone I ever care to see, and if I did, I'd knock some sense into his stupidity. You already help your dad—just be there, listen, take care of Kara when you can."

The beach ended and the bluff reached its calloused fingers into the sound.

Dean backed me against the sea wall. Waves crashed.

His mouth was on my neck, then a warm breath in my ear. "You don't have to worry about things like that with me. I'm loyal. I'm yours. And I'll protect you," he promised, his hands inside my clothes.

I heard his zipper, the gulls, and the wash of the tide.

He moved himself up against me.

I closed my eyes.

On our return to Sound View, we strolled past the Painted Princess Tattoo Parlor. Dean had his arm over my shoulder. He raised an eyebrow.

"Want to?" he said.

"Will it hurt?" I asked.

"Only a little."

The man at the desk of the Painted Princess was shirtless with a shaved head and a giant Puerto Rican flag inked across his back. He rested an elbow covered in dragons with long, unfurled tongues on the counter.

"*Hola*—whatcha you want? Hearts? *Nombres?*"

"Stars," Dean said. "With flames. You know, *fuego?*" He squeezed my hand.

I squeezed back.

Dean told the guy, "I have cash."

Together, we flipped through pages of a binder and chose the images we liked best. Then the guy who took Dean's money sketched our tattoos on the back of a dirty envelope, to practice before he opened up the needles.

Dean went first. The skin grew rashy and raised around the five-pointed star inked on his bicep and along the band of flames that looped the circumference of his arm.

The tattoo artist looked over his glasses. "You keep it cleaned," he said.

Dean winced.

When it was my turn, I told the guy, "Tiny comet," as he tenderly turned my foot to examine my instep.

"*Cometa pequeño*," he said.

I clenched Dean's hand and bowed my head, holding in a shriek as the outline of the comet's tail left my skin feeling singed.

Hobbling to our blanket, my arm hooked through Dean's, we walked through the crowd and I was disappointed to find Jimmy still there waiting for us on a night that was supposed to belong only to Dean and me. "Let's party," Jimmy announced when he saw us, extending two plastic cups full of warm beer as a greeting.

Dean flexed his bicep and showed his buddy the meteor blazing his skin. "New ink," he said.

I pointed to my foot.

Jimmy hollered. "Party hearty, homies." Then he gulped his beer and belched the first four letters of the alphabet.

Dean and I held our drinks high for a toast. He winked at me, and I winked back.

"Cheers," he said.

"Cheers," I agreed. We drained our cups.

Dean carried me piggyback following a procession of brassy Harleys, making our way to his pickup.

In the cab, I squeezed between the boys while Van Halen's "Why Can't This Be Love" blared from the speakers. We peeled out of the lot and raced down Hartford Avenue with the windows down. The wind tangled my hair and whipped it into my eyes, while the boys lit cigarettes inside cupped hands. It was summer and hot, and with night falling, we cruised Route 156.

At a stoplight in East Lyme, under a sky the color of raspberry sorbet, Dean kissed me. Everything inside me expanded, then settled back. I loved him, I knew—his tan skin, his hair of spun gold, the way his arms were defined into hills and valleys, the salty taste of his lips, how he always smelled of cigarettes, coffee, Juicy Fruit, and rain. I loved his spontaneity, how he would suggest a tattoo, how he snuck me out of my house for beach walks late at night, how I would find flowers that Dean bribed the custodian to hide in my locker after hours, for no reason at all.

He was fearless with his high-speed driving and fake ID for beer runs. I loved that danger in him, how he blew through red lights, drove down one-way streets, and lit his cigarettes in cupped hands next to *No Smoking* signs. Whenever he had a chance, Dean broke the rules, but sometimes he would say, "I'm gonna do something crazy, but not with you. Not with precious cargo on board." And that was what I loved most about Dean, his protectiveness of me. I knew he meant it when he said, "I'm loyal. I'm yours." And I believed he would always adore me and guard me, that I would always be his girl.

After stealing a second kiss, Dean hit the gas when the light turned green. We picked up speed and headed east on Old Shore Road. Jimmy tapped my shoulder and asked, "No kiss for me?"

Jimmy Pistritto was the opposite of Dean, with dark curls and pockmarked skin. He had known Dean since the fifth grade, where they were both put in a classroom for kids who couldn't read well. Dean told me that Jimmy had been a fat kid, but he had grown into someone thin and tall, funny, and, at times, frightening and mean. He wore suit jackets over T-shirts with stonewashed jeans and took on a 1980s gritty *Miami Vice* sort of persona.

Jimmy watched as Dean put my hand under his and showed

me how to shift from second gear to third, third to fourth, fourth to fifth.

Racing around the curbs, we hit a speed that felt destined for flight.

In minutes, we reached Rocky Neck State Park, across from which we turned into the Bayberry Motor Lodge, our wheels grinding over the gravel lot.

Dean said, "Remember Eddie Gabes, the kid who looks like Theo Huxtable from *The Cosby Show*? He and I went through drivers ed together, got our licenses on the same day. He and his mom work and live here in the summer. They get free HBO and she lets him keep a cooler full of beer."

Dean knew someone everywhere. But I had hoped we'd be alone that night, climbing the bluffs that formed stony vistas over Niantic Bay, making out on the swings at McCook Park and sharing Frosty Treat cones by the train tracks. I hadn't counted on Dean bringing Jimmy with us, or on meeting up with Eddie Gabes.

When I lied to my dad about where I was staying, I had imagined a different kind of night. My expectation was a date, an evening that was about sleeping (and not sleeping) all night long beside Dean. I hid my disappointment when I understood that he had a different plan. "Looks awesome" is what I said, my arm around Dean's waist as we walked into the motel office, which resembled a giant tollbooth.

Inside, Eddie Gabes blared Run DMC's "You Talk Too Much" and continued to dance unabashedly when we stepped in.

"What's up?" he hollered over the music pounding from a silver boom box.

Eddie's mom walked up behind her son to introduce herself. She didn't look old enough to be anyone's mother as she snuffed a cigarette out on the tile floor with the toe of a neon pump and turned the music down. "Don't you kids destroy anything, you hear?" She turned to me and stuck out her hand. "Keep the boys in line."

"Nice to meet you," I said.

Mrs. Gabes's nails had rhinestones in the polish.

"I'll be right there in number two, in case these boys get dick-brained." As she spoke, she leaned into the hand she held above her hip. She was sexy and she recognized the power it gave her. When she reached for the door, she shouted, "Everyone better be eighteen."

Dean answered, "What do I look like, a baby snatcher?"

"Yes," she called over her shoulder before she slammed the door.

We all watched Mrs. Gabes walk across the lot, her tiny ankles wobbling in her heels as she let herself into a room on the other side of the building. Before she closed the door, she gave a little wave.

Jimmy bit his fist. "Goddamn. I'd die if my mom looked that good."

"Well, she don't," Eddie told Jimmy. "Nothing to worry about there."

Eddie had his mother's good looks and dressed like a rich kid, even though, like the rest of us, he was not.

"You got my shit?" he said to Dean, who nodded and handed him a heavy black gym bag.

I knew better than to ask what was inside but guessed that it was more stereos. Jimmy and Dean had developed a system for scouting out car doors with manual locks that had upgraded pullout radios in the dash. A friend had sold them a lock pick that looked like a long silver ruler. It slid along the passengers' windows into doorjambs to finesse the locks until the door handles popped open. A month earlier Dean had told me, "That's the last of it," after he sold the radios to a pawnshop to pay off his gambling debts, promising that the stealing was over.

But when he gave the bag to Eddie, he reached for my hand and squeezed it, a sign to me that my worry showed and to let it go.

Eddie stashed the loot in a closet behind the registration counter and pointed at Jimmy. "Dude, what's with the suit coat? You look straight-up hellacious."

Jimmy was dressed in a blazer with the sleeves rolled up and had his usual pastel T-shirt underneath to go with his precisely torn jeans. He put his hand on his chest. "This shit is mint. I just took Kelly Jenkins to dinner. She couldn't keep her paws off it."

Kelly was Dean's girlfriend before me; he had dated her when I was far too young to even think about boys. "Kelly was a sweet girl," he told me once, "but not the brightest bulb in the shed. Not smart like you, Claire." Despite his reassurance, I felt a twinge of jealousy at the mention of her name. Kelly was older, with hair like Kim Basinger, a cascade of blond curls falling down past her waist.

Eddie said, "Jimbo, you're going out with Dean's old girl? Isn't there some law of the brotherhood that says you can't do that shit?"

"Good thing I'm not in the brotherhood," Jimmy said and punched Eddie's shoulder.

Eddie was one of the few black kids in town, but he was lighter skinned than Jimmy, who was Sicilian.

Eddie looked to Dean. "What room do you want with your lady?"

"Number seven, Ed. 'Cause we're getting lucky."

Eddie smiled at me. "The stabbin' cabin." He tossed Dean the keys.

"Let yourself in," Dean told me. "I'll be there soon."

For a minute I felt afraid, wondering if the guys were in on a secret I wasn't privy to, but I couldn't fathom what that secret would even be.

Family cars with inner tubes roped to the top were parked in a line along the perimeter of the property. In front of Cabin 7 there was a cat smell, but otherwise it was clean. The lock, rusted and hard to turn, led to a bed whose comforter crinkled like paper on a doctor's table when I sat down. My newly inked foot throbbed. Elevating it on a stack of pillows, I turned on MTV and watched Downtown Julie Brown count down the top ten videos.

In the big mirror across from the bed, I studied myself and teased my hair as I waited, unbuttoning my shirt lower than I usually wore it. At that very moment, Jimmy barged in. "Hello, *Mommy*," he said.

Instantly, I grew embarrassed. "Where's Dean?" I asked, knowing Ms. Gabes would never hear me if I screamed.

"Who cares?" Jimmy said. "You got the Mac Daddy right here." He flopped down on the bed next to me. "Gonna get some uh-uh from Dean?" He straddled me and pinned my arms down so tightly that it hurt, humping me over my jeans.

I struggled beneath him and yelled, "Get off me, Jimmy!"

He kissed me sloppily on my mouth, trying to stick his tongue between my clenched teeth. Then he rubbed his face across my chest and bit my breasts, hard, leaving my shirt wet with his spit.

"I'd do you right now if Dean weren't my best friend," he threatened, yanking his pants low to show me his excitement, then tossing his jeans at my face and stepping into a pair of swim trunks. "Slut," he whispered, "you love it." Then he left, making a *V* with his middle and index fingers, sticking his tongue between them, and slamming the door.

All I wanted then was to be at the end-of-the-school-year track team sleepover party with Lauren Lombardino and my other classmates, at the party that I had lied to my father about attending.

I pulled the curtains open and watched the pool at the center of the motor court, where Jimmy made his way to the end of the diving board, bobbing on his tiptoes and smoking a cigarette, while Dean and Eddie sat with their feet dangling over the edge, beers in hand.

Shortly thereafter, Dean walked through the door. "The guys want you to jump in the pool naked. I told them no fucking way." He handed me a can of Miller High Life.

"Jimmy's creepy. He scares me," I admitted.

Dean pulled me close. He adjusted the pillows under my foot, examined the instep where it throbbed, and leaned me back onto the comforter with great care, tracing the nape of my neck with the back of his hand, his skin already tanned that second week of June.

"Shouldn't we go hang out with your friends?" I said.

Putting a finger to his lips, he told me, "I want to be with you."

"I feel weird with them out there. You sure?" I whispered.

"No place I'd rather be."

He moved his hands under my skirt to finesse my panties over my knees, holding them cautiously on each corner as if they were made of tissue paper, slipping them over one foot, then the wounded other.

I turned toward the window where I saw the sunset reflected off the pool and closed my eyes.

Dean worked a kiss from my ankle to my thighs. And as we grew frenzied, I opened my eyes to find Jimmy's toothy smirk and dark stare leering over us. Catching my glance through the windowpane, he pretended to suck an invisible dick.

"Stop," I told Dean, pushing him away and pulling my skirt down. "Jimmy's peeking."

"What?" Dean jumped up and threw his hands in the air. "You want me to kick your ass now?" he hollered through the glass.

Jimmy hollered back, "My bad."

Dean ran out the door, shoved Jimmy up against the window, and yelled, "You disrespect my girl again, I'll fuck you up. Got it?"

"I *said* sorry, dude," Jimmy told him, stumbling away as I watched.

Dean slapped the back of his head, saying as he went, "This conversation isn't over, asshole."

Jimmy threw him the finger and bolted across the lot.

Dean returned to the room, pulled the curtain shut, and eased back down onto the bed. "Sorry," he told me, wrapping his arms around me, seemingly guilt-stricken as he circled his hand around my waist and pulled me close. "I'll talk sense into that kid. He'll never disrespect you again."

Dean kissed me, an apology. Then, with great care, he caressed the inside of my knees with the tips of his fingers.

"Massage?" he offered, sliding my skirt back up toward my hips.

Rolling me onto my stomach, he rubbed my neck and shoulders. On the television in front of us a gum commercial told everyone to kiss a little longer.

Dean took off his jeans. I buried my face in the pillow.

"Relax," he whispered.

And, as I did so, the doorjamb squealed open, the knob smashing into the wall. A second later, Dean's body fell away from me. He moaned in pain, his body thudding as it hit the floor.

Startled, I rolled over.

Standing there, his hand clenched in a fist, stood my father in the Hawaiian shirt and black pants he wore to bartend at the Sound View Beach Cantina.

"Get dressed and get your ass in the car," he told me.

Red with shame, I tugged my skirt over my knees and wiped a stream of tears on the back of my hand. I looked down at my throbbing foot, which had bled all over the mattress.

"Daddy," I pleaded.

Dad dragged Dean outside by his hair.

Speechless, I peeked through the window where Jimmy had spied.

In the lot, my father slammed Dean against the side of his car. Uncle G sat in the passenger's seat, looking straight ahead, wearing his poker face. My father kneed my boyfriend in the gut and knocked him to the dirt.

Jimmy and Eddie were nowhere to be found.

I threw open the door of the motel room and called to my father. "Daddy, don't!"

His rage scared me.

"Please," I whispered, "don't hurt him."

My father kicked Dean after he was down. "Claire, I told you to get your ass in the car."

Petrified, I walked past them both and opened the door to the backseat, certain that Dean was no longer breathing.

Uncle G said, "Apple doesn't fall far." But I wasn't sure if the dig was directed at me or my mother, or maybe even Dean.

My father yelled, "Fucking piece of trash." Then he called to my Uncle G. "Get the stuff."

As I glanced into the rearview mirror, my uncle walked behind the car and swung the trunk open. Behind him to the left, Jimmy and Eddie crouched beside the pool in the shrubs, looking on. G slammed the trunk and stood beside my father, holding a can of paint, a brush, and a roll of duct tape.

Dean was in the fetal position on the ground, his lip bleeding and his shirt torn. My father knelt beside him, first tying Dean's hands with duct tape, then tearing another piece with his teeth to hog-tie his ankles.

"Don't ever fucking touch my daughter again, or I will kill you."

"And I'll help," G said.

While my uncle stood watch, my father cut off Dean's boxer shorts with his timeworn Army knife, always kept in his pants pocket.

Naked and shuddering, Dean begged, "No, please."

G pried the paint open with his keys. My father dipped the brush into the can.

Dean whimpered, "I'm sorry, sir."

Dad slathered the green bottom paint he used to cure the hull of his fishing boat across Dean's crotch, while Dean tried to fold himself in half to protect his genitals, pleading, "I'll leave her alone, I promise."

Uncle G held his legs down and still. Dad finished, took the gallon, and chucked it across the parking lot, the paint splattering across the motel door and the hood of a parked car.

We drove off, but as I looked back, I saw Jimmy still crouched in the bush, while Eddie ran toward Dean. My tears fell into my lap and my nose ran as we drove in silence.

Dad pulled up in front of our house and said, not looking at me, "Don't ever lie to me again."

Uncle G glanced over the seat and pointed at my tattooed foot. "Someday you're gonna look at that and wish you could take it all back."

Thinking they were headed in behind me, I got out of the car and limped to the door, but G and my father drove away.

Home alone, I dialed Dean's number over and over. There was no answer at his house, and I wondered if I would ever see him again. I thought too of how I had forsaken Dean, and, afraid of my father's rage, how I allowed him to brutalize the very boy who had always protected me.

Too upset to sleep, I considered my bathing suit on the line in our side yard and yanked it from the clothespins. I changed in our outside shower and hobbled along the beaten path between houses to the sand beyond the glow of our porch light. In the dark, I plunged into the inky cold of the Atlantic. Swimming until I could no longer touch the bottom, the saltwater setting my inked foot on fire, I floated on my back, relying on the tide to push me in. My body grew cold enough to turn my insides numb, and once my teeth began to chatter, I kicked the water and propelled myself home.

When my mother pulled in the next morning to drop off Kara, I ran out to greet them. I could feel my mother scrutinizing me, deciding if something was wrong. "Honey," she asked, "do you need to talk?"

"Yes," I said. And because the apple didn't fall far, I told her everything while Kara watched the Smurfs on the small black-and-white television upstairs.

My mother did not judge me as I spoke. She did not interrupt my tears. She sat on the back deck and listened, her words sparse and practical. And when Kara appeared at the screen door, Mom gently pushed her away and shut the sliding glass door. It was clear to me then that I was being treated like an adult by my mother, the two of us on equal ground.

"Boys do stupid things sometimes," she said, talking about Jimmy. "I'm pretty sure Dean will never allow anything like that to happen again."

She paused, looked out over the yard to where Dad's boat sat on a trailer, and added, "The problem with bottom paint is that it's designed to keep the barnacles off a boat. The only way to get it off is with turpentine and a cloth, one inch at a time. You might need to help Dean. You can use my house. There's a bathroom on the first floor, just off the mudroom to the right. Craig and I will be out late tonight and tomorrow."

As she shifted, a huge diamond on her hand caught the light and scattered it. Catching my worried glance, she tucked her jeweled hand under her knee, playing down her excitement for me.

She said, "The address is 101 Quayside Lane."

"I know where your boyfriend lives." I swallowed. "Husband. Whatever."

She bit her lip. "Be careful not to—"

"Get pregnant?" I finished for her.

"That too," she said. "But also be careful not to get into it with your father. He's obviously gone over the edge." She inched close to me. "These things happen," she said, smoothing the hair out of my eyes. "Growing up is hard sometimes."

But I soon found out that those things *don't* happen, and never again would I understand so clearly the kind of intimacy that comes from helping someone through his shame, as I did when I bathed Dean in my mother's boyfriend's tub with a bottle of turpentine and a tiny rag.

Kneeling in the tub beside the boy whom I had given myself to, a boy who had both thrilled me and loved me, terrified me and protected me, I removed the bottom paint from his skin, leaving his penis raw and sore, touching him cautiously, and silently doing my best to dissolve his humiliation and my own.

Dean sat in the water with his hands over his face. He said, "If you were my daughter, I would've done the same thing."

As I bathed him, I sensed a feeling unknown to me, a touch so delicate and careful that my hand itself became an instrument of lovemaking, and while I cleaned him up, I begged his forgiveness for what had been done to him. I also knew that, like things between my parents, things between Dean and me would never be the same.

CHAPTER FIFTEEN

FERVOR

FLURRIES SCATTERED OVER LONG ISLAND SOUND as Jonah and I turned down Willard Street, slowing to a stop in front of my childhood home. Parked out front, I imagined ringing the bell to find Dad there at the breakfast nook, drinking his morning coffee in a flannel robe and a pair of shearling slippers.

I exhaled, trying to expel the overwhelming ache of missing him, and as I did so, I thought of the words of the infamous cosmologist, Carl Sagan:

In a hundred billion galaxies, you will not find another.

I slipped my hand into my coat, touched the plastic yellow lighter that I had tucked into my pocket from my luggage, and trusted it to be a token of good fortune.

From where I'd parked, the old Cape looked as dingy and forlorn to me as it did the night Kara and I let our mother and Craig Stackpole drive us away with our skirts and sweaters, scrunchies and hair bands, Kara's Barbies, and our joint teddy bear collection tossed haphazardly into four black trash bags, which we dragged like cadavers down the front steps before hefting them into the trunk of Craig's car.

Leaving that house felt like leaving my father forever, a deep-seated homesickness that has never gone away, even to this day. But there, looking at the place, I remembered every detail of that day we were forced to abandon our home.

Mom had told us, "Take just what you need, clothes and things, your toothbrushes, keepsakes. Everything else, your beds, your bedding, those things we can replace."

Then she tossed our jelly shoes and leg warmers, our diaries and cassette tapes, into the garbage bags while her husband paced the halls with his Walkman on and his hands sunk deep into the pockets of his golf shorts.

Still I can conjure the memory of her voice that summer day, gentle and raspy from crying. "We'll get you new things," she assured us, nodding her head fiercely, which set her dangly earrings into a metronome swing above her tanned shoulders. "We'll go shopping. We'll make it fun."

But there was nothing fun about backing out of the driveway in that big luxury vehicle with white leather seats. It was the car against which my father's body had leaned after the gun kicked back, and for the rest of my high school years, I searched for Dad's bloodstains every time I reached for the handle, part of me wanting to find a gruesome sign of him there.

Idling so many years later beside the begrimed snowbanks with my son, I wondered, as I so often have, if our mother had been relieved in some way to have Dad gone. Unlike Kara, who grew to hate my father for his final act, I attrib-uted my remaining sadness over his death to the decisions my mother made. It's not that I believed Mom would have chosen my father's death, but having him choose it for her meant that she would never have to battle him for custody, and that in some ways she could have her dream—her two girls under an extravagant roof with a new husband, in a completely different kind of life, a life she believed was better for us because we would no longer want for the things we needed.

My mother sold this belief to Kara and me time and time again as we grew up and headed out on our own, encouraging us to search out and embrace the help of a successful man, a partner who could provide us with the security we would need to raise families, rather than insisting we be strong and smart on our own merit and pave the way for ourselves.

"I'll buy you a new car and pay for your apartment if you stay in Connecticut and go to community college instead of going away to school" was my mother's reaction when I showed her the Women Chemists Committee letter I received my senior year of high school, announcing my scholarship to an undergraduate program in basic science.

And always I longed for something more than the simple security my mother promoted, but as I contemplated leaving Miles to return to Connecticut, to that former life there with Dean, I also never wanted Jonah to know the kind of grief I felt when I recalled my parents' divorce. Nor did I want him to know how much happiness my parents' split hijacked from us all, but reasoned that maybe if I left Miles while he was young, Jonah would never remember.

The sea smoke beyond us rose off the water and dimmed the morning with fog. The old Willard Street garage door rattled on its hinges, a stark bulb illuminating the spot where my father once parked. Searching for some sign of Dad inside, I found only a man my age, a brown bag in hand, walking to his car and slamming the door behind him. In the front window of the house, I made out a woman in a purple robe holding a little girl who waved to her daddy as they saw the man off. Any sign of my own father was gone.

K&P Forever, I thought to myself, looking down at my mother's former wedding band stacked next to my own. I clenched the wheel tighter, my knuckles gone white.

"Fuck you, Mom," I whispered.

Pulling away from the house, I drove toward the creek while Bruce Hornsby sang "The Way It Is" from the local radio station, and I sobbed in a way I hadn't since I first held Jonah, whose birth, for me, was somehow like losing my dad all over again. From the onset of my pregnancy, I pined for a boy who would grow into the man my father wanted to become but never got to be. But to hold my infant was to acknowledge that my father would never meet my precious son in his likeness, nor ever see me as a mother, the most substantial role of my life. That moment felt like yet another that my mother's affair had hijacked, and I grew fearful of what my own relationship with Dean might steal from my son.

I crossed the Singing Bridge and drove over the gravel roads woven through the marshlands, ambling toward the Quayside and watching my window of time to set the blaze dwindle.

Passing Sea Glass Beach, where Mom spent countless days of summer, I wondered as I always have if I could have stopped my father from taking his life by coming home early that night from the fireworks, instead of sneaking up the back stairs thirty minutes past curfew. Had I been on time, maybe we would have passed each other along the banister, and I could have asked, "Daddy, where are you going?" And he would have said, in his authoritative tone, "A better question, Claire, is where have you been?"

I've replayed that imaginary detour a thousand times. The one where instead of heading to the barn that Fourth of July, Dad instead cries on my shoulder and we sit on the back porch together under the crescent moon to look for meteor showers, singing "Lucy in the Sky with Diamonds" over and over, as we once did, until Kara, in her My Little Pony jammies, fumbles with the screen door and herds us in for bed.

Shuddering, I cranked the heater, wary of leaving Jonah in the car despite the January chill. The temperature read below freezing, yet it was safer to leave him outside in the car to wait than to bring him inside with me. Eyeing the thermometer on the dash, I churned with guilt and dread and shame, topped with the headiest excitement, as I turned down the narrow road.

Across a street to the left of 101 Quayside Lane, blocking the view of the address, was the former Ansel Sterling estate, renovated in 1988 to become the White Sands Country Club for the Quayside Beach Association. I remember how we picnicked with our father on the docks there that day my mother remarried, watching her photo shoot with Craig from afar. Behind the tennis courts, I parked where the club's staff left their cars before punching the clock at the clubhouse office. Next to me was an orange Volvo station wagon with a bumper sticker that read "Surf or Die," the long board tied to the roof covered in three inches of snow.

Idling, I scanned the lot and hoped to find someone there who would put a stop to everything I was about to do for Dean, for my father, for me.

But there was no one. And according to Dean, the club began brunch at 8:15 a.m., so with my 8:00 a.m. arrival, the waitstaff would be on the floor taking orders, and the cooks and dishwashers likely in the throes of the Wednesday morning rush in that breakfast spot popular with the locals in the off-season. If he had planned it right, I would not be seen by anyone.

Through a scatter of flurries, for the first time in more than twenty years, I faced the Quayside property, its imposing arrogance and hulking narcissism calling forth my old rage as I noted the single lamp on the second floor illuminating the room where my mother straddled Craig Stackpole's slim frame on top of his banker's desk. An ominous, haunted sensation washed over me then in the shadow of the place, and the despair unnerved something in my gut. I shivered. A metallic taste coated my tongue.

"Mommy needs to do a quick errand," I told Jonah.

Procuring my son's breakfast from the diaper bag, I knew I was no better than my mother with my online flirtation and my lies to my husband about where I was, who I was with, and what I was doing. But standing there in the shadow cast by the house, I wanted that job done—not just for Dean, but also for my father—and to reclaim the parts of me still preoccupied by the torment that began there.

"Mommy needs to go inside," I said, pointing to the address.

"I will be right back. You're going to eat your muffin and look at Elmo."

I handed Jonah a book and a giant pastry that he held with two hands.

"Milk, Mama?" he asked sweetly. He bit into the muffin and, with a mouthful of it, announced, "Big cake!"

I admired my boy. His features matched my husband's—the eyes, the nose, the cleft chin—but his coloring, that milky Irish skin, was my father's, just like my mother once said. In his face, even more so as he would grow, I could see his grandfather, the Grandpa Peter he would never know.

And there, that morning, I watched Jonah take another bite of his muffin and understood the possibility that I could go to jail, that for the second time in my life I could lose everything that mattered. But if I didn't do it then, I also knew I would never repossess those broken parts of myself, to be whole not just for myself, but for my son. Caught in a maelstrom, I questioned it all. Exhilaration. Repentance. Loss.

Then I moved forth.

"Mommy loves you," I said to Jonah, just as my father had told Kara and me when he saw us off for the last time.

Breathing deeply, I reached for the giant canvas boat bags on the passenger seat stuffed with latex gloves, a mask, and thirty-five aerosol flea bombs divided between them, then patted my pockets to double-check that I had my accelerant and the yellow lighter, my lucky charm.

"Five minutes," I told Jonah and pulled on my gloves. I was anxious, but Dean promised I would be able to see the car from the house.

When the Quayside is gone, I won't be haunted anymore. I'll be a more clear-headed mother, I convinced myself. Then, I leaned over the console, squeezed my son's hand, and tucked the edges of a stroller blanket into the folds of his car seat. I tugged his hat down over his ears.

I told him, "Mommy will do better. After this, Mommy will stop being sad and we will be happy together."

Jonah nodded his head. "Cake," he said, offering a bite to Elmo.

I locked the door and sprinted toward the house, anxious.

At the place where the barn used to stand, I paused.

"Daddy," I said aloud to my father's ghost, "we never saw the comet."

Snow squeaked beneath my boots and tears blurred my eyes, but I keep running. The aerosol cans clanked together in the bags. I worried about leaving tracks, evidence, my shoe size, but when I reached the walkway to the house, I found that Dean had shoveled the stairs as he promised, heavily salting the path on his way out the door.

I smelled the ocean, the muck of low tide mingled with chimney smoke and the morning's bacon grease from the White Sands across the street.

With my gloved hand, I turned the knob on the mudroom door I'd closed behind me the day I graduated from high school. I looked back at the lot where the car was parked. My body trembled. Inside the entry, I whiffed gas seeping from the lines Dean had punctured before hightailing out of there, as we had planned. His perforation of the main lines running from the basement up through the kitchen motivated me to move quickly, to hold up my end of the promise.

I stepped across the creaking floorboards and checked the grandfather clock in the corner. The hour hand quivered with each tick of the second hand.

Like a burglar, I moved toward the granite island in the center of the kitchen. I pulled on a gas mask.

"Hurry," I whispered to myself.

Dean had spread a thick layer of grease that coated the kitchen surfaces. It lent a slick, waxy veneer to the hardwood floors in the hallway and the stairs leading up to the second floor. I steadied myself so as not to slip, turned the gas dial on the range clockwise, turning it on, and stepped away.

Outside the window above the kitchen sink, I looked for my car flecked with flurries and worried about Jonah.

Moving fast, I tucked flea bombs into corners of the large room. Pushing their tabs to activate the propellants, I arranged eight cans total to ensure the kitchen as the epicenter of the blaze.

I checked the time—two minutes down—and slipped from the galley into the dining room.

There I pulled another set of foggers from my bag and recalled my mother leaning against the stone hearth, her long, dark hair to the middle of her back, Craig's hand on her ass at Christmas. The memory incensed me as I remembered staring at a holiday roast, its red blood pooled onto my plate fifty yards from where my father had bled to death in the barn.

My phone vibrated in my pocket, interrupting a memory I was eager to shake. I looked at my phone. A missed call from Miles, back in Wisconsin.

Shame overwhelmed me. "Keep going," I told myself.

From the dining room, I took the stairs two at a time to the second level. At the landing, I veered into the former guest room that became mine, now Dean's office, as my breathing quickened and moistened my mask. I primed six more aerosol cans, then moved to the next bedroom, once Kara's, to position six more. In the master bath, I perforated one fogger, and I placed four additional cans in the adjoining guest room.

Beside a hallway fireplace with a propane insert, I dropped another propellant and then entered the master bedroom, scattering the aerosol cans along the perimeter. I set the last one where the telescope once stood.

I caught the view. Out the window, haze edged off Long Island Sound and onto shore.

The last time I stood there, I was home to visit Kara, who had just graduated from college. She was twenty-two to my twenty-four, and while we polished off the last of my mother's white wine, we stood there looking out that bay window. Kara had adopted Craig as her new father long ago, making me cringe and feel more separated from my sister every time she called him Daddy.

We had snuck into the forbidden master suite while Mom and Craig were away, each of us taking a turn to peer through the giant, white telescope after TWA Flight 800, a Boeing 747, exploded and crashed into the Atlantic Ocean off the coast of Long Island, killing all 230 people on board. Through the scope we searched for the burning wreckage plummeting like meteors across the night, as Channel 3's Gayle King broadcasted images of debris burning on the water in a ring of jet fuel. During the few weeks I was home from graduate school, before my research started and before Kara started her first advertising job out of college, we hunted for charred bits of plastic, which took precedence over our usual hunt for blue and green sea glass. We filled special receptacles left on the beach by the National Transportation Safety Board until their investigation was completed and authorities took them away.

I pushed the final tab on the last fogger and wondered about my sister now, still living in Connecticut with her family, hoping that maybe I could reach for her again once the haunts of that house were gone. I peered out the window again, noting my car in the parking lot across the street, and readied to race back to Jonah, wanting to be done with all that was wrong with my being there.

Downstairs in the kitchen, fumes emitted a noxious veil of combustibles, already the perfect atmospheric condition for flames. A broom-handle torch—made by Dean, tipped with crumpled newsprint and bound together with packing tape—waited on the island.

Remembering my chemistry, how the radiation and the convection of a fire are more important than the conduction, how fine fuels combust more rapidly than coarse, I knew that the walls and ceiling would burn more eagerly than the floors, the flames moving up rather than down.

Carrying the torch past the bathroom, the place where I once bathed with Dean, I moved into the breezeway, the point from which I would ignite that final expedient—the torch.

The clock chimed: 8:15 a.m.

I pictured Jonah out there crying in the cold and the patrons of the White Sands Country Club cutting into their frittatas. I calculated the handful of seconds it would take me to get back.

Unfastening my coat pocket, I pulled out the lighter and gave it a shake.

Terrified and eager, my breath became some dog's summer day pant. I thought about respiration and its "carbonic acid," the midcentury's archaic term for CO_2. How in Michael Faraday's *Lecture V: Oxygen Present in the Air—Nature of the Atmosphere*, he investigated the taper giving rise to soot, water, and a noncondensable gas with singular properties capable of snuffing out the very fire that produces it. Carbon dioxide was foe to the flame, he proved. So I held my breath and flicked the lighter again with my thumb, and my whole body quivered.

Small glints jumped from the wheel, but with the first few strikes there was no flame.

I took a deep breath, held the yellow lighter to my ear, and shook it again, noting the slosh of fluid inside. I struck the wheel once, twice...ten...twenty times more, turning over the switch until my thumb felt raw.

The clock chimed again, twenty-five past eight, my window of time to ignite the thing becoming slim.

I raced frenzied into the kitchen and slipped on the grease coating the floor. Rummaging through drawers, I sifted through silverware and sandwich bags, pushed back spatulas and Tupperware, envelopes and elastic bands, searching for matches.

I threw open the cupboards, rifled past foodstuffs and paper plates, dishes and cups. Empty-handed, I turned the corner into the dining room and patted above the mantel, claiming a single, silver matchbook, the logo of Patty's Irish Pub lettered across it.

Panicky, aware of the time and potential witnesses, the patrons at the White Sands Country Club finishing their brunches, I grabbed Dean's handmade torch and steadied its handle between my knees. Opening the fold of the matchbook, I scraped the last remaining matchstick across the flint to kindle the newsprint bound with tape. The flame fizzled out with the incoming draft of the door. I choked back a sob.

Taking a deep, quivering breath, I tried the yellow Zippo again, one last time, flicking it to initiate a single, glorious flame. Igniting the torch, I dipped an arm of blooming fire through the cracked breezeway door.

Light poured from the wand like liquid and doused the kitchen in brilliance.

My heart vaulted.

Above the island was a flash, a glare that temporarily blinded me.

I covered my eyes, opened the exit door, and ran.

Outside, the melted plastic trailed behind me. At my back, there was a wall of heat, followed by the sound of gunshots— one pop after another, a series of rapid-fire explosions.

Against the wind, I raced past the spot of my father's suicide and to my son. I whispered, "I love you, Daddy. Forgive me."

Cold froze my nostrils.

Behind me I heard another boom, then the hiss of a thousand snakes.

Rounding the shoveled lane into the parking lot, I reached my rental car. Swinging the driver's side door open, I jumped in, buckled my belt, and looked in the rearview to comfort my son.

"You okay, baby?" I said.

But when I turned to greet him, Jonah was gone.

A moment of sheer terror held me motionless.

"Jonah?" I called out, paralyzed, my pulse throbbing in my neck.

I crawled over the console into the backseat. His half-eaten muffin and Elmo book were tossed onto the floor. I rubbed my hand across the empty car seat where his blanket was draped over the side. I popped the trunk and peeked foolishly inside, slamming it and circling the car, then the parking lot. Again, I yelled my son's name in a voice that did not sound like my own, but more like the cry of an injured bird.

In the distance there were sirens.

"Where are you?" I screamed, retracing my steps to be sure he was not hiding, reminding myself that Jonah was not big enough to have unbuckled himself and walked away, or *was* he?

Panic rose in my throat. Across the street, flames of blue and beetle-green waved from the house's second floor and the black smoke roiled into a dark cloud.

God is punishing me, I thought, my dread welling faster than smoke.

Inside the White Sands Country Club, I was consumed with panic, standing at the hostess station where I frantically tapped my fingers on the desk. "I need your help," I told the teenage girl dressed in a skintight sweater dress.

She chewed the end of a pencil and held a telephone between her shoulder and ear. "One minute, please." She smiled.

"It's an emergency," I almost screamed.

"We've already called," she said, holding a finger to her lips. "The people at table five saw smoke."

"No," I said, taking a deep breath. "Not that. I'm looking for a little blond boy. My son. Did you see him?"

She covered the receiver with her hand and calmly mouthed,

"Nope." She jotted down a reservation, covered the receiver again, and whispered, "Have you checked the powder room?"

I ran to the ladies' room and threw open every door. "Jonah!" I hollered.

At the men's room door, I said, "Hello?" No one answered. I flew past the urinals and checked the stalls. I ran out and around the dining room and scanned the aisles of tables. I even dropped to my knees to peer under the booths. Nothing.

Peek-a-boo, I imagined him saying.

"Jonah!" I said aloud, half sobbing. "Where *are* you?"

I hurried back outside. All I could think of was the cold and the fire trucks pulling into the lot, soaring around the corner, not seeing my small son, and me, his own mother, responsible for his death. Or worse, him having grown impatient, pushing through the front door, searching for me inside the burning house…

"Jonah," I screamed.

My breath collapsed. I jumped into the car and circled the lot one last time. Then I pulled over and folded my hands in my lap for a prayer that I suspected, given my deeds, would go unanswered.

Across the street, the fire revived and quickened. Cruisers pulled up along the curb.

From my jeans, I took my phone and dialed Miles's number.

"Hello," he answered on the first ring.

I couldn't catch my breath. It was hard to speak, and my face was soaked with tears. "I can't find him!" I shrieked. "He's *gone*."

"Slow down," Miles said. "Who's gone?"

"Jonah, it's Jonah. Oh God...I left him in the car. For a minute." I turned on the wipers to clear the slush from the windshield. "Now he's missing."

Across from me, 101 Quayside Lane burned like the firing chamber of a spaceship.

"What do you mean?" My husband's voice did not waver. "Is your sister there? Could she have run inside with him somewhere? I'm certain he isn't strong enough to unhook his own seat belt, Claire."

An unfettered darkness billowed from the second-floor windows, their glass already blown. EMTs lined the snowbanks. I turned onto the street and passed, while firefighters broke down the front door.

I looked behind at the empty backseat. "I'll call you back," I told my husband.

Driving too fast down windy roads, I watched as fleets of oncoming squad cars soared by. Farther from the main drag the traffic slowed, and I sped down a lane behind the Bee and Thistle Inn, where I found Dean's car.

"Please God," I said, leaving the keys in the ignition, my heart thumping away. I rounded the front desk and raced upstairs to our rooms.

Throwing the door open, I found Jonah jumping on the bed, a green balloon in one hand, a cookie in the other.

"Mama," he cheered gleefully. "Mama. Up!" He leaned against Dean to steady his landing and let go of his balloon. He reached for me.

I tossed my phone on the bedside table and scooped Jonah into my arms, holding my son so tightly he yelled, "Ouch!"

My terror withered into tearful gratitude as I inhaled his sweet, syrupy smell.

Glaring at Dean, I whispered: "You *took* my son?"

Dean pushed his sunglasses up onto his head. "Didn't you get my note?"

"Note?" I said.

I kissed Jonah's neck, his face, his ears, his eyes, his hair.

Dean voice's deepened with concern. "I left you a note in the car telling you to meet us here. You were scared about his safety. Figured I'd take some worry off your plate."

"Didn't find a note," I said, backing away from Dean, clenching Jonah tight. "You terrified me. I thought he was gone. I called my husband."

"Oh man, Claire. I'm so sorry. Last-minute decision. I'd gotten nervous that you were right, that it wasn't safe, you know, so close to things. Went and grabbed him, popped the lock. He seemed happy to see me." Dean turned to Jonah. "Right, buddy?"

On the bed between us, next to the set of blueprints, a Slim Jim similar to the lock pick Dean used to break into cars and steal pullout radios when we were kids jutted out from his duffel bag.

"Don't be upset. Good intentions," he reminded me. "Too cold to leave him out there."

Dean paused and walked around the bed, holding the balloon in his hand. He offered it back to my son. Jonah declined.

Dean told me then, "I'm glad to see motherhood hasn't changed you. You're still so daring."

"You're dead wrong," I said, knowing in that moment that

Dean wanted me to be the girl he remembered, the one who would set her son down in the next room and give herself to him again right there. But that girl—like the years that had passed, like the house—was history. And as much as I had gone back East anticipating his desire and how I might let it fill me, setting my loneliness free, becoming that old version of myself for Dean, his jimmying the lock and taking Jonah from that car had clarified how terrifying his unpredictability could be.

Dean rubbed my shoulder. "It's over, babe. You did a fucking amazing job. There'll be nothing left. Have a drink with me? To celebrate."

"You should go," I said, scanning the room to take inventory of our things.

Dean tugged a bottle of champagne from his bag. "It's not cold enough," he said. "But it'll do." He popped the cork and sipped the foam from the bottle.

"Really," I said, "I need to leave here, forget this place and go home."

Dean told me, "You are home, babe."

He poured two glasses and held one out to me. I shook my head no.

On the bedside table, my phone vibrated.

Dean gulped down both glasses of champagne, picked up my mobile, and looked at the face of it before he handed it to me. "Your husband."

Across the screen was a text: I just talked to your sister and your mother. Where are you? Where is our son?

Something inside of me went undone. Dean walked to the door and jingled his keys.

I texted my husband: Will explain later. Jonah in my arms. All is well. Still in CT. Home late tomorrow night.

When I looked up, Dean was watching me. "I'm staying with my mother. If you need me—"

"I won't," I said.

Jonah rested his head on my shoulder.

"You might," Dean said gently, "and I'd take you both."

He squinted against the morning light coming through the window and held out a hand, reaching for me. "You can't go back there, Claire. I saw it with my own eyes, you sitting alone in that front room two nights in a row, eating dinner alone in your pajamas, drinking all that wine by yourself. That's no kind of life. Especially not for you."

Fear, cold trickles of it like ice water, roiled through me. "What do you mean? What do you mean, you saw me?"

Dean stepped nearer to Jonah and me.

"In Madison. I watched you. I was there a couple days before I rang your bell. And most of the time we were chatting on Facebook, I was parked right outside your window."

I shook my head, staggered, wanting to believe that Dean had come to Wisconsin to support me, like he always had, to see who we might be together again. My speech stuttered. I asked, "Did—so did you know when you came that you wanted… this? That you wanted me to set fire to the house?"

"I did." Acknowledging the expression on my face, he came closer still. "But don't take that the wrong way, Claire. I was also curious about your life. And so I scoped it out for a couple of days, to see how interested you'd be in getting out of there, before I asked you to do this crazy thing. A payback for me."

Dean and I were again close enough to kiss, yet all I felt was deceived. He rubbed the knuckles of his hand along my face and grabbed my free hand. I clutched Jonah tighter with the other.

"The truth is," he told me, "I got hung up on you. I'd pictured your life so differently—this woman married to a doctor, a perfect little family. I didn't believe you could be as lonely as you said. But then I saw it with my own eyes, even worse than you let on, fucking *heartbreaking* to watch a woman I loved be overlooked and wasted. I had to take action, do *something.*

"I wanted to make things better for you there, Claire, but it didn't work. Miles still ignored you after the lab fire. You said it yourself. And then I knew the right thing to do was get you home with me, and that if we burned down the Quayside and got in the clear financially, you and me—Jonah—we'd all get everything we needed."

Gasping for breath, I was so struck with revulsion that I struggled to gain my composure.

Dean remained calm, sucked air through his teeth, and cuffed the sleeves of his shirt. "You told me that you dreamed about that lab exploding, Claire. Remember? Said you dreamed about some scientist getting a formula wrong and taking the place down."

Deeply disturbed, I finally recognized that Dean's dark side had run riot, his reality had skewed since I last knew him. I whispered, "And so you did it?"

"Only when I knew no one was there, that no one would be hurt. I did it for you." He looked at me tenderly. "And now you've done the same for me."

I turned my back on him, wracked with tremors. Hating myself for what I had done, all of it clear then how Dean had staked out my life and burned down my husband's lab, hood-winking me to come back home and commit a felony. And it was even worse than that, I know now. The sickening grasp of it still floods me sometimes when I realize how I played the pawn in Dean's design, his agenda for the arson made without my knowledge, his seduction a form of trickery to gain my participation in a crime he had already staged. And for the first time, I was afraid of him. Terrified, even.

He grabbed my arm. "Wait, Claire."

I wrenched it away, set a tearful Jonah on the bed, and snatched the hotel phone from the nightstand, preparing to call for help.

"Get out!" I said.

"You're overreacting," he said softly. "That's all behind us now."

"I could go to *jail*," I screamed.

He shook his head and backed toward the door. "If questions were asked, if it ever came to that, I would take the fall to protect you. You know that, Claire."

Jonah continued to weep, calling, "Mama, up."

"Out," I demanded. "Please leave."

He moved toward the doorway and said, "Thank you. For everything." And as he backed through it, he blew me a kiss.

Nauseated, I bolted the lock behind him. My head fell against the door and I bowed with remorse over what I had done. I lifted Jonah from the bed and sobbed with him as I carried him into the bathroom. In the mirror I examined our reflections under the fluorescent lights, noticing the singed ends of my hair and the soot on my chin.

Jonah's eyes were draped with heavy lids and he nuzzled his face against my neck, blinking his eyes and catching his breath.

"I'm sorry," I whispered to my son. "Mommy is so sorry."

I kissed his face. I kissed his hands. I took each big toe and brought it to my lips. I exhaled and considered Miles. I wondered how he could ever again trust a mother who let her son go missing, a wife who slept with another man, a woman who had loved fire since her youth.

I hated myself, and with no belief I could ever deserve forgiveness, I wept, muttering, "Stay calm."

"Calm," Jonah repeated. He patted my face.

Forcing deep, slow breaths, I stripped us both down for a shower and washed the residue of pesticides off my skin. Through the steam, I watched Jonah blink water from his eyes, and while we clung to each other under the warm spray, I cried for my father, I cried for my crime, I cried for all I was ashamed to be capable of—knowing there would be a reckoning for the lies I told Miles, and that it was coming fast.

CHAPTER SIXTEEN

DISSOLUTION

THE NEXT DAY, AFTER I PACKED OUR THINGS, I looked out over the Atlantic from the inn one last time and touched the window seat where I believed that Dean and I had reclaimed each other, or so I thought at the time, hollowed now by my understanding of the trick it all had been. As we headed out to the airport, I contemplated cruising through Mystic with Jonah to steady myself, thinking that seeing the house Miles and I had reconstructed might help me to regain some footing in reality.

But as I traveled east, driving along the waterfront, I feared that seeing the place might only make me more distraught. I abandoned the visit altogether, looping around in a Dunkin' Donuts parking lot. I detoured instead to Marty's Clam Shack, a place my father loved to go, raving about their shrimp boats and clam cakes every time we went.

It was deserted except for a few locals eating chowder from steaming bread bowls while one of the two employees attempted to keep the winter chill at bay by lining the windows and doors with plastic wrap.

Paranoid about the fire and disgusted with myself, I pulled Jonah from his snowsuit. I chose a spot in the far corner of the room and eased him into a high chair bellied up at the end of a yellow picnic table, where we swayed with the dock upon which the restaurant floated. A cold breeze rose through the cracks in the floorboards, nullifying the meager efforts to keep the place warm, while outside seagulls landed on the roof of the take-out window. From where we sat, the view framed by Millstone Nuclear Power Station and the Niantic River Bridge, Jonah and I could make out a long line of silver passenger cars as they rattled their way from New York City to the New London station.

Above our heads, faded buoys and dragnets trapped plastic lobsters, and just beyond the restaurant's bay window, waves crested over Black Point's breakwater, besieged by the tide. Dark cumulonimbus clouds hovered over the ocean, and I knew they meant thunderstorms, which in the winter in New England come in the form of sleet or freezing rain. I wondered if our flight out would be delayed, and if one day I might return again to find some peace in the fact that the Quayside was gone.

In my father's honor, I ordered his favorite plate for Jonah and me to share: the Captain's Platter of fried fish and fries, something I would never usually consider, and waited for our number to be called.

"For Grandpa Peter," I told Jonah, envisioning Dad hauling the entire vat of tartar sauce to our table and scooping an embarrassing heap of it onto his paper plate. This he did on countless summer nights when he brought Kara and me there for an early supper, hoping to beat the droves of summertime tourists who swarmed the place for boiled lobsters and ears of sweet corn.

Over the microphone, a teenaged girl in a hat that looked like a paper airplane called our order into the empty room.

Failing to steady the anxious warble in my belly, I carried the red baskets of fried fish to our table and showed Jonah how to use the "dip," as he called Dad's favorite condiment. I drenched a piece of fried haddock in the tartar sauce and broke it into tiny pieces with a plastic fork.

Jonah's face grew bright with recognition. He clapped his hands together.

"You like it?" I said. "Yummies? Can you say *tar-tar* sauce?"

"Dada!" Jonah screamed.

In that instant there was a tap on my shoulder and a gasp as I turned to face an elderly woman who resembled my mother. Standing beside her were Miles and my sister, Kara's hand resting on my husband's shoulder.

"Oh my God," I said.

With only a glance at me, Miles went to Jonah and lifted him from his seat.

"No!" Jonah screamed. "Down."

Kara, more glamorous than I remembered, frowned at me. "So you were here, and you didn't even call?"

"Easy," my mother told her.

Mom's hair was cut into an angular bob gone almost completely silver. A fuchsia pashmina was draped over her shoulders. "We've all been worried sick about you, honey," she said.

Miles finally turned to me, more lost than I'd ever seen him. "Claire, *why* are you here exactly? What's going on?"

I watched my husband bounce with Jonah, who settled into his daddy's embrace, and told him, "I'm fine. I just—I wanted some time alone. To get away. To come home." Sounding defensive, I repeated, "Really, I'm fine."

Miles looked down at his feet and took a deep breath through his nose. He wore the Cleveland Browns ski cap I kept tossing into the Goodwill pile, and as he shook his head in disagreement, the orange pom-pom bobbed from side to side, an indicator of his skepticism.

Kara patted his shoulder and looked out over the ocean.

I turned to my mother, the only one person who stared at me directly.

"I had to come back to figure some things out," I told her, my voice rising with alarm. "I would have called. But, I needed time."

Mom forced a smile and straightened the posture of her slight frame. "We're all just glad we found you both safe."

Weighted down by her winter coat, my mother seemed frail in comparison to the version of her I remembered from sixteen months prior, the last time I saw her on the day Jonah was born. For a moment, I wondered if she was sick, or if she noticed the same yardstick of time as she studied my face.

"I knew she would be here," Kara said to my husband, talking as if I were in another room. "Mom saw a quote about missing home on Claire's Facebook feed, and, well, this was her dad's favorite place."

"Our dad," I said. Then I asked my mother, "How could you see that? I declined your friend request. And why are you here? Why aren't you in Florida?"

"Privacy settings," Kara murmured. "And we're glad she helped us find you. Miles called, worried sick."

"I wasn't spying, honey, really. Just concerned is all. It's been too long." My mother wrapped her arms around me and held me so tightly that I could barely breathe. In her hair I smelled the cold and the hint of a woodstove. She exhaled.

Kara turned toward us, another great beauty like my mother, with a stunning mane of dark hair. "Mom and I were really worried about you after Dad died, Claire. Then all these years of silence, your withdrawal from us. We should have reached out a long time ago. Whatever's going on now, I feel like it's our fault too."

I underwent a jolt of panic when Kara said this and I broke from Mom's embrace, registering that the reason my mother was not in Florida had everything to do with me.

I searched Miles's face for a sign of what would come next and grew further paranoid, my own guilt eating away at my resolve. I peered out the window and scanned the lot for medics ready to haul me off to the crazy house, fire investigators with questions, or maybe even Dean coming to condemn me.

But outside there was only the russet sea grass left over from a season past, the sward bent by the gusts blown in off the ocean, and alongside it, stark rows of birch trees standing at attention.

We were the only distraction from the desolation of winter in that seaside town. There were no signs of emergency vehicles, no officers waiting to post blame, just the awkwardness of the five of us situated around the yellow picnic table, staring at baskets of fried fish and the oversized vat of tartar sauce.

Miles told Jonah, "Missed you, bud." Then he looked at me. "It's true. We're all just relieved to see your face."

Dark circles shadowed Miles's bloodshot eyes, the same look of exhaustion he got after his nights on call. And although he generally kept his reactions turned inward, which made reading his emotions something like turning an auger through a thick layer of ice, I saw the fissures in his calm as Miles paced beside my mother and sister. I saw the tension in his jaw and the anxious shift of weight from one foot to another that marked his concern. I worried about how much he already knew.

Jonah covered his father's eyes. "Dada! Peek-a-boo!"

Wanting to be part of their playful diversion, I told my husband plainly, "I'm sorry I lied to you."

"There's nothing you can't tell me, Claire. Nothing."

Outside, storm clouds stirred above the whitecaps.

Forewarned by the ominous sky, I thought back to the night Miles and I met, not a single cloud over the quarter moon, and how we kept buoyant, treading calm and flat waters. But there on that floating dock upon which the restaurant sat, all I felt was a kind of sinking.

Shocked to encounter my mom and sister in the company of my husband, I told him, "I know this whole thing must look crazy to you, but I'm okay." But as soon as I uttered the words, I realized how unwell I sounded.

My mother interrupted by kissing Jonah's cheek and saying, "Such a big, beautiful boy." Jonah played shy and Mom continued to pretend our reunion was some sort of planned lunch date, not an awkward unearthing of my whereabouts.

"Sit," she ordered the group, taking a seat on the picnic bench.

Kara, Miles, and Jonah did as they were told.

I continued to stand.

Mom said, "Kara, tell your sister how you have been."

Kara refused to play along. Blinking back tears, she wringed her long, slender fingers around a pair of leather gloves. "I hate that I never hear from you, Claire. Then this. Whatever this even is."

Mom cut her off. "Kara is headed to Key West with Craig, her three girls, and me. Her husband, Luke, travels a lot for business, so we try to take Kara when we go someplace special."

I nodded vaguely. Miles studied me and took Jonah's small hand in his fist.

Sleigh bells on the clam shack door rang, and an old man in a winter cap came through, ushering in a gust that sent our paper cups and plates across the floor. Miles, with Jonah in his arms, and Kara in her high-heeled boots chased after them, leaving Mom and me alone.

Mom murmured, "Miles called me before you left for Connecticut. He told me he wasn't sure it was a good time for us to meet. I, of course, had no idea what he was talking about, but I didn't want to make waves or get you in any kind of trouble, so I immediately booked my own flight and arranged to stay with Kara at her house in Essex, since it's only six miles away from where I imagined you'd be. And ever since my arrival, I've been driving up and down Route 9 like a crazy person, scouting out all the places where I thought I might find you. Guessed you were missing your father."

"I miss him every day," I told her.

Mom put her arm around me. "I carry my own guilt about his death, honey. I miss him too. Every day I blame myself."

"Do you?" I asked.

"I do." She squeezed my hand and paused, choosing her words. "And, honey, one other thing before Miles comes back. He called me a second time, saying that Jonah had gone missing. He had a lot of questions, but I shared only that we hadn't yet connected. He loves you and is very concerned. We all are. Anyway, I came to help, but I have to admit I'm worried too."

She slipped the front page of the *Hartford Courant* from her purse, unfolding the newsprint to reveal a five-by-seven color photo of 101 Quayside, the image of the house cast in orange flames.

Mom set an article from the *Hartford Courant* on the table in front of me and said, "It's gone."

I read the headline and a guilt-ridden flush came over my face.

Blast Levels Quayside Beach Historic Home
January 12, 2012

A fire yesterday morning at 101 Quayside Lane that injured three firefighters, one seriously, is under investigation with the Connecticut State Fire Marshal. Members of that office reported a gas explosion that destroyed the historic four-story home, said William McMahon, East Lyme's code enforcement officer.

The 5,500-square-foot historic property has lost $530,000 in value since the housing market crashed, and East Lyme police have stated that this fire may be the bizarre last chapter in a divorce battle over who would end up owning the depreciated building.

"There was a bang followed by a loud sizzle, and then everything shook. We ran to the porch, thinking the explosion was a gunshot," said Clyde Reynolds Parker, a 67-year-old neighbor and president of the Quayside Beach Association. "That house has suffered nothing but bad luck. A suicide in the barn followed by another fire in July 1986, and now this. We're just relieved no one is dead."

Late yesterday evening, owner Dean D'Alessio was taken in for questioning after Mario DeVito, the Hartford Police Department's deputy commissioner for public information, said that an unusual number of accelerants had been found on the premises.

Neither D'Alessio nor his estranged wife could be found for comments.

CHAPTER SEVENTEEN

RETICENCE

I THINK CLAIRE AND I NEED A LITTLE MORE TIME TOGETHER," Mom told Miles and Kara when they returned to the table with coffees and a hot cocoa for Jonah.

Kara sat, looped her arm around Mom's waist, and rested her head on our mother's shoulder for a quick hug. Their eyes were the exact dark hue of ash, their bee-stung lips glossed like race cars. As long as I can remember, my sister and mother have shared a beauty at different ends of the timeline.

"Take as much time as you need," Kara told Mom. "I'll help Miles get Jonah into his snowsuit and collect his things."

The newspaper article was tucked under my arm, and the heat I felt holding it was like the warmth of the fire itself. Standing there beside my mother, I suspected that all my lies were transparent.

Miles collected my winter hat and gloves and scarf. "Some water, babe?" He rubbed my neck and handed me a cup.

I gulped the drink back.

With his brow furrowed, Miles took my hand and his thumb lingered on my pulse. Discreetly attempting to get a read on me, he looked into my eyes with a gentle nod.

Tucking Jonah's Matchbox cars into the diaper bag, Kara told him, "That Jonah is so stinking cute. And I agree that they should *not* fly home without you."

Miles set my wrist back into my lap and told me, "Maybe you should ride back to the hotel with your mother now, so you can talk. I'll rebook your flights so we can be together on the plane. I'm not letting you or Jonah out of my sight."

Kara bit her lip and scanned the room as if the answers were hung on the walls amid the series of watercolor seascapes. "If there's anything Luke and I can do, we're happy to help. You're all welcome to our guest room if you don't want to stay at the hotel. I'd love more time with your little cutie."

I nodded and said, "Thanks."

Watching Kara direct Miles's search for Jonah's lost mitten, I could believe that my sister was an attentive mother to her three girls, and I felt the guilt of having denied Jonah an aunt and cousins out of my own distaste for Craig, who had legally adopted Kara as his daughter once I left his house for college.

Admiring my son's industrious stacking of cups, Kara murmured, "I miss this age."

"It's the best age," I agreed, smiling my best sane-person smile, keeping my hands folded to stop their trembling and wondering how long it would be before my family uncovered my crime.

Miles kissed my cheek and put Jonah in my lap. "You've got the car seat, Claire, so the little man should ride with you and your mom. Kara can drop me at the hotel and take your mom back to her place when you meet up with us there. That way, you'll have a little time alone in the car with your mother. Tonight, you'll rest. I'll take care of you." He gave Jonah and me a long, tight squeeze before joining Kara, who stood off in a corner and whispered into her cell phone.

Chewing the cuticles of my free hand, I held Jonah close and scanned out the window again for police cars. Mom wound her scarf around her neck, took the newspaper from my arm, and tossed it into her bag. "Let's skedaddle," she insisted.

Departing, Miles and Kara strolled a few paces ahead of us, their hands tucked into their pockets. They talked about the kids.

"I'd like them to know each other," Miles said. "For Jonah to have cousins and really develop a relationship with them."

Kara stopped to wait for Mom, Jonah, and me.

"Claire," she said, "it makes me sad, all this distance between us." She gestured to Jonah, who squirmed in my arms. "Look what I'm missing. You're my only sister. He's my only nephew."

I set Jonah down beside us. He held on to my leg then pulled the keys from my pocket to play. "I know," I said. "I'd like to meet your kids too. So much time has gone by."

Kara held up her phone. A picture of her three daughters, all wearing pink T-shirts, lit the screen. The one in the middle, her smallest girl with the biggest grin, was lacking a tooth.

"They would love Jonah," Kara said. "I know you'd prefer not to see Craig, but he is really good to Mom and my girls." She shook her head, aware of the mistake in mentioning his name. "Anyway, we could make arrangements for a visit, maybe take a vacation together—just you and me, Miles and Luke, Mom and the kids. It would be good for everyone."

Abruptly, Kara hugged me, her hold so tight that it cracked my back, our first embrace since her wedding, over a decade ago, the last time I saw her. And as we clung to each other, I smelled the musky oil in her hair, the vanilla of her perfume, and I couldn't stop the tears that streaked my face as I squeezed her back.

Miles said, "We can discuss some more definitive plans after the dust settles."

When Kara let go, she wiped her own eyes, then mine. Mom moved between us, her girls, and looped her arms around our waists. "Claire, I hope you know that Craig would also like to see you, like your sister said, maybe get to know you a little better and meet our grandson."

"You know, Mom, I've always felt like you and Kara just replaced Dad," I said, the old resentments welling.

"You need to let go of that, honey," Mom said softly as she stroked my hair. "Is that why you came home? To seek some kind of retribution?"

I took Jonah's hand and started toward the exit. "I don't know why I came. I just want to forget all of it."

Together the five of us walked the rest of the way to our cars in silence. Then Kara called, "Claire, I'll drop Miles at the hotel, wait for Mom, then I need to scoot. Get my kids off the bus. Maybe you two can figure out a time when we can all get together."

Reaching my sister's black sedan, my husband held the door open for her as she climbed into the driver's side. She looked back and shouted, "Take care of yourself, please."

Miles walked around to the passenger's side of her car and called to Jonah, "See you in a few, little buddy. And make sure your mommy drives safe."

Jonah waved at his daddy.

Miles and Kara drove off.

Across the lot, I lowered Jonah into his car seat and handed him the earbuds for his portable DVD player. While I struggled to fasten his lap belt, Mom opened the back passenger's door and said, "Let me help you."

Checking the latch on Jonah's belt, our hands fumbled with the buckle and Mom took my wrist, her grip tight as a tourniquet.

I looked at her. "Got it," I said.

She didn't let go. "That fire, Claire?"

I stared at her, the skin around her eyes like crumpled crepe paper, soft and creased. But I remembered her much younger, my age, that morning the *Challenger* split in two, her ponytail swinging behind her, her green boots crossing the creek, her white coat hung from the end of the telescope, and how after discovering her, I allowed Dean to pull me from my clothes. How Dream Academy played in the tape deck, and how then, my insides aflame, I bloomed with a rage that never left me alone.

She whispered it again, a statement this time: "You burned down the Quayside."

On her nose, small beads of sweat formed despite the cold. She scrutinized my expression over the top of the car, waiting for me to bite my lip and give myself away. My guilt became a copper taste in my mouth and a drone in my head. I slammed Jonah's door closed, dropped into the driver's seat, and turned the key.

As she got in, Mom pulled a slip of paper off the passenger's seat and handed it to me. "Need this?"

The scrap was Dean's mislaid note, its message brief: *I've got your boy. Meet us where we started.*

Rattled, I crumpled it up and stuffed it under my seat.

Behind us, Jonah watched the screen of his DVD player and hummed "The Itsy Bitsy Spider," twisting his fingers up the spout.

Looking over the leaden horizon, I clenched the wheel and

calculated the atmospheric instability of a storm clustering along the squall lines, while eerie cumulonimbus clouds obscured the last of the sunlight.

Mom rested her hand over mine. "That fire?" she said again.

Savage and unexpected, my sobs welled up, irrepressible.

Impervious, Mom kept hold of my hand. She let me weep.

My speech ragged in between my gasps for breath, I told my mother the truth, as I always have. "I wanted that place gone a long time ago, Mom."

She squeezed my fingers and didn't say a word.

"What you did there. With him. With Craig. It killed Daddy. So, yes," I admitted, "I burned it down. I burned it down with Dean."

Mom's composure remained unchanged. "I know Dean," she said. And looking at some far-off marker she asked, "And all those years ago, my car on Willard Street?"

Seagulls circled over us and guffawed like hecklers.

"And your car," I confessed.

Mom remained the shatterproof survivor of torment. Her grip on my hand did not loosen; her voice did not falter. She asked, "And the barn? And Miles's lab?"

I knew even those acts of arson were of my own design, my fantasies actualized by Dean.

"Pretty much. Yes," I said, owning them all.

Mom said simply, "Okay, then."

A bad kind of flutter welled from my gut.

Jonah, still watching his movies, kicked my seat.

"We better get to the hotel," Mom advised. "Before Miles worries."

"Please don't tell him," I pleaded.

"Never," she said. "But did you buy anything incriminating with a credit card? Anything linked to your name or address? There are cameras at every checkout these days."

"Dean bought it all," I explained. "I was in the car. And all our plans, the blueprints, and receipts, I'm pretty sure they were destroyed by the fire."

The buttons of my mother's duster were undone, her fuchsia scarf looped around her neck. She continued without judgment on her face and presented something like gratitude for me having confided in her.

"That's a terrible burden to carry alone," she said.

I put my head against the steering wheel and cried anew.

Mom wrapped her arms around me and whispered, "We'll get you better. There are good people who can give you the right guidance or medicine, if you need it." Then, with her free hand, she guided my chin and forced me to face her. "And, Claire, honey, I'm so sorry you lost your father." Her eyes flooded with tears, and the pencil lining them smudged. "He loved you. Think of how much you love Jonah. He loved you that much. Maybe more."

She kept me there a minute in her grasp, pushed my own tears away with her thumb, and went on. "You know by now, honey, that marriage is hard. Even under the best of circumstances, it's work to keep it together, to ride out the storms. Your dad and I were so young when we started. And those were such strange times."

Her voice cracked, but she caught herself and cleared her throat.

"We were babies, Claire. Your dad was nineteen. I was seventeen when I moved in with him, only eighteen when we married. Young and foolish. And we tried; we really did. But Peter was so haunted after his affair, blamed it all on being drunk and careless. Then he drank because of his guilt, because of hurting me. And I wasn't attempting any sort of tit for tat. It wasn't like that. I met Craig, I liked him, and I didn't know how to leave your dad. I did it poorly, I know. But after his betrayal, and with all the drinking and the layoffs and his inability to hold a job, I felt entitled to another kind of life. And I wanted a better life for you and Kara too."

I looked at her, confused. "What do you mean, *his* affair?" I wiped my face on the sleeve of my coat. "What the hell are you talking about?"

Mom shut her eyes and bit her lower lip, the same pained expression I'd adopted as my own.

I moved closer to her ear, even though Jonah couldn't hear me, and whispered, "You're trying to tell me *Dad* cheated?"

She shook her head, her eyes still shut, and said, "I assumed you knew. I thought Uncle G, or certainly Rex, told you before you went off to college. Rex mentioned it to Kara years ago now."

I searched the rearview for Jonah to ground myself, my sense of home and my father's identity slipping from my reach.

"I don't believe you," I told her.

Then the tears that fell were hers, soaking her cheeks and pooling in the corners of her lips.

"You don't have to believe me," she said. "But it was a couple months after you were born. I demanded to know what was going on—why your father was so quiet, so detached. I threatened to leave back then over it. That was when he told me. He broke down and admitted everything. It was just a fling, he said, some woman at a bar. He said they were both drunk, a one-night stand. He begged forgiveness. Told me he was certain he would die if he lost me over it. If he lost you."

Mom looked up at the sky and blinked hard. And paused. "He never forgave himself for my hurt. And, I guess, I could never forgive him, either."

I said nothing but felt the confidence I had in who, and what, I believed my father to be rupture into brutal reality. The sanctity of my last childhood hero was lost, but this time lost not to space or progress or adventure, but to temptation—a kind of betrayal I had thought Dad only victim to, not capable of, not realizing his imperfections, that he was a liar and a cheat, just like my mother.

Just like me.

I contemplated how I had surrendered a relationship with my own mother over half-truths, always blaming my father's broken heart solely on her, never once considering that maybe Dad had hurt her first.

I shifted the car into drive, attempting to understand how I had been so single-minded to assume the sole catalyst of my mother's affair, carrying my adolescent reasoning into adulthood.

Mom opened the passenger's window and angled her face into the wind. Her silver hair shot up toward the sky and her fuchsia scarf flapped across the dash, the only color in the winter twilight.

At an intersection in Niantic, I slowed. The Amtrak train made its way south over the platform toward the bridge. To Jonah's delight, we were waylaid at the only crossing in town.

"Choo-choo!" he shouted, headphones still on.

As the first car passed, an engineer held up his hand like the greeting of an Indian chief. '

Jonah's giggles clipped at the tension between my mother and me.

Passenger cars scuttled past.

"Claire," Mom said, "I thought you knew."

The snow picked up, and with a head full of misgivings, I turned on the radio for the forecast. On AM radio, a voice I grew up listening to on car rides with my father broadcast the evening report.

"And tonight, along coastal regions, winds will be out of the northeast, lows in the twenties with an eighty percent chance of sleet. Highs tomorrow morning are estimated to reach thirty, under clear skies. And up next, in other late-breaking local news, as the housing market continues to go up in smoke, insurance fraud officials say more area homes are going up with it, as property owners turn to fraud as a means to cope with the economic crisis, both locally and around the nation.

"Here in Connecticut, forty-three-year-old Dean D'Alessio of East Lyme pleaded no contest to arson charges this afternoon after his five-thousand-five-hundred square-foot property burned to the ground subsequent to becoming yet another victim of depreciated home values. More on this story with AM 1080's Diane Smith, after these messages."

The station broke to commercials.

Warning lights beamed from the tracks. Our faces—my

mother's, Jonah's, and mine—glowed red, and I felt as if I was again cast in flames.

The caboose rumbled past.

My mother said, "Dean took the blame."

"Protecting me," I told her. "Like he promised."

The gates blocking our path ascended.

Jonah shouted, "Bye-bye."

We bobbled over the rails and I was overcome with a complicated sense of relief and heartache, knowing that Dean had set me free—unscathed—while recognizing that few truths, if any, were exactly what they seemed.

Reaching behind my seat, I clutched my son's small foot, my devotion to him my only certainty, and I pondered the strength of a mother's love—what we sacrificed for it, what it kept us from, what it empowered us to do—and I forgave my own mother for everything.

At the hotel's parking garage, before we stepped out into the cold, Mom and I tucked our shared secrets away and made promises.

She said, "If you're not too tired, if Miles doesn't have plans, we could have dinner tonight, or maybe coffee with your sister before you head out. I think maybe we need more time." She waited. "I could visit alone sometime too."

I hugged her.

"It's gonna be okay?" I whispered the question into her scarf.

"I hope everything will be," she whispered back. "Miles loves you."

I tasted Mom's perfume, the dense bawdy musk of it, and told her, "Thank you for coming."

She held my face in her cold hands, rested her forehead on mine, and said, "I love you. You are my daughter. And all we can do is learn from our mistakes." Then she gestured behind us with her chin to Jonah. "And I love that little boy of yours too. Like you girls did for me, he will teach you what you need."

As Mom and I walked toward Miles, who was pacing along the hotel entrance, Jonah ran out ahead to greet him. Kara beeped from the hotel turnabout where she was parked, talking into her cell phone. I considered the weight of secrets—my father's, my own. I thought about how Dad's betrayal surely poisoned his heart and how revealing that must have broken my mother's, mutual wounds that would never heal.

Mom and I looked over at Kara.

My sister yelled from the open window of her car. "Mom, I really need to get the kids. Luke is stuck at the office." She pointed to her watch and blew me a kiss good-bye. "Claire, please be in touch. Come back. Stay with us. Mom, we've *got* to go."

Mom held me by my shoulders and stared into my eyes. "I love you, and I want to help you get your head straight. Whatever you need," she told me. Then she squeezed me tight.

She was slight under her heavy coat, all bones. And backing away, she took off her scarf and looped it around my neck. "Better color on you." There were tears in her eyes. "Take care of yourself and your boys." She tossed me a final kiss and mouthed *good-bye*.

Miles greeted me with a quick peck on my cheek, Jonah in his arms. And the two of them reeled me back into a complicated reunion that was mine with which to contend.

"You were gone a while," he said. "How did that go?"

"Good," I told him.

"Good?" he repeated and set Jonah down.

"I'm ready to accept her as she is."

"I'm glad," Miles said.

The three of us walked through the hotel lobby, Miles and I racing after Jonah as he picked up speed.

The hallway dead-ended at the elevator doors.

Miles picked Jonah up so he could push the elevator button. Then, in his daddy's arms, the little guy squeezed his father's nose.

Miles yelled, "Honk," and the two of them busted up laughing at their old joke.

In the elevator we were alone. Jonah smacked at every button to illuminate it on the panel, but when the doors opened on the third floor, Miles stepped out, held his hand against the opening to let us pass, and told me, "I'm glad you feel like you can accept your mother. Maybe you can accept me too? Forgive me a little. Teach me what you need?" He pulled the hotel key card from the back pocket of his jeans to confirm our room number, then continued, "Maybe, Claire, you can help me bring back that silly, sweet woman who used to love me? I miss her so much. I miss you."

"I'd like that," I said.

Inside the room, the bed was turned down and containers of takeout Miles had brought up from the hotel restaurant while he waited for us sat on the desk in the corner. On the television, an animated movie that Miles had chosen for Jonah played, with the volume muted. His gestures were sweet and made the onus of what I'd done even more unbearable.

Miles unzipped Jonah's coat, then he helped me ease out of my parka. I imagined the lighter tumbling from my jacket pocket onto the floor and the questions that would be asked, so I took the coat from my husband to double-check the empty pocket linings, making certain that bit of evidence had been tossed with the rest of it in the Dumpster behind the inn.

"Dinner?" Miles offered, opening up plastic bowls of pasta and salad. He buttered slices of bread.

Silently, we sat together and shared bites, all three of us eating from the same fork.

Drained, I kicked off my shoes and crawled across the white sheets. Miles followed me, nestling Jonah between us. We huddled together.

"Sweetie," Miles said, resting one hand on Jonah and one hand on me, "I'll do whatever it takes."

"I'm sorry I ran off," I apologized again. "I'm sorry I lied to you." Exhausted and ashamed, I fell asleep before I could offer him anything more.

CHAPTER EIGHTEEN

VESTIGE

B ACK IN SNOW-COVERED WISCONSIN, AS I SAT across from my husband with Jonah in my lap, Miles said, "I'm so glad you're home." Then he, a better partner than I have been, promised, "I'm not letting you give up on us yet."

Forgiveness is not a practice I have mastered, but I believed that when Miles came searching for me in Connecticut, he was determined to fix what was broken, to forgive me for lies he knew not the extent of, and that in his own quirky way he wanted me for keeps. I pardoned his part in what was missing between us, but harder for me was exonerating myself from the secrets I hadn't yet shared with Miles, those betrayals I made privately with Dean.

And I'll probably never forgive myself for my father's death, even if the reasons for it came from a more complicated reality, a truth revealed to me perhaps only because I took the risk of going east with Dean. And yet, despite those festering wounds that fed my father's brokenness, I'll always wonder if I might've stopped him, had I made curfew the night he took his life—always feeling part owner of his suicide.

In light of it all, home with my own family somehow intact,

the Quayside gone, I hoped Miles would decide to grant me a second chance to have what I'd yearned for as a girl—a life where maybe no one gets exactly what they need, but one where we all get to have each other.

Pushing my soup bowl aside, I told my husband, "I'll do better."

"You *are* doing better," he said.

"*We* can do better," I reiterated. "We still need more laughter. More intimacy. Some bigger connection to each other."

Miles lit a candle on the kitchen table. "You mean romance?" he said, raising an eyebrow, part teasing, part serious. He set the flame between my wineglass and Jonah's sippy cup, next to the stack of unopened mail.

Seated beside us, Jonah scribbled on an envelope with a crayon.

I sipped from my drink and beheld the flicker cast from the wick.

"I hear you," Miles said. "More togetherness. More fun. Got it." Then he jumped up, opened the freezer, and added, "And we all need more *ice cream*!"

Jonah clapped his hands.

I told him, "None for me."

And while Jonah and Miles delighted in eating chocolate gelato straight from the pint, I thumbed through a pile of glossy magazines and medical journals.

Scrolling the table of contents in the latest issue of *Astronomy Magazine*, I noted a brief article on Alpha Centaurids' meteors, in which the author noted:

This shower will stream six to ten meteors per hour along Alpha Centauri, the brightest star in the constellation

Centaurus, named for Greek mythology's half man, half horse, the beast who dominates this part of the sky and denotes all that is wild, savage, and lustful.

Miles blew his nose into a dish towel.

"Lustful," I whispered, eyeing my husband.

I chucked the magazine into the recycling bin. Then, as I sorted the remaining junk mail from the bills, I came across an envelope with the return address of 61 Willard Street, East Lyme, CT 06333.

An uneasy flutter rose in my chest. I slipped the letter into my lap. Trying to keep the shrillness from my voice, I asked my husband, "Should I take Jonah up for bed, or do you want to?"

Miles tossed spoons into the sink. "I've got it," he said and lifted Jonah, with his sticky face and a fistful of crayons, up from the table. Our little guy rested his tired head against his father's chest and waved, "Night night, Mama."

With slow, deliberate steps, Miles ascended the stairs and rubbed the small of Jonah's back. Awaiting their slip beyond the banister, I kept the letter tucked between my knees, where it seemed to radiate heat. Once I heard the water running and Miles singing, "Brush, brush, brush your teeth," I tore the envelope open.

Dean's script was composed in blue ink on yellow-lined paper jaggedly torn from a legal pad. There was a doodle of waves in the margin above which he had drawn a star, streaming across a cloudless sky.

Dearest Claire,

I tried to respond to your last message but it seems I'm blocked from your contacts. I don't dare call now that I'm under investigation, so figured the safest bet was to bust out the old pen and paper to reassure you that I've fully protected you from things here.

Following this note, I'm sad to say I won't contact you again. I have to let you go. I realize that now. It hurts to admit this, but I know you want to give Jonah a life neither of us got to have. I'll confess, though, that seeing you made me feel a whole lot of regret and desire, also some warmth that you look so in love with that kid. I'd be lying if I didn't tell you that it made me wonder what a life with you would've been like, what our son might have looked like, who he would have grown up to be, what I gave away. It's too late to second-guess those things, I suppose.

But the point of me telling you this is that me seeking you out was never about the fire alone. As I watched you, things evolved into this hope that we might set the world on fire together, somehow. That matters not so much, I know, because you'll sacrifice what you need to be there for your family. It's honorable, Claire. In fact, it's one of the things I love about you the most.

On this end, nothing is entirely clear.

My attorney thinks that since the Home Depot's records verify my purchase of accelerants, I could get five years of probation and, worst-case scenario, a charge for negligence with fines for property damage, potentially serving six months to a year, tops. But he claims arson is the hardest crime to peg, even with prints, which they don't have. And because those products cause these types of problems all the time, pretty fucking flammable, we're arguing their usage in my home the obvious culprit for the damage, all of it an innocent, albeit foolish, accident.

Regardless, the place is gone. Be free of it.

And should that last message you sent mean I'm wrong about anything I've said here, you know where to find me, at my mom's place on Willard Street. I'd happily open the door.

Forever yours,

Dean

I set the letter down and regarded the gift Dean's devotion granted me—the repossession of my life in Madison, a protected secret, something I could hide forever, if I chose. But I knew that my return to Miles wasn't as simple as Dean signing off. I was branded too by the burden of those choices I'd quietly made. So much had happened. I had fallen for his scheme, and I had fallen for Dean. I'd believed in the seduction enough to commit a felony. And even if those confidences were never exposed to anyone, vaulted in the place of kept secrets, I knew I'd live with the emotional consequences forever.

Through the baby monitor, Miles's voice narrated *Goodnight Moon* to Jonah upstairs in the nursery. His speech was a comfort: "Good night stars, good night air, good night noises everywhere."

"He's a good man. Hang on to him, Claire," my mother had said about Miles, now that there was a different kind of secret between her and me. She encouraged me to resurrect my marriage and to figure out what Miles and I had to do to rebuild.

I pressed Dean's letter to my lips, then held it over the candle at the center of my kitchen table and pushed the stationery into the flame. The yellow notebook paper curled back, the envelope charred into dust, and while it all burned away, I remembered Michael Faraday's closing words from *The Chemical History of a Candle, Lecture VI*:

> **Now I must take you to a very interesting part of our subject—to the relation between the combustion of a candle and that living kind of combustion which goes on within us. In every one of us there is a living process of combustion going on very similar to that of a candle, and I must try to make that plain to you. For it is not merely true in a poetical sense—the relation of the life of man to a taper—and if you will follow, I think I can make this clear.**

Fanning the air with his dish towel, Miles descended the stairs just as carefully as he had gone up them. He asked, "What's going on down here?"

"Firebug," I said. Between my index finger and thumb, I

held the last corner of the envelope. The table in front of me was speckled with ash.

My husband carried our wineglasses to the sink and returned to sponge off the surface where I sat. Removing the candle from the table's center, he held it out before us, like a lantern, and took my hand to lead us through the dark.

Our shadows fell across living room, down the hall, and into the playroom, where he knelt in front of the blanket fort I had built for Jonah. Crawling beneath the draped bedspreads and flannel sheets, he waved at me to follow him.

Inside, he rested the candle on a plastic bin of Legos and inched us toward a stack of throw pillows and the dozen or so teddy bears lined up against them. Leaning me back, setting a stuffed dolphin under my head, he pulled off each one of my slippers and socks. He worked his hands over my toes and massaged the instep of my foot, where my tattoo of the comet had long ago faded into a bit of blue, like a bruise.

With his hand ascending my legs, Miles kneaded my calf and my thighs; he caressed my belly, moved his hands over my breasts, and then up over my shoulders. Straddling my waist, coming up onto his knees, he pushed me down and kissed my lips, my ears, my neck, and my face. He kissed me like he meant it, with an unusual urgency, like a man whose future was at stake.

"Start over with me?" he whispered.

And as we fumbled with each other's buttons in the soft, expiring candlelight, I felt the good fortune of the familiar.

"Okay," I said. "For Jonah."

"For all of us," he said. "Promise me?"

I considered how life *can* exist without flames, how the oceans prove this, and guessed that planets beyond our own someday would too. I lay there, while Miles searched for me, waiting for my pledge to commit to our marriage again. I rationalized how fire, that kind of fire I had with Dean, was not something needed for survival, but more a chemistry affixed to our own human behavior, to desire. Then, I considered burning—how when a blaze is snuffed by wind or by rain, humans still flourish. How in the wild prairies, when conditions change and the rains dry out, combustion rekindles and new flames sometimes burn again.

My eyes followed the subtle movements of Miles's silhouette along the blanketed ceiling of our makeshift fortress. "Yes," I said finally. "I'll start over with you. But first there's a lot I have to tell you. Some things I'm ashamed of. Bad things I've done."

He ran his hands through my hair. "Okay. I want to hear it, Claire. But whatever it is that's happened, we'll get through it."

I wasn't sure we could get through it, and even twelve weeks from that moment of tenderness, it still feels uncertain. But there, under the blankets with Miles, I tallied the lies I'd told, the bad choices I'd made, including the fire in Miles's lab, something I was ultimately responsible for, and I grew anxious, knowing that without the truth, there was no way we could continue.

My tension mounted as I fumbled for the words to explain myself, to confess to my husband. Instead, I thought of the quote I'd impulsively messaged to Dean before I boarded the plane back to Madison:

Like a comet, our dust casts an infinite trail, leaving and returning still.

It was my hint at possibility, that maybe someday, somewhere
I would find Dean again, and also an indirect attempt to express
that he was not to blame for everything. But the second I sent
it, I was embarrassed and ashamed, knowing that those were the
last words I would ever say to him.

And so, when Miles kissed me after my confessions were
made, I succumbed to him, recognizing and remembering the
security of our love, imagining we might find a way to recon-
struct a life together, one that would remain uninterrupted
from then on. The hope for that better life and the promise of
rekindling the simmer between us made it possible to commit
to that risky business of beginning again.

But starting over is no easy feat and even our counselor, Anna,
has admitted that as much as what happened at the Quayside
set me free from my history—from Dean—it also has left me
captive to the guilt that hollows out my insides and bangs panic
into my chest, keeping my moods toggled to the spectrum of
Miles's clemency or grief. And over the past twelve weeks since
my return home, the misgivings I've caused Miles have not
mended but spewed into something septic.

His belief that he could forgive me *everything* failed to take
into account that the "everything" I disclosed was a more con-
voluted and complicated betrayal than he could've anticipated.

So despite making love in that makeshift tent through tears, while Miles whispered "How could you?" and "No, no, I want you to tell me" and "Of course I'll forgive you," I found him, nearly three months later, out in the snow, drinking Scotch and stoking a fire of his own.

Late this past Friday I startled to the sound of a dog barking, to find the bed empty beside me and, out the window, the curling tail of drifting smoke. Tiptoeing, I headed downstairs, where the back porch was lit and Miles sat outside, bundled in the late March cold, the never-ending Wisconsin winter still upon us.

I slid the glass doors open and called, "What are you doing out there?"

Miles did not answer.

Smoke billowed up from a fire before him.

"Honey?" I said.

He shook his head.

I stepped into my boots.

He sipped from a tumbler. And I approached.

The fire flashed orange and blue, and Miles stoked it with a stick as I came closer.

Kneeling beside him, I followed my husband's stare to the center of the blaze, where the white cover of our wedding photo album charred black, its plastic coating shrinking back, while the flames crackled and hissed.

My heart panged. And to steady the tremble in my knees, I sat on a log beside him, the ground still frozen beneath my feet, the snow glistening. I hugged my arms around my chest to fend off the bluster and withhold my hurt, remembering the ivory dress I wore on our wedding day, the eyelet fabric that fit slim and spilled out into a train, the baby's breath in my hair, and how Miles beamed as I stepped toward him under a gazebo on the village green.

I said, "How can I make things right?"

Miles stared straight ahead. Brought his glass back to his lips. I couldn't help but notice his absent wedding band and wondered if maybe I should leave him alone. But I also felt deserving of his anger, whatever form it might take, and so I stayed. Waiting.

From him, there was only silence.

"Miles?" I said.

He reached between us into a slouched canvas bag and lifted another album into his lap. He tapped his naked ring finger on the word *HOME* typed in gold across the book's center.

I set my hand on his wrist. "Honey," I said. "Don't."

But he pitched it underhanded into the flames. Hot embers spattered at our feet.

"Don't leave me," I whispered.

And as the cinders cooled from orange to ash, burning up with our wedding album were the pictures of our home renovations in Mystic, the before-and-after shots Miles had meticulously captured with his Nikon in early-morning sunlight, images he had developed himself after the reconstruction was done. The photo book was a gift he made for me the first Christmas in our newly restored house.

At the epicenter of the flames, the album seemed to go liquid. The smoke billowed, black.

I reached for my husband.

He shirked.

The fumes were toxic; the flames went blue-hot.

"I'm sorry," I muttered.

With his face twisted into a grimace, Miles tossed the last of his drink toward the glare. Then he stood and, walking away from me, boomed, "Shame on you, Claire."

These past two days, nothing is certain. Miles's address of me wavers with a constant swing of emotions—a pat on my knee this morning in bed, then a moment later, a stern glance in my direction.

Outside, the place where the photo books burned looks like a rabbit hole in the snow, and I think about Alice falling down the dark center of it, chasing after the White Rabbit into that troubled and peculiar Wonderland.

At the breakfast table, I warily join my husband and son, where I unfold the Sunday paper to read the forecast, hoping for a thaw.

Miles makes coffee.

Jonah dips a paintbrush into a watercolor palate.

The one hundred forty days of snow cover we've had this winter are tallied in the *Wisconsin State Journal*, the calculation in agreement with Punxsutawney Phil's prediction that we should be in our last stretch of a long, brutal winter. I remind myself that this kind of early April freeze is a metaphor, the frozen snow protecting and insulating the grasses and seeded grains beneath it while they await better weather for their bloom.

Jonah taps his brush on the edge of a glass.

"Pretty," I tell him of his work.

Miles sets a steaming mug in front of me, and I echo the mantra Anna keeps tacked to her clinic door in an attempt to steady the race of my heart every time my husband stands close to me: "Live in the present. Be in the now." Because to do otherwise means worrying about the future or hating myself for the past, both of which send me spinning with fear and guilt and sadness.

Of course to "be in the now" also means to live where the consequences are, while in the meantime I attempt to forgive myself enough to go forward and be a good mother to sweet Jonah, who happily paints three tiny rainbows beside me.

"For Mama, Dada, and Jonah," he says. He arcs red, green, yellow, and blue across the white paper as I have taught him.

Miles flips the pancakes. Then comes close again to study his son's work. He tousles Jonah's hair and whispers, "Artiste."

Next week, our big boy will be eighteen months old. And since he will be old enough, Miles has encouraged me to enroll Jonah at the university day care, reassuring me that it's an amazing place. Once Jonah starts "school," as we're calling it, I'll begin a new job as an environmental consultant for Midwestern Energy Manufacturers, who face ozone compliance issues. Miles found the posting and said it was not an option, that I *had* to apply. After three interviews and a few follow-up phone calls, I was shocked to be offered the position. It'll be my first employment since my pregnancy, and starting it, I'll be scared to death.

The fear is not just about how I'll need to work double time to make up for knowledge not gained during my eighteen-month sabbatical at home, or about leaving Jonah in the care of someone else, although those concerns make my thoughts spin: *What if there's an emergency? What if Jonah doesn't nap? How will we all get out the door in the morning? What if I misread the printouts from the spectrometers?*

But even if all those worries come to pass, taking the position means accepting that I will never be a NASA correspondent like my friend Gillian, acknowledging that for me it's a girlhood dream passed by. And with that acceptance, I also can't keep from wondering if Miles pushed me into the job so that I can become financially and emotionally independent—so that he can eventually leave me on my own.

This morning I struggle to stay hopeful, knowing that in time these answers will reveal themselves. Until then, I'm toiling through things with Anna to see what work I have left to do on myself, on our marriage, hoping Miles will continue to slog it out with me—hoping to get more clarity about what I learned and what I can still change.

On the table, Miles sets out the breakfast plates.

I breathe deeply. I sip from my mug. "Can I help?" I ask.

Miles shakes his head no and lays a platter of pancakes in the center of the table, and as he leans forward, Jonah smiles and paints a splotch of blue on his daddy's nose. Proud of himself, our little boy reaches out and wraps his arms around us both.

In meteorology, dark matter is a term used to describe all that appears to be missing from the universe, things there but unseen. The existence of dark matter is inferred only from the gravitational pull it asserts upon observed objects. No doubt, I'll always feel the pull of what I can no longer perceive—my dead father, the demolished Quayside, perhaps even Dean.

But I also understand now that Miles could never have saved me from the pull of that dark matter, nor the loneliness the past imparted to me. During that brutal time in our marriage—the move, the isolation—through all of it, I was weak and strong-armed by the force of a history that was, quite simply, stronger than me.

So like the little girl in the Khoisan legend, I tossed red-hot embers from my fist, but in my version of the story, what I illuminated was that dark matter from my past. I do believe I learned from the flames at Quayside and all that brought me there, that I was vulnerable to those childhood holdovers like we all are, and that to linger in their wrongs means to blight the life out ahead.

I can only hope that one day Miles will trust me again. And, God willing, if I am given that second chance, I want to be, for all of us, the mother and the wife and the scientist he loved—one I hope he still does. What I learned from all of it is that maintaining the wellness of my son, my husband, and myself—who we three are together, with respect for who and what we sometimes need to be independent of one another, not losing ourselves inside each other's ambitions or affections—is what counts most. And I do believe now that no matter how strong the pull of the past, I can persevere in the present and do my small part to restore the wounded sky, righting the troubles instigated long ago when that old comet Halley went passing by.

READING GROUP GUIDE

1. We see Claire depicted as vulnerable throughout much of the novel—not just as a new mother and homesick wife, but also as a person who bears the weight of her past. What strengths do you see emerging out of Claire's vulnerability?

2. In what ways do you see Claire's guilt over her father's death manifesting itself in the plotline of the novel?

3. Is Claire ever able to see Dean for who he really is, or do you think people always fall victim to seeing the most redeeming qualities in their former lovers?

4. This novel demonstrates how influential the virtual world is, not just in Claire's life, but also in Dean's ability to find her. How are relationships affected by our constant use of social media and virtual communication?

5. Claire is very clearly the central character of this book, but is she the character you feel most connected to? Why or why not? What other characters do you find most compelling?

6. At the end of the novel, we are led to believe there may be a possible resolution between Claire and Miles. Do you think this is the best thing for them? Or do you think they would be better off on their own?

7. This novel plays with the intersection of the present and the past. How hard is it for the characters in this novel—Claire, her mother, her sister, even Dean—to evaluate people from their past?

8. Many marriages are changed with the arrival of children. Do you think having a child changed Claire's expectations for her marriage to Miles? If so, in what ways?

9. Miles is obviously the breadwinner in the story, so Claire stays home to raise her son. Do you think the stakes of their marriage would have been different if Miles were the one to surrender his career to raise Jonah?

10. In the final chapter, Claire has resolved herself to "living a life without fire." What is she talking about here?

11. When Jonah goes missing in the story, we realize that everything is at stake for Claire. How does that scene influence our feelings toward her as a mother?

12. In this novel, motherhood and professionalism are clearly in conflict with each other. In what ways is Claire's plight universal?

13. How does Claire's father's infidelity affect Claire's under-standing of her mother and herself?

14. Do you think there is hope for Claire and Kara sustaining a relationship? Do you have a sense that they will ever be closer, like they were as children?

15. If you were Claire, would you have been able to light the match at the Quayside? What was her ultimate motivation? Do you believe Claire will be able to put her haunting to rest now that the Quayside is gone?

A CONVERSATION
WITH THE AUTHOR

In *What Burns Away*, which character do you feel most connected to, and why?

The story is Claire's story, of course. She is the one we have the most access to—her loneliness, her loss, and her confused identity. Initially, when I first wrote the book, I found myself most deeply connected to her and the ever-changing world of new motherhood, its required self-sacrifice. And because I too was still in that place, coming to terms with having a young son and what it meant to put a teaching and writing career on the back burner, I found myself identifying most closely with Claire and her sense of isolation. But, through the process of revision, I've grown deep affection for Miles, who is so focused on providing for his family that he nearly loses them altogether. Throughout the rewrite, I lingered most in scenes with him, most especially the one after his lab has burned, where we see Miles, perhaps for the first time, as vulnerable as Claire. Understanding how Miles is made powerless during that crisis, I've become tender toward him, especially in those moments where his professional polish and impenetrable drive crack. Once things go undone in the lab, and later when he comes searching for Claire and Jonah in Connecticut, I worked hard to reveal Miles's tender underbelly and his emotional responsiveness so readers understand that he too is struggling. And finally,

at the close of the book, Miles undergoes what I feel is a real reversal. There beside a fire of his own making, burning their wedding
albums, it's my hope that the reader will note the subtle parallels
between him and Claire's father—men aching to reclaim broken
marriages they, too, have failed to nurture, maybe realizing belat-
edly their own role in the relationships' unraveling. But for Miles,
it is not yet too late.

What was your inspiration for writing _What Burns Away?_
For most of my adulthood, while I was perusing a writing
life, I also worked full-time as inner city schoolteacher—first in
the South Bronx, then in San Jose, California's Eastside Union
District, followed by downtown Boston. I had many complicated
students who came through my classroom doors, including three
teenage arsonists, one of whom was a fourteen-year-old girl, who,
aside from loving fire, was also, like me, infatuated with the sky.
Although this young woman was deeply troubled, having survived
a traumatic childhood, losing her parents to addiction and bounc-
ing between foster homes before she struck the match that would
take her out of my charter school and back into a juvenile deten-
tion center, we spent afternoons bent over star charts and reading the legends of Halley's comet, working on her research paper,
awed by all of it, together. I always wondered about that young
woman after she was gone, imagined where she might be and how
I could have saved her somehow. I also wondered who it was she
might become. So there's a bit of that student in Claire, along with
a bit of my own family. My maternal grandfather, Jim Horan, who
died tragically in a car wreck shortly before my birth, had been a
Hartford firefighter. Despite his absence during my upbringing,

his work was what my mother and her four brothers most often talked about around our holiday tables. Often, those discussions led to the legendary Hartford Circus Fire of 1944 and Grandpa Jim's understanding of the fire science that led to the devastation there.

What advice would you give to aspiring fiction writers?

Touch it every day—just a sentence or a word. Take a walk with your story, think about it as you rock your baby to sleep, do everything you can to hold on to the thread of your story, because once you drop it, it's hard to find again in all the chaos of everyday life. I say this because there was a long stretch of time when I wondered if I would ever finish Claire's story, juggling teaching responsibilities, then orchestrating my own cross-country move, all with a very busy and often missing husband and a young child in tow. But I'd say too, if nothing else, scribble new notes daily in whatever handful of time you can find. Along the way, I wasn't getting a lot of encouragement for my writing, but there always remained a part of me that needed Claire to stay afloat, to have something all my own, and for me, her story and her voice had become real. It sounds hokey, but I really did want to know what it was she was supposed to teach me, so I keep returning to the narrative to find out. I think aspiring writers need to take those simple steps. Some days it's literally writing one word or one sentence, on better days it is one paragraph, and later, all of it comes rushing out in pages. And most important, of course, is that while writing, you must read—obsessively. By this, I mean reading like a writer, studying the crafting of a book, wondering about the choices the author made, and considering all the ways the story was constructed.

Did you do any particular research about arson to write this book?

I always thought I didn't like science. It was not my strong suit in school. But as a kid I liked to set fires, small ones out behind the local drugstore, bonfires on the beach, and at home, even now, when someone lights a candle, I can't keep my fingers out of the wax. I knew there was a science to fire, a chemistry about it, but none of that science really spoke to me until I found Michael Faraday's old lectures from the Royal Institution of London. And, really, I just loved reading them. I thought the experiments were dazzling, and I performed a few at home. I loved that trick of dipping arsenic into a flame and watching it go blue; for me, so much of that chemistry felt new, even though I learned some of it in school. So, yes, I started to research fire science, learning how fires behave, studying how they move through enclosed rooms. Then, in my backyard, while my son napped and my neighbors mowed their lawns here in Madison, Wisconsin, I lit Ping-Pong balls on fire and made flamethrowers with aerosol cans. I studied combustion so I could understand Claire's draw to those flames.

Why did you choose to set the novel in two different settings? Do you see a particular contrast between the East Coast and the Midwest?

I'm a New England girl, and although I have lived all over the country, there's been very little of my life, until recent years, that I have spent without an ocean. When my husband and I moved to Madison three years ago, I thought, "There's a lake. It's water. It's all the same." But what I learned that first winter was how different weather patterns move across bodies of water, how the snow on a lake lasts longer and drifts in ways I have only ever associated with sand, whereas it's the wind off an ocean that delivers a nor'easter, with snow that melts quick and floods to cause coastal erosion. To me it was noting these differences in those two kinds of unforgiving winters that make both the Midwest and New England equally spectacular in the severity of their storms. The commonality, of course, is the desolation of those long winters, that kind of beauty you have to search for—a cardinal in the underbrush or the ice coating naked birch branches. I suppose too that it was my interest in those weather patterns that ultimately led to my choosing atmospheric chemistry as Claire's career.

Your main character Claire is, at times, a seemingly unreliable narrator. Did you find her character hard to write, and why did you choose to depict her this way?

I think an unreliable narrator is especially useful when developing a story in which the characters' work/life balance is all off. Claire is a more unhinged version of how I think many new mothers feel after the birth of their first child, especially older moms like myself, who had lives that were once defined by their careers. Then—*wham!*—there she is at home, doing the hard work of rearing a child, mostly in isolation. The balance is off for Claire and Miles once they become parents, and thus, I wanted Claire to reflect that imbalance, taking those normal unanchored emotions to an extreme and to become the kind of unreliable narrator I have always found alluring in fiction.

What do you love most about writing?

What I love most about writing is not knowing where I am

going. When we were kids, my parents would take my sister, Kristen, and me on what they called a "mystery ride" in our old wood-paneled station wagon. We never knew where we would end up, but often there would be ice cream. I loved those drives the same way I love writing—how you can be on a road you vaguely recognize, unsure of your final destination, until the very end. I was really lucky to find my wonderful agent, Jennifer Gates, and her copilot at the time, Lana Popovic, who took a ride with me on this book. *What Burns Away* was in an early draft when I first sent it to Jen, and I felt like by the end of our revision process together, and again after we got my editor Shana Drehs in the car, we were all four arriving at the close of the novel and that journey together. The editing is *really* rewarding for me, as much so as the conception of a story. So even when it means cutting away scenes, or letting my characters fail despite my desire to protect them (which was hard for me with Claire), I love that process, that journey through the narrative, getting to the end and writing the whole work over again, informed. Because so much of writing is done alone, getting feedback from smart readers and working out the story's flaws, for me, is where the magic really starts to happens. That journey through the revision process is my greatest pleasure as a writer.

What relevance do you see socioeconomics having in the novel and, in particular, Claire's story?

Claire's crossing from a blue-collar world into a more privileged one is relative because she fails to assimilate anywhere. Through her narrative, we learn that Claire was the first person in her family to attend college, and we understand that there was little push from her mother to do so. Therefore, the professional identity she created for herself was of her own drive. Writing her, I understood too that although Claire longs for the past and that old house on Willard Street, she is no longer a part of that world. Gone from her in all ways, Dean remains the only true representative of that place, drawing Claire to him because not only is she ostracized culturally and regionally from her history, but also because she fails to find a sense of belonging in her husband's privileged world of medicine. It is that play on socioeconomics that furthers Claire's isolation and ropes her into Dean's scheme.

How do you see Claire's virtual affair working toward or against her as a catalyst for change?

Claire is so caught up in what is behind her that I worked hard to emphasize her disillusionment with what is in front of her. My hope was to leave Claire susceptible to the kind of seemingly "safe" virtual affair she embarks upon. Thus, it seemed only logical to make Claire's first exchanges with Dean virtual to make it plausible that she would indulge the flirtation. Of course, she mistakenly believes that an online affair is both private and risk-free, allowing the exchange to grow more and more intimate until she falls victim to the dream of living another life, like her mother did, like Emma Bovary after La Vaubyessard ball. It was very hard for me to let Claire eventually fall prey to an *actual* affair. In the earlier drafts of the book, I kept stopping her short before anything unfolded physically between her and Dean. But ultimately, as I revised and worked through the edits, I felt that a virtual affair alone was not consequential enough to push Claire toward a reversal. So, I put her and Dean in a room alone together just to see what would happen. And once I set them there inside the inn, entangled with

the memory of who they were, wanting each other but also wanting to reclaim their youth, I simply could not apply the brakes. I
believe too that Claire's betrayal of her husband, and most especially
of herself, was one of the most emotional parts of this writing. To
let your narrator fall and know she may not recover is a hard thing
to do when you are emotionally invested in the character. Yet, I
do see Claire's failure to stay faithful to the marriage as part of what
forces her to look inward and reclaim herself, and as the thing that
finally sets her free of the past's hold on her.

**Self-forgiveness and atonement are major themes in this
novel. Who do you believe has done the most genuine aton-
ing in this story? Who has the biggest sin to forgive?**

The mother-daughter relationship between Claire and Kat is
especially interesting to me in terms of forgiveness. How they
reach for each other after all those years of hurt, Claire having
carried a sense of responsibility for her father's death, then learning that the history between her parents was more complicated
than she ever could have imagined. But what was most incredible
about writing a dually troubled love story (Kat and Peter, Claire
and Miles) is examining all the different types of love and the
angles that love can manifest, alongside the remedies for heartache, forgiveness being one. For me it is Claire who does the
most damage in this story—her anger is often misdirected, both
toward her mother and her husband, and her facts are skewed,
yet it is also she who is forced to make the greatest reparations
toward self-forgiveness. I set out to render Claire's marriage to
Miles as a sort of destroyed fairy tale, which is why I love the
cover so much—that image of a storybook set safe in a shadow

box with matchsticks. And as Claire embarks down a path of moral ruin, unable to appreciate the realities of her life, becoming full of nostalgic fancy after reconnecting with Dean, she grows only further discontented with her domestic monotony. Claire is unable to accept her current situation and attempts to escape it through deception. This, of course, only brings her further harm, ultimately risking the marriage altogether and jeopardizing the well-being of their beloved Jonah. For these things, it is Claire alone who must atone. And it is Miles who must forgive her if they are to step from the wreckage and build again.

In the novel, we find many quotes that deal with the sky, most especially Halley's comet, and in the opening chapter you write: "Nineteen eighty-six was the occasion of Halley's comet...and it seemed everything that happened that year was caused by the sky." Can you discuss why you chose to use the comet's pass as a literary device?

I myself came of age in that time of Halley's comet—and I remember learning its celestial folklore in school. I was completely obsessed with it. So when kids at my grammar school started wearing Halley's T-shirts and chewing Halley's Comet Rock Candy, checking the time on their Halley's Comet Swatch watches, I was all about it, even though I was equally fearful of the legends associated with that strange, bearded star. I studied the omens associated with comets, how the pass of a comet like Halley's often coincided with the births of two-headed calves, the deaths of kings, and the fall of empires. Later, as a teacher, I used my students as an excuse to dive back into those legends, imparting celestial folklore as part of my eighth grade curriculum. From the very onset of Claire's story, I knew that I would weave in elements of natural phenomena to demonstrate how life is often marked in seeming response to the natural world. I've always been fascinated by astronomical patterns that repeat themselves, and Halley's comet returns on a cycle that approximates the human life span, which makes it a wonderful device for marking narrative time in a novel—especially one where aging is a part of the through line. Here, the use of the comet punctuates the novel with a historic, scientific, and inevitably personal meaning.

Most of the characters in this story are at the onset of middle age. Can you discuss why you chose that as a narrative stance in the novel?

I have always loved coming-of-age novels, and for me, middle age is the second coming of age. That moment of realizing your youth is more behind you than in front of you gives a person pause. You have to decide what to let go of. You must redefine yourself and decide how you want to live out the rest of your life. It is the middle-age "awakening," particularly in women, that I am interested in as subject matter. There is something about redefining yourself professionally, familially, and sexually that fascinates me. What was once sexy, what once felt like desire, is driven by different external factors. There is also a new embrace of simplicity or fancy, depending on who you are, and an unshrouding of former definitions of self. Because middle age is something we can't stop—because it is simultaneously happening to our husbands or our lovers—there is a redefinition of beauty too, finding what is left underneath the obvious youthful pretty. I loved writing a character in this space, acknowledging these things about herself. The process of that surrender for Claire is both brutal and transformative, and that is why I felt compelled to capture it.

ACKNOWLEDGMENTS

I AM INCREDIBLY GRATEFUL TO THE MANY FRIENDS who helped me in the writing of this book, most remarkably those early readers who gave frequent advice, direction, and the necessary tough love: Don J. Snyder, Debra Monroe, Dagoberto Glib, Suzanne Matson, Jan Elizabeth Watson, Sarah Braunstein, Dina Guidubaldi (toughest of all), Jaquira Diaz, David DeVito, Lucie Scholz (medal of honor for most reads in record time), Julie Michaud, Antonya Nelson, and, most especially, Bill Roorbach. To my Madison Fiction Writer's Group: Susanna Daniel, Michelle Wildgen, Jeannie Reynolds Page, Jesse Lee Kercheval, and Judith Claire Mitchell, thank you for guiding me through the editing process with love, wisdom, and enthusiasm and for making Madison, Wisconsin, my writing-life home.

The Bread Loaf Writer's Conference filled this story with fresh perspectives and new writerly friends to inspire the final revisions of this book, the Sequoya Branch of the Madison Public Library provided me with a beautiful workspace, and Mary Ellen Marchant took loving care of my son so I could live inside this story.

Most certainly, I would be nowhere without my editor, Shana Drehs, who understood Claire's motivations from the start, and the rock star team at my publisher, Sourcebooks, took wonderful care of me, especially Lathea Williams and Anna Michels. It was the talent, wisdom, and friendship of Jennifer Gates, my beloved agent, and the savoir faire of Lana Popovic that pushed me to discover the depths of Claire's story. Jen, you took a chance on me, for which I am forever grateful to you. And for everyone else at Zachary Shuster Harmsworth who read and gave feedback, I am so truly appreciative.

For all those summers in the mideighties full of Frosty Treat and the family beach walks inside the setting of this novel, thank you to my sister, Kristen Falcon-Shannon, and our loving parents, Kathleen and Patrick Falcon. Philip Horan, your memory still lives with all of us on that stretch of sand, evermore.

Finally, to the man who devotes himself in equal measure to his work and our treasured Noah, while challenging me to live outside my comfort zone, Michael Field, you told me that one day I would thank you for all that is unconventional and crazy in our lives. My gratitude, darling; *here it is!*

ABOUT THE AUTHOR

Melissa Falcon Field was born in Hartford, Connecticut, and earned her BFA in creative writing from the University of Maine at Farmington and her MFA in fiction writing from Texas State University. She has been a recipient of the Katherine Anne Porter Writer-in-Residence appointment and attended the Bread Loaf Writers' Conference. Currently, she lives in Madison, Wisconsin, and spends summers along the coast of Maine. *What Burns Away* is her debut novel.